Christina Consolino

Rewrite the Stars

Black Rose Writing | Texas

First printing

This is a work of fiction. Names, characters, businesses, places, events, and incidents are either the products of the author's imagination or used in a fictitious manner. Any resemblance to actual persons, living or dead, or actual events is purely coincidental.

ISBN: 978-1-68433-650-0
PUBLISHED BY BLACK ROSE WRITING
www.blackrosewriting.com

Printed in the United States of America
Suggested Retail Price (SRP) $18.95

Rewrite the Stars is printed in Garamond

*As a planet-friendly publisher, Black Rose Writing does its best to eliminate unnecessary waste to reduce paper usage and energy costs, while never compromising the reading experience. As a result, the final word count vs. page count may not meet common expectations.

For my mom,
Mary Ann Serafini Consolino,
who always wanted to rewrite the stars

Praise for

"Rewrite the Stars offers a touching exploration of the complex and divided nature of the human heart."
–Jenny Jaeckel, author of *House of Rougeaux*

"A fabulous read that will keep you intrigued until the very end."
–J.E. Irvin, author of *The Strange Disappearance of Rose Stone*

"The story, told expertly by Consolino through the voices of Sadie and Theo, is emotionally gripping and touching, creating deep connection and sympathy for the reader with both characters."
–Elena Mikalsen, author of *Wrapped In The Stars*

"*Rewrite the Stars* gives the reader an insider's view of a marriage in the midst of falling apart."
–Karri L. Moser, author of *A Home for The Windswept*

"An absorbing read, from start to finish."
–Anne Valente, author of *The Desert Sky Before Us*

"A slow burn of a novel, with flames licking higher page by page. This beautiful and eloquent novel explores…depth, grace, empathy, and intimacy."
–Erin Flanagan, author of *It's Not Going to Kill You and Other Stories*

Rewrite
the
Stars

I want to see you.
Know your voice.

Recognize you when you
first come 'round the corner.

Sense your scent when I come
into a room you've just left.

Know the lift of your heel,
the glide of your foot.

Become familiar with the way
you purse your lips
then let them part,
just the slightest bit,
when I lean in to your space
and kiss you.

I want to know the joy
of how you whisper
"more"

— Rumi

Chapter 1: Sadie

On the morning my life began to unravel like the hem of my worn-out sweater, I found an old love letter from my almost ex-husband in the bottom drawer of my home office desk. The paper, at least fifteen years old, felt thin to my fingertips, like the lace on the bodice of my wedding dress. Inside the folds of the sheet, Theo had printed a few lines of text in his block scrawl—some words he'd written on his own, some he'd borrowed from our favorite poet, Rumi. *You have disturbed my sleep*, the text read. *You have wrecked my image. You have set me apart.*

Times had changed.

Without you, I can't cope.

And yet, they hadn't.

The letter's edges scraped my fingertips one last time before I placed the paper into a file folder near my computer. The summer humidity made the drawer stick, and I pushed it closed, upsetting the small pile of bills balanced on the desk. Water sloshed from the tall glass near the computer—Theo had probably left it out all night—reminding me dishes still needed to be washed and put away. Moving toward the door, I kicked a toy car with a missing wheel. The vehicle crashed against the wall and came to rest near a singing-alphabet snail that had been waiting for new batteries for two weeks. *From sweet love letters to dirty glasses and broken toys.*

Insane giggles from the next room interrupted my progress, and the scene unfolded before me: Theo on hands and knees, three rambunctious children scattered across his back. Make that *hand* and knees—he possessed enough strength to balance on one hand. His arm muscles rippled against his favorite blue T-shirt as he tickled the children's bellies. One tumbled off Theo and onto the carpet, while the second attempted to pull his shirt. The youngest, a pile of curls and drool, peered up at her father, joy radiating from her eyes as her pudgy fingers gripped his waistband. She clenched her teeth and yanked with a linebacker's strength such that in one fell swoop, a portion of Theo's shorts sprang away from his body. The kids rocked onto their heels, clapping their hands and howling, pointing at their father's underwear. In return, Theo growled, his voice echoing across the great room rafters. The guttural noise sent the children to scatter from one toy-filled corner to the other and then back to him again.

I pinched my lips, stifling the laughter, before my gaze met Theo's. It had been a long time since I'd witnessed such life in his eyes and in his actions. In fact, I couldn't remember the last time he'd played with the kids so effortlessly. On many days, an ordinary day's struggles wore him out long before he had a chance to interact with the children. Wiping away a tear from my cheek, I smiled—breathing in the happy moment, reveling in the charming family image, hoping to hold on to the contentment enveloping me as I went about the rest of my full day.

"I've got this." Theo craned his neck to look at me as the children began another round of assaults on his back. "You're overworked and underpaid. Go do what you need to do."

"But it's Father's Day. I can't do that to you."

"Do what? Leave me with my children? I'm right where I want to be." Theo—in one swift move—flipped his body over, grabbed the children, and clutched them to his chest. The move surprised me and gave me hope that Theo still existed. He did *have this.*

A mental check of my to-do list: most of the day consisted of tasks to be accomplished at home—doing laundry, decluttering the mud room, sorting old toys for the Vietnam Vets pickup scheduled for the next week—except for grocery shopping. "Okay, but at least let me take Lexie to the store. She loves to see her grocery store friends. Plus, Charlie and Delia have been complaining about their lack of Daddy time."

A year ago, when Lexie turned six months old and Theo had been struggling with PTSD for eleven months, we called it quits. Somewhat. Theo and I as a unit didn't work, mainly due to his symptoms. He'd turned inward, and nothing I had tried brought him back. At that time, we stopped sharing our day, stopped touching one another, and eventually stopped sleeping together. Theo refused to see a therapist with me on a routine basis, claiming we'd be "better off with different expectations of our future together."

After much thought and debate, and because we still both respected one another, we decided to be frank and tell the kids of our separation. The PTSD made sure Theo needed our help, so he still lived in an addition at the back of the house. But with the older kids at all-day summer camps and school the rest of the year, Charlie's and Delia's time spent with Dad was at a premium.

He didn't hesitate. "All right. Take Lexie and go get the grub. It's Father's Day, and I'm *not* doing the cooking!" He convulsed with laughter as the kids' fingers found their way into his armpits.

"Ha! Like you ever do." I winked at him.

Not wanting to waste a moment, I pried Lexie from Theo's legs and nuzzled her belly with my nose, drunk on the scent of my eighteen-month-old daughter. She giggled and squirmed and, like an inch worm, wriggled to the floor, then caught my hand in hers. With a quick swipe of the car keys and diaper bag and a check that a snack was accessible in the refrigerator, we wound our way through the back hallway to the garage.

"Do we know what we're getting?" I asked Lexie, who held the paper between her thumb and forefinger. She lifted the list in the air and waved it like a flag before crumpling it in her tight, gooey grip. When I pried the list from her hands, her grin stretched as wide as her face.

Once I'd buckled Lexie into her car seat, I grabbed my favorite cotton sweater from the seat beside her. "Okay, sweetie, to the store we go!" I tugged my sweater onto my arms and adjusted the buttons across my chest. It wasn't until later, as I hung the sweater on the drying rack in the laundry room, I noticed the loose thread at the bottom hem.

•   •   •   •   •

"Lexie, please. Sit still. We're almost finished here." I handed my stack of coupons to the cashier, then rummaged in my purse for my shopper's card.

A sharp squeak of a cart's wheels fought for attention with the piped-in music streaming from the store's speakers, and I threw a quick side-glance to the offender behind me. Too concerned my grocery order was holding up the line, I noticed nothing about him.

The cashier took her time scanning my coupons. *Swipe. Bing! Swish. Swipe. Bing! Swish.* Thankful we'd saved a good deal of cash on this trip, I turned again toward the man behind the cart, hoping my face held a silent apology for the delay. This time, I saw all of him: warm brown eyes sparkling under the fluorescent store lights, perfect bow lips curving upward, and a dimple flickering on his right cheek.

"Hey, no worries," he said. "It's Sunday, and I don't have anywhere else to be." A slight drawl clung to his words—a simple protraction that drew me in and made me want to hear more. Butterflies collected in my stomach as I stared at him.

Lexie's babbling helped me focus on the task at hand: squaring myself in front of the cashier and sliding my credit card through the reader. With a single, piercing gaze of his eyes, this man had rattled me. What was *that* all about?

"Happy Father's Day to you!" the cashier said to him, interrupting the spinning inside my head. She gestured to the belt that he should empty the cart of its items. "You should take the day off and spend time with that sweet daughter of yours."

The man nodded and moved his squirmy child away from the edge of the almost-full grocery cart before looking at me.

"When you have kids, there is no day off, is there?" The words escaped before I could think better of it, and a current of heat ran through my body, from my stomach to my heart, then to my neck. I averted my eyes: partly to mask the blush, partly to look at the credit card reader as the need to ground myself overwhelmed me.

"So true, so true," the man replied. "How many do you have?"

"Three. She's the youngest." Lexie reached for the receipt, which I gave her. Much to my chagrin, words continued to flow. "The others are eight and eleven. What about you?"

"This little bug is three, and I have a son who's seven. I'd have liked more but..."

"You get what you get, and you don't get upset?" My ears warmed, a not-so-subtle indication another blush had spread throughout my face, and I moved Lexie and strapped her into the front of the cart.

"Said like a true mom." Crinkles formed at the corners of his eyes as his mouth turned upward.

Something in his tone—a hint of admiration or respect—hit me out of the blue, reeling me forward, making me want to hear more. "Do you have plans for Father's Day?" I asked.

"Not a whole lot, which is exactly the way I'd have it. And you?" He pulled his wallet from his back pocket with his right hand—no chance to see if he wore a ring or not.

"Dinner with the family."

Family. Not alluring man at the grocery store.

The conversation needed to end, and I had to be the one who ended it. Walk away, I willed myself. Walk away. "Hope you enjoy the afternoon," I said and added a quick "Thank you!" to the cashier and the bagger, nodding my head in the man's direction. My short heels clicked on the blue and white tiles like old-fashioned typewriter keys, so desperate was I to flee before I said or did something regrettable.

Disbelief at my reaction washed over me. Noticing strangers at the grocery store. Flirting, stammering, and blushing at the view of a handsome man. Sadie Rollins-Lancaster—a woman with three children at home, a woman who still lived with a man she once loved? These behaviors weren't normal.

Our cart bumped over the crevices of the parking lot, and my world moved in slow motion. One half of my attention on the purchases, the other trained on the sliding doors of the store, I loaded my groceries into the rear of the minivan and babbled with the baby. After securing Lexie in her car seat, I pulled the seat belt strap over my midsection, clicked it into place, and checked my mirrors before putting the vehicle into reverse. "Be real, lady," I said to myself. "You're stalling."

At that moment, the man exited the store, and like a stalker, I followed his movements as he ambled toward his car. He performed the same mundane motions I just had as he chattered to his child. My heart skipped at his deep voice, carried by the wind to my open car window, and my pulse quickened at the sight of arms that would hold his daughter with ease.

"I can't believe this." Muttering to myself, I slammed my hands against the steering wheel and then jerked on it, pulling out of the parking space. "Really!"

"Wha?" Lexie asked. A glance in the rearview mirror showed my personal cherub, a beautiful example of how well Theo and I blended. A tear of regret sprang to my eye.

"Nothing, honey...I...I love you."

Pretending the high-noon sun blinded me, I hoped the man didn't catch me taking one last, longing look in his direction before I turned right out of the parking lot and onto the road. My entire body hummed, and I drove home on autopilot, my mind numb, the warm June wind whipping my hair through the open window.

Chapter 2: Sadie

Monday morning, at the beep of my alarm, I rose, padded down the stairs, and brewed the coffee. Charlie would remember to make his lunch if I placed his containers on the counter. At eleven years old, he was self-sufficient but still required daily reminders. Once everyone was awake, we'd review the day's schedule, and then I'd drop Charlie and Delia off at day camp. As I opened the cabinet to pull down the kids' vitamins, my eyes landed on the store receipt from the day before. I stopped, palms against the counter, to steady myself.

*Hey, no worries. It's Sunday...*that voice again in my head. Another kaleidoscope of butterflies frolicked in my stomach, and a heat spread across my cheeks. Placing my cool fingers against the skin of my face, I concentrated on the coffee. A quick inhale of the fragrant brew should have helped. But still, thoughts of the man distracted me—his eyes, his arms, his smile, his...

The quiet lull of NPR always guided my mind in the right direction, so I flipped on the kitchen radio. And for a while, the distraction worked. Between bites of cereal and sips of coffee, I finished dishes from the night before, threw a load of laundry into the washing machine, and scooped the cat litter. After finding all the documents I'd need for work and placing them in my briefcase, I looked at the clock. Time to wake the children. Charlie, Delia, and Lexie would anchor my mind in the right place. And if they didn't help, a conversation with Theo about paying his share of the latest in a long line of bills would do the trick.

But my encounter with Grocery Store Man haunted me the rest of the day— at work and at home—and well into Tuesday. That evening, after the kids were tucked into bed and Theo was busy watching sports in his portion of the house,

I called my friend Kate, hoping her kind, familiar voice might push my thoughts back on the proper track.

"I'm not sure what to say," Kate said. "Is there something I don't know? Something going on with Theo? With you? Is everything okay?"

"No, nothing's going on. I mean, we're status quo. Living together but not living together. Same old same old, really." Unconventional situation? Yes. But it worked for us.

"Hmm." Silence from Kate never boded well.

"I'm human, right? Maybe it was just the moment." I twirled the ends of the light afghan wrapped around my legs for warmth against the ceiling fan's cool currents. My mind drifted to images of the man—pictures I'd never seen, but somehow formed in my imagination with ease. A rippled chest. A pair of muscular thighs. A broad, naked back. How had my thoughts become so tawdry so fast? How unlike myself: *Were* Theo and I all right? Was this situation working for us? For me?

"Or it wasn't..." Kate's clipped voice admonished me from afar.

"We might not be officially divorced yet, but I'm not dead."

"I know."

Kate's simple words had touched on something poignant. Was the universe trying to tell me something? Distracted by a handsome man in one moment. Was I ready to move on? Was Theo? We hadn't talked recently about moving on, or moving out, for that matter, but the topic seemed to follow in the natural progression of things.

"If we aren't into each other any longer, why can't we be into someone else?" I said.

"I never said you couldn't..."

What a daunting thought, to start over again, hoping to find love when you weren't confident in your abilities to do so. If I had trouble finding it the first time, what made me think I'd find it this time? Would I repeat the same mistakes?

"I'll chalk up the rise in blood pressure to the heat, okay?" I fanned my face with my steamy April Wilson novel and kicked off the blanket, heated from the thought of Grocery Store Man. *Crap.* "This has been a warm June, right? And it won't matter. I won't be seeing him anytime soon. Coincidences happen here all the time, but Kettering isn't *that* small of a city."

Kate and I said goodbye, and I sat there, thoughts tumbling in my head. Over the years, young children, a full-time job for me, a job and military service for Theo, and the daily grind of chores had taken up most or all our time. We had embodied the two proverbial ships in the night. He'd get home, and I'd swoosh out the door, usually with a child in hand. Or, I'd be ready for bed, eyelids drooping shut, and he'd be coming home to eat dinner. It wasn't that I hadn't *wanted* to spend time with Theo, but I was too tired to do so. During those times when I had so much to do with the kids and with work and when I tried to get everything done at home, too, we'd grown apart. And then we'd been hit by Theo's PTSD.

Was I a different person now? Could I balance everything, including a new relationship, not comprehending what that might entail? Gah, jumping ahead of myself again. A simple flirtation with a stranger at the grocery store meant nothing. What didn't mean nothing, and what I needed to answer was, what did I want?

Even though Kate and I had known each other for years, I hadn't been ready for the conversation she and I *should* have: the one where we discussed what might be going on with me. This flirtation, while new, was the last of a series of new behaviors indicating my dissatisfaction with my current life. Behaviors like having highlights traced into my hair, buying knee-high leather boots, and wearing leggings at work instead of traditional slacks. Doing something radical with my look—such as getting a nose ring—had appeared on my radar, and I passed my evenings after the kids went to bed sipping wine and reading romance novels. Deserted beaches, margaritas, and olive-skinned fan boys dominated my thoughts while driving into work. And I noticed men at the grocery store *and* stalked them in the parking lot.

The Sadie I'd always been was missing, it seemed. But instead of owning up to those behaviors, I'd convinced myself they were mere whims—at worst, a midlife crisis. On that overstuffed chair, thinking of Grocery Store Man and everything else, I understood something bigger, more profound, loomed at the root of those behaviors. Maybe I *wasn't* happy. Maybe this situation—mine and Theo's—*wasn't* working for me.

Tired of my thoughts, I folded up the afghan, then padded into the kitchen to get myself ice cream—a habit I'd started before the kids were born any time my stress level increased. The frosty air from the depths of the freezer rushed at my face as I searched for the quart of ice cream living there, beneath the bags of frozen vegetables, toaster waffles, and ice packs. My favorite mug sat on the top rack of the full dishwasher, waiting to be cleaned. Shaking my head about my inability to get everything done, I reached for a glass bowl that belonged to Charlie.

A simple bowl, made of thick, clear glass, it sported a hint of blue tint, much like the color of Charlie's eyes. The bottom of the bowl fit into Charlie's hand, and a blazing sun—a perfect symbol for the child—embossed the side. As I scooped the raspberry cheesecake ice cream into it, the day eight years before, when Theo gave Charlie the bowl, came to mind. Charlie, three years old at the time, hadn't adjusted well to Theo's time away from home. One day, on a visit home during his first deployment to Afghanistan, Theo brought the bowl, nestled between his strong fingers. He explained to Charlie he wouldn't always be there, but the bowl would be—all Charlie had to do was use it, and Theo would be with him. From that day forward, nothing separated Charlie and the bowl, at least when it came to his morning cereal.

Despite the importance of the glass bowl to Charlie, he wouldn't mind sharing. After finishing the ice cream, I washed and dried it. As I reached to put it back on its shelf, the still-damp bowl slipped from my fingers and tumbled toward the quartz countertop. It landed in the crook of my elbow, which saved it from destruction. Inside my chest a storm brewed and sweat beaded on my brow; had I broken the bowl, Charlie would have never forgiven me. I turned out the lights, placed a hand to my beating heart, and thanked the universe for lucky saves.

Tiptoeing across the wood floor of the hall, I glanced at Theo, sound asleep on the recliner, the flicker of the television in the background, and my thoughts turned to my conversation with Kate. Those thoughts accompanied me to the bedroom, where cool sheets welcomed me into their embrace; sleep could not come too soon.

That night, a dream sequence so vivid, so detailed and colorful, occupied my mind. Flashes of skin, warm lips on my neck, kisses trailed down the column of my throat to my breasts and below; chocolate-brown eyes under a full moon, a human heart cracked in two pieces; drops of scarlet blood collecting in a puddle on a blue- and white-tiled floor. I awoke with a start in the dark, heart bumping, breathing ragged.

When I stepped into the shower the next morning, I wasn't certain where I was or to whom I belonged. My mind envisioned the trappings of a campy Harlequin novel: Grocery Store Man and I would meet again, realize we belonged together, and despite all the odds, certain obstacles, and assumptions, end up together as true soul mates.

"Fate isn't that kind, you dimwit," I said to myself. Clenching my eyes shut, I hoped to force away the images that still danced in my mind and wash the dream down the drain. My life might fill the pages of many a book, but it was not, had never been, and never would be, a romance novel.

Chapter 3: Theo

"Something has changed with Sadie. I just know it."

Doc narrowed her eyes at me. "What do you mean by changed? You're still living together at home?"

"Yes, that's the same. What I mean is..." How to say it? Something different in her posture. Something different in the flush of her cheeks. She hadn't mentioned anything to me or the kids, but she'd been more... "She's been more distracted. Less focused on us."

"And how does that make you feel?"

Why did therapists always use those words? Those terms—spoken over and over—were so cliché, and what did they expect the person to say? Did she think I'd tell her everything as I sat in the suffocating air of this cave? While the dusty blue walls were soothing, the lighting...well, it could stand to be improved. How did it make me feel? It made me feel...

"Angry."

"About what?" Doc asked.

Angry summed up my life since being discharged—honorably, but still discharged—from the service. Angry I'd been in Afghanistan in the first place. Angry I'd seen what I had when I was there. Angry that Sadie and I didn't make it. Angry I couldn't hold onto my old job as a web developer because too much screen time set me off. Angry, angry. Fucking angry. No other word sufficed. "Everything."

"Theo, one-word answers will get you nowhere in this office."

Maybe, but so far Doc hadn't kicked me out. Biweekly therapy appointments—one-on-one, addressing cognitive behavioral therapy—had been on my schedule for the last six months. I kept some of them; others, I didn't. Everything would get better once I'd worked through it. I *knew* that, but days existed where I didn't care. Life was too painful sometimes. That's partly why Sadie and I had split.

Doc tapped her fingernails against her clipboard, a sure sign she was debating about where to go with the conversation. Always the type of therapist not to push—I appreciated her approach. But she also knew I would sit and say nothing for the remainder of the hour if I felt like it.

"If you're not ready to talk about your anger, then let's get back to Sadie. How is she doing?"

Sadie was an independent woman. The sort who gave birth naturally in the morning and was home, doing dishes, writing emails, and dragging kids to the library by the evening time. Nothing stopped her. Nothing bothered her. At least in my estimation. Her resiliency, her competence, her strength: those qualities had been attractive early on. They'd also been why I had to walk away, why we had to end the marriage—not that we had gone through with it yet. I didn't want to hurt a woman like her any more than I already had. She deserved so much more than I could give to her then or now. More than I could *ever* give her.

"She seems to be holding it together. As usual..." A piece of lint on my jeans drew my attention, and I flicked it to the floor.

Doc finished my sentence for me. "But there's something different about her."

"Yeah. Maybe next time I come in, I'll know what."

Understanding what was wrong with Sadie meant I'd need to "spend time self-reflecting"—Doc's words, not mine. I faced more time at home now, only working part-time at a local fitness center's front desk (thank goodness for old friends and a bit of structure), but that didn't mean Sadie and I had reconnected. A huge gap still existed between us. And since we were no longer together, no incentive existed to bridge it.

Doc's voice cut through my thoughts. "Are you finished for the day?"

"I am."

Sometimes Doc went with it and let me call the shots. Another thing I appreciated about her. She sighed, closed her notebook, and cocked her head to the right, a slight gesture I'd learned to interpret.

"Game on," she said and rose from her chair.

Most of my life was atypical now. Living with a woman who wasn't quite my ex-wife (but would be if I signed the papers). Spending time with a therapist who used ping-pong as part of her repertoire. They both fell into the "atypical" category. *So be it.*

The paddle's cool wood tingled against my hand. It gave me something tangible to take my anger out on. Doc lifted the ping-pong ball and shook it in the air, helping me focus. I knew the drill: breathe in through my nose and out through my mouth five times, and then we'd begin. Lame, but a process that helped, especially on days when I couldn't (or wouldn't) talk and let out what was inside. Doc raised her paddle and tapped the ball once. She didn't know it yet, but she was going down.

•   •   •   •   •

The next morning, I clocked-in at eleven. Being employed at the fitness center had taken time to get used to. Web developer hours and gym staff hours varied widely, and my deployments had brought variety—albeit the dangerous kind—to my days. At the center, life ran at a different pace, more like corn syrup than water, and nothing screamed *urgent!* on a daily basis. Except for a broken workout machine or an out-of-order water filter. In the summertime, the number of clients depended on the weather. On those days when the humidity hung like a haze in the air, more people sought shelter from the air-conditioned space. On other days, the lazy, sun-high-in-the-sky-so-blue kind of days, the whole city seemed to have gone away for vacation, leaving the place with so few clients, each hour took so fucking long to get through. Starting a shift so close to lunch time meant the day should be busy—we saw an uptick in patrons for the noon hour—but the more I had to do, the more my mind would be occupied.

Just as I'd logged myself on to the fitness center's employee system, a thwack near the front doors drew my attention. My gaze flicked from the doors to the windows, to the right hallway and the conference room on the left, back behind me and then again in front of me. Under the glare of the sun streaming through the windows, someone had dropped a backpack, and another person had stopped to help, something too few people did these days. I'd seen the guy with the backpack before. He came to the gym each day to lift weights and run on the treadmill. But the other guy was new. Dressed in a suit, almost as if he didn't quite belong there, he finished helping with the pickup and then headed my way.

"Morning." The man tipped his head in my direction.

"Morning to you as well, though there's not much left to it."

The man wriggled the watch on his wrist and smiled. "You're right. Thank goodness, because it's been a long one."

He had to be here for only one thing, so I got to the matter at hand. "What can I help you with?"

"I'd like to check out my options. I have a bit more time these days. The kids are getting older and easier to manage, and you know how it is." He patted his abdomen. "I need to stay on top of this."

I'd never been into free weights and all that, but as a reserve military member who faced who knew what when deployed for six months every two years, I had always kept in pretty good shape. Plus, the gym had been a sanctuary of sorts many times since leaving the service.

"What type of membership are you looking for?"

"I need a place to come and work out with hours that fit my schedule. I'm not one for classes or training."

"The basic plan is your best bet then." I handed him a brochure with the fine print and spaces to fill in his personal information and signature. "It's twenty bucks a month, plus taxes and fees, and we're open twenty-four hours a day. The basic plan doesn't give you more than entrance, but it sounds like you might not need any extras. And of course," I added, "we have free Wi-Fi. I like to point that out because people tend to call back and ask us about it."

The man smiled again. "That's great, but honestly, I'll be coming here to get away from work. Maybe you get that."

"I do." Over the last few months, I'd learned to be polite to the clientele. Part of Doc's reason for approving this job involved the low-stress environment. She also appreciated I'd be forced to speak to other people each day. "Let's bring you back to the land of the living," she'd said.

Without my prompting, the man went on, something that happened often in this place. "I own a company that helps other companies be better. We look at their branding, their workforce, their mission, web design, all that stuff. Try to make them do what they already do, but better."

"Huh."

"It's going quite well, and we're expanding...so much we're hiring right now. If you hear of any web or software developers or marketing professionals, please tell me."

A shiver began to crawl underneath my skin. I had enjoyed my former job, but it was too interwoven with my time overseas. "In a former life, I could have helped you."

"Really?"

"Yeah." I left it at that, but this guy, while not pushy, told me what he was looking for and why, then dropped the subject. I'd likely never pass the information to anyone else. In fact, the info would worm its way into my brain and stay there. I should have cut him off before he'd given me the details.

The silence that usually stretched between me and anyone else seemed heavy as I entered his information.

"Have you tried that new microbrewery?" he asked.

Beer and Zoloft didn't mix, but the art of a craft beer had always held my interest. "I haven't, but I've heard good things."

"It's been busy at work, but it's time to head over. Heard the layout of the place is fantastic. Loads of space, only a few televisions to watch the Browns lose."

I smirked at his comment. "Not a Browns fan?"

"Not a football fan, but I do love *Tech City*."

"One of my favorites," I said. Doc would be proud: holding my own in a conversation with someone unfamiliar. Maybe my ability to relate and connect with people was prepped to resurface.

I tipped my head when I handed him his receipt and credit card. "This can be automatically renewed if you like, but I'd advise you to wait and choose that option once you've decided if you like the place or not. Things have changed in the last few years with the new owner. All good, if you ask me, but the place runs a bit differently than in the past."

"Sounds great." He leaned in and extended a hand, then looked at my name tag. "Thanks for the information, Theo. It was nice to meet you. I'm sure I'll see you around."

Handshakes these days seemed too intimate and took too much of my energy, but Doc had me working on trying to reinstate my manners and proper etiquette. This guy had given me no reason to feel awkward. And this space? Familiar, calming. "Thank you. You'll like it here, man." I looked back at the screen to catch his name: *Andrew MacKinnon*. "Andrew. You'll like it here."

Chapter 4: Sadie

Time to dwell on Grocery Store Man didn't exist over the next week. Between the kids' swim classes, my job, and the many doctor appointments I'd scheduled for the summer months, my mind was occupied by so many details—only one of which was Charlie's camp presentation, something he told me about one late afternoon at the end of June.

"Mom, I'm not sure about this camp." He walked into the kitchen as I prepped vegetables for dinner. "It says here on the activities list...we need to do a presentation."

"Okay. What's wrong with that?"

Charlie snatched a piece of red pepper, popped it into his mouth, and took a seat. "It's weird, that's all. We work on it during the summer and into the fall, but we don't present our project until sometime before Christmas."

This was the first summer we'd signed up for a camp sponsored by the middle school, and while Charlie enjoyed his days there, the staff seemed to do things differently from other camps he'd attended in the past. A few more weeks of adjustment time might be required.

"No issue, Charlie. That gives you plenty of time to research the subject and to create as nice a presentation as possible. Do you need help?"

He scrunched up his nose and shook his head. "No...it's..."

Charlie was the type who chatted incessantly, about anything. Minecraft, math, music. Insects. Grammar. Latin verb conjugation. You name it, he'd talk. Charlie had big (and small) ideas and liked to share them. His lack of articulation meant he needed me. I sat next to him on a kitchen stool and rubbed circles on his back.

"What is it?"

"We're supposed to do this project called *My Dad, My Hero*. We have to feature a dad or a grandpa or some other male influence." He used air quotes around the word "influence," which almost sent me into a fit of laughter, something Charlie wouldn't appreciate.

I cleared my throat. "And what's the problem?"

"The problem is...it's..."

"Your dad was in the service, honey. He fought for his country, and he saved a lot of lives, even though he might have been scared. That sounds like a hero to me. Doesn't it to you?"

"Yes, but—"

"But what?"

Charlie shook his head and chewed on his fingernail. "Never mind. You're right. I need to...I need to find all the pictures we have of us, going as far back as I can find. This is a pretty big project."

My misstep—not letting Charlie finish his sentence—had pushed him to turn inward, just like his dad. But what was I to say to him? Theo was a hero, wasn't he? Even if he didn't quite have his life together right now in the way he or I wanted, he'd bravely faced an adversary that most wouldn't. And definitions of the word hero varied.

"Honey, life right now is complicated for your dad. Remember that. But if you put your mind to it, this can be a great project. Okay?"

"Okay."

"Tell me if you need any help."

"I will."

I rose from the stool and ruffled Charlie's hair. "Now let's go tidy up before dinner and get rid of those 'landmines' your dad says he's always stumbling over. Then we can go get frozen custard after dinner!"

Charlie's eyes lit up, and he nodded his head. "Race you to the family room!"

•   •   •   •   •

Two warm and sluggish months crawled by and soon mid-August was upon us. One night after dinner, when Lexie and Delia were tucked in bed and Charlie had escaped to the family room, I mentioned to Theo I'd had a difficult day. Kate had given me grief about not attending a karaoke night at the bar. And not only had I stepped on Charlie's latest cardboard creation, but both Lexie and Delia had experienced episodes of projectile vomiting, the dregs of which ground nicely into the minivan's new rugs.

"Please, Sadie. I'm tired. Too tired to listen to you whine," he mumbled.

His simple statement echoed. I *had* whined, although admitting that to him would never happen. I pivoted from the kitchen sink to look at Theo, who had placed his elbows on the worn dining table and his chin in his hands. His eyes held frustration in them—perhaps his day had been just as discouraging as mine—but at that moment, little sympathy existed within me.

"I didn't go into work today," he continued.

Understanding hit me. He *had* had a day. Not going into work was the last resort, according to his therapist, something reserved for the days when he malfunctioned around people or felt like he'd come undone.

"Do you—"

Theo held up his hand, palm outward, and shook his head. Shutting me out seemed to be Theo's way. I'd hoped he'd made progress these last few months, but...

Turning back to the dishes, I scrubbed against the glass of Charlie's favorite bowl and plunged the piece into the rinse water. I traced the tempered glass with my fingers, moving bubbles away, and felt a rough edge that gave me pause. Had the bowl hit the countertop that night months ago? The light above the sink revealed a small, glistening crack that winked at me. A flaw large enough that if I didn't fix the bowl soon, the whole structure's integrity would shatter. What an obvious crack; how long had it been there?

Against the screech of Charlie's video game in the family room, I placed the dish into the drainer to dry and made a mental note to fix it in the morning. Another item to add to the ever-growing list. Outside the kitchen window, the sun continued its descent into the horizon. The clouds hung low and the sky's canvas faded to a soft, muted purple, a beautiful sight from which I might gather strength. If I—

A cry erupted over the monitor, most likely Lexie. The vomiting episodes, while brief, and taken their toll on both girls. Lexie's discomfort might mean we'd be launching into another round of sickness, soon.

"I'll go check on them," Theo said, then rose from the table and pushed in the chair. For one split second, the chair's leg caught on the seam of the area rug, and I feared both Theo and the chair would tumble to the floor. Instead, Theo righted himself, adjusted his shoulders, and trudged to the bedroom.

He was a ghost of the man I had married fifteen years prior, on the hottest day of the year. That afternoon, no one could have convinced me we wouldn't be together forever. We'd written our vows of extraordinary love for one another, and we'd refused to add a phrase about *for better or for worse*. Which young couple wants to imagine a dismal future? And that future, *our* future, had been full and bright...

Until Theo's PTSD.

So there, in the thick of what wasn't even by far the worst we might experience, I questioned my future—

"Sadie, I need help cleaning up Lexie." Theo's voice filtered through the monitor. Despite his mental state, Theo still had his physical health, but situations involving bodily fluids were more difficult to accomplish, and cleaning up a mess alone would be next to impossible for him.

I wiped my hands on the damp dishtowel and draped it over the handle of the stove. Now clearly wasn't the time to bring up the topic of signing the divorce papers, but should I try to speak to him about these newfound feelings? Learning about my reaction at the grocery store might be too much for him to take, even if it was one of his good days.

•　　•　　•　　•　　•

Two months, one week, and a day after I ran into Grocery Store Man, and when I thought Kettering really *was* that big and coincidences no longer happened to me, he and I met again, this time inside my office building.

"Which floor, miss?" A voice reverberated as I strolled into the elevator with my head down, looking at the report in my hand. That *drawl*. I lifted my gaze.

"It's you!"

The man narrowed his eyes and tilted his head until a wave of comprehension rolled over him.

"Bloom Market? Kettering Plaza?" He pointed at me.

"Father's Day." I nodded, my index finger against my sternum.

"Right." Adjusting his necktie as he cleared his throat, he looked away to the dark corner of the ceiling. Soft Muzak trailed out of the speakers above our heads.

The whole situation dripped with hokeyness. A few years before, I'd edited an article on the best places to meet a mate. The author had included convincing evidence that the number one place to meet a potential spouse was on the job. Where did the grocery store fall on the list? At a respectable number four.

I stepped closer to Grocery Store Man, my back to the corner of the elevator, and the tall doors closed. My agitation grew, and I tugged at the corner of the report in my hands. "So, did you have a nice Father's Day?" Part of me wanted to know, another part of me wanted to hear his voice, and the last part of me wanted him to keep talking so the awkwardness engulfing the small space would dissipate.

"Actually, I did." He shoved his hands into the pockets of his dress pants. "We had a nice barbeque and a relaxing day. And Sydney's balloon stayed inflated for hours. It's the little things, right?" The smile I'd tortured myself with for the last two months flooded his face, as if the mere thought of his daughter brought him joy.

My shoes suddenly held my interest, so afraid was I that my tears would fill my eyes. "Yes." *Little things Theo no longer seemed capable of: Being able to pick up the children from school or having the energy to get out of bed by himself. Walking the kids to the bus stop and having confidence his neighbor isn't really a threat.*

I caught him staring at me, his body poised, as if he wanted to ask a question. Holding his gaze seemed impossible as I fixated on the pronoun he'd used. *We? Does he mean the kids and himself? Or does that* we *include a wife?*

"Umm. Which floor did you want, by the way?" He reached out to the panel of shiny buttons on the wall.

What sort of man made me forget what floor I needed? Was he trying to get rid of me? My tight lungs struggled to inflate. "Seven, please."

He used his left hand to push the button—confirmation of no wedding band on the ring finger. I clenched my eyelids shut. What in the hell was wrong with me? Any progress I'd made over the last two months with trying to forget this man evaporated like my sense of humor on a hot, humid day. But as long as he didn't get off on my floor, I would be fine. To calm myself, I tapped a rhythm with my foot to the awful rendition of Elton John's "Rocket Man" filtering through the speakers.

The elevator's abrupt stop jolted me out of my seventies time warp, and the smooth, gray doors slid open. Without looking backward, I stepped forward onto the shiny tile floor and tossed a brief wave behind me. Introducing myself was out of the question—the less I knew about this man, the better.

●　　　●　　　●　　　●　　　●

I closed the door to my small office—junior book editors didn't command much space, if any—and hung my summer sweater on the silver coat rack standing in the corner. Rounding my desk, I bumped the corner of it with my hip, and the expletives I rarely used at home rushed into the air. The flesh of my hip—now likely bruised—felt tender against the pressure of my fingers as I waited for my computer to power up and my email to load. Only a few messages in the inbox needed my attention: one from HR about up-to-date health insurance forms; a second from a client confirming an upcoming meeting; a third from a book vendor regarding a delivery date. Nothing urgent.

I exhaled and wiped my brow, then flopped into my chair and assessed my desk. Pens and pencils leaned in the canister to the right of my computer, and my desk calendar sat ready and waiting for any changes I might make. The tick of the clock on the wall reminded me—no, mocked me—that the workday was about to begin, and yet, I sat, unmoving. Would Jackie have more information about why Grocery Store Man might be in the building? Unable to wait until later in the day to ask, I hurried from my chair and rapped my knuckles on the wood doorframe of the office next door.

"Good morning, Jackie! How was your weekend?"

My friend and coworker lifted her head from the hammock she'd made with her hands, and her puffy eyelids and blazing pink cheeks greeted me. The half-moons under her eyes stood out as dark as a football player's eye black. Jackie had returned from maternity leave the week before, and finding the balance between editing and parenting was proving to be elusive, or so she had confided in me a few days prior. Her daughter, Clara, screamed like a banshee much of the night, and Jackie needed more sleep than she was getting.

She waved her hands to draw me into the office. "I swear that kid uses my boobs as pacifiers. Why can't she fall asleep by herself? How hard can it be?" Jackie said. "And no judging...this," she gestured to the steaming mug in front of her, "is decaf. I would never pass on caffeine to Clara on purpose."

I held my hands up in front of me, palms facing Jackie, as I moved farther into her office. "No judgment from me, I swear! I've been there myself three times, remember?" The memories of my sweet babies brought warmth to my chest. "You might not want to hear this, but life will get easier. She'll learn to sleep alone, and you'll get your body back. Right now, though, *you* are what she needs. What can I do to help?"

"I know, I know." Jackie pushed her bangs off her forehead and tucked her hair behind her ears, then rubbed her eyes and sipped her coffee. "I'm finding all this *so* much harder than I expected. And Pete is trying, he really is, but he can't nurse the baby." Jackie's phone trilled. She placed her coffee cup on her desk, picked up the receiver, and replaced it on the cradle without answering.

Clearly the fatigue was getting to her. "Theo and I went through the same thing. By the third time around, I thought I had a great system. The doctor told me every child is different. Charlie and Delia were so much alike, I didn't believe him. Until Lexie..." Thoughts of the kids would overtake my mind, but this was Jackie's well-being, not mine, and my offer to help her was sincere. "However, this is about you." Taking the chair across from Jackie, I lowered myself into it then straightened a pile of mail on her desk. "You can hear those stories later— if you haven't already—when you've had a bit more sleep. Seriously, what can I do?"

"I appreciate the thought. Really, the only thing I need is more shut-eye. Any thoughts about an evening shift?" Desperation radiated from her glazed eyes, an all-too-familiar emotion.

"Sure. Let me talk to Theo, and I'll get back to you. I can run on little sleep these days." It had been weeks since I'd had a night of restful slumber thanks to my grocery store run-in. That morning, my own weariness had flooded my body, but the charge of seeing Grocery Store Man in the elevator had eradicated any leftover fragments of sluggishness.

"Oh really? What *is* your secret? I need some of whatever it is." Jackie closed her eyes and drew in a deep breath through her nostrils. She picked up the mug and took a large sip of the coffee.

Jackie and I had worked together for eight years. She'd become my confidante and go-to friend and had helped me navigate onerous times when Theo shut me out and during our quasi-separation. If I confided in her about my current problem, she might be distracted from her fatigue. I leaned in toward Jackie's desk.

"Well...I've been dwelling on an encounter I had...two months ago. With a man."

A torrent of coffee blew in my direction before Jackie moved her hand to her mouth. After lifting herself from her leather chair, she walked to the door of her office and closed it. "I am *so* sorry," she said. One napkin would not be enough, so she passed me two, then leaned over the desk, which she tapped with insistent fingers. "First, why didn't you tell me? Second, that was the last thing I thought you'd say. Does Theo know?"

"You were busy with Clara, and it's not entirely what you think. I have *not*...you know. I couldn't do that. I mean, we're not divorced, but he's living in the house and, well, that would be awkward, wouldn't it? But if I had to be honest, I might be able to say...oh crap, this sounds sappy..." The words clinging to the edges of my mind sounded so tacky, so trite, but I spoke them anyway. "It might be an affair of the heart."

"Oh. My. Word! *That's* a great title!" Jackie sat back in her chair, an enormous smile filling her face, and spread her hands before her. She narrowed her eyes like she'd already formulated a book cover in her mind, the words *An Affair of the Heart* emblazoned at the top.

Revealing the whole story needed to occur before Jackie's overactive imagination thrashed out of control, so I recounted my grocery store interlude and the elevator episode. Jackie's eyes took on a dreamy quality as she blew on her still-hot coffee. The smell of the beverage wafted over to me and wrapped me in comfort I wanted to keep with me forever.

"I still can't believe you didn't tell me. But this is a serious issue if you're checking out other men. Are you ready to move on? That's a conversation for another time, of course. In the meantime, you should write this up and send it to *Love Stories Today* or one of those other magazines. Don't they publish short stories? Who knows? If you have the time, you might be able to expand it into a real romance novel. I'd read it." She beat her fingers on the outside of her mug and stared off behind me, lost in thought.

Leaving Jackie's office took top priority—otherwise, she might grab me as her next pet project, something she was well known for around the office.

"I doubt I'll be writing the piece up anytime soon, but now I need to run." I rose from my chair and turned toward the door.

"That's it? That can't be it. Wait!" Jackie stood and stumbled over the breast pump bag at her feet. Next, she would try to drag me back into the office.

"Is that spit up?" I pointed to a nonexistent stain on her lapel. She glanced down, taking her eyes off me for only a moment, leaving me just enough time to sprint out the door.

Chapter 5: Sadie

Most of the time I considered my past choices sound. The decision to buy the house, the decision to have children, even the decision to marry Theo—they were all *right*. But so was the decision to serve him divorce papers.

The first seven years or so of our marriage had been filled with much love, laughter, and joy. Theo made a point to come home for dinner even when he had a big project, and the love notes I had placed into his lunches each day fulfilled a much-needed connection. When the marriage was good, it was good: we'd find time every two weeks for a date night, even after Charlie and Delia had come along.

"It's important to remember who we are. You and me," he'd say to me as he pulled me in for a hug and lingering kiss. "You. Me. Forever."

And of course, even though we'd gotten busier and spent less time with one another, we had a beautiful family with three adorable kids. Theo's job kept us more than comfortable, and my place in publishing would allow the kids to go to college and beyond. We had a spacious house, two cars, and organic food on the table.

But the last tour and his PTSD diagnosis had changed everything.

Sure, Theo was *alive*, but he wasn't really living. And despite everything I'd tried to do for him—practice patience with him, listen attentively, create routines, minimize his stress and possible triggers, give him his space—as difficult as it was to serve him those papers, I'd do it again in a heartbeat, wouldn't I?

Those thoughts drifted through my head as I checked in on the children before heading over to Jackie's the following Friday night.

"Good night, sweet pea." Lexie's cheek warmed my lips as my kiss landed there. The light from the functioning monitor winked at me, and I adjusted the blinds to keep out the bright, toxic light that would creep in before seven in the morning. I extended a gentle hand over the crib rail and onto Lexie's quietly breathing form, feeling her stomach rise and fall, a soft snore escaping her parted lips. The preciousness of that child always amazed me. Our miracle. The one who came after Theo turned inward but before life turned too complicated.

And Delia. She lay tangled among the flowered sheets of her twin bed. Pulling the blanket up to protect her from the conditioned air would be futile—the edge of the cotton fabric twisted around her ankle such that the blanket wouldn't budge. Delia slept like Theo did, in one enormous, chaotic mess. "You are just like your father," I whispered in the near-silent room. Hot tears pricked at my eyelids as I made my way down the carpeted hallway to Charlie's room. A light peeked out from beneath the door, a sure sign my oldest child would be perched on his bed, graphic novels spread before him, eyeglasses on the tip of his tiny nose. With the edge of my fingernail, I tapped and then opened the door. My sweet Charlie looked up with a gleeful expression of genuine love. He was still young enough to want his mom to tuck him in at night.

"I've got to go now." I moved toward the bed and sat on the mattress. Charlie shut the book he was reading and adjusted his glasses.

"Where are you going?"

"I promised Mrs. Mills I'd help her out for the night. Little Clara is only ten weeks old, and they're all having a rough time."

"Lots of crying?" Charlie stacked his books on the nightstand, making sure each one lined up with the one above and below it.

"Yes. And little sleeping. Remember how it was with Lexie?" I leaned over to fluff his pillows—a nightly ritual I'd started when Charlie first began sleeping in a big bed. Forgetting about it that night wasn't an option.

"Oh yeah. I never thought a baby would be so *loud*. Thank goodness she's out of *that* stage."

His words sounded so mature. I knew it had to do with everything he'd experienced over the last couple years, but at eleven years old, Charlie was still too young to be shouldering the burden. He was such a *good* kid: good brother, good son, and good person in general. Aside from the clutter in his room and his tendency to shove items into his pants' pockets (and forget them there), I'd been more than lucky with Charlie. Changing his childhood experience—making sure I didn't place too much responsibility on him when it came to Theo's needs—needed to take center stage.

I placed a kiss on his forehead and then on his cheek. Charlie wrapped his thin arms around my neck and snuggled in against my body.

"I love you, Mommy."

"I love you, too, Charlie."

"I love you too."

Charlie added the last "I love you" as he always did, like it was a reflex, then fell back against the pillows, pulled his comforter up, and curled against his favorite stuffed salamander. My heart was full, warm, and content as I rose from the bed, turned out the light, and closed the door.

•　　•　　•　　•　　•

The headlights of my car illuminated the outside of Jackie's Cape Cod, marking a sharp contrast to the dimness within. During my conversation with Charlie, a moment of indecision had washed over me: I loved my family and really didn't like not being at home for them, but Jackie and Pete were counting on me.

Using the key Jackie had provided the day before, I unlocked the front door and shut it behind me. Quietly, I tugged open the foyer closet door, hung up my thin sweater, and removed my flip flops, which were slick from a hard summer rain. The tick of the clock on the mantle in the living room and the whir of the air conditioner threaded themselves throughout the silence. Another noise, a consistent and even thrum, pulled me toward the kitchen at the back of the house.

"Oh dear."

Jackie sat slumped over the kitchen table, asleep, breast pump still siphoning the liquid gold from her chest.

"You must be tired, honey, if that motor hasn't jostled you out of your dreams." I rubbed circles on Jackie's back, trying to wake her without scaring her, and she raised her head to meet my gaze. Imprinted lines from the table ran across her forehead, and relief flooded her features. "Go, sweetie. I'll take care of all this." I patted her back once more.

"But the milk!" A panicked look flew across her face as I reached to turn off the breast pump's motor.

"Really, I've got it. I'll check the current stock of breast milk in the fridge, and if there's enough, I'll freeze this batch. Sound like a plan?"

"Yeah, sorry. And thanks." Jackie handed me the parts of the breast pump, taking care, despite her fatigue, to keep every drop of milk within the bottles. She readjusted her pajama top, ran a hand through her matted hair, and hugged me.

"By the way," Jackie mumbled, "Pete and I are sleeping in the basement tonight. It's practically soundproof in there, and with the baby *and* the rain, that's what we need. Silence." She trotted with soft footsteps to the basement stairs. The click of the doorknob rang as she shut out everything behind her.

The large kitchen sink held all the washable parts of the breast pump plus a few random glasses that remained on the counters. The hot water poured into the sink, and the detergent slithered from the bottle; upon contact with the water, the cascade of blue liquid transformed into a layer of foam. An errant bubble escaped from the cluster, rose above the sink, and wound its way past my face before falling against the kitchen window, instantly bursting. "Such fleeting beauty..." The bad habit of talking out loud had worsened with age, reaching gargantuan levels in those moments when I spent time alone.

A slight rustling echoed over the transmitter of the baby monitor. "Before I get started, I'll check on Clara." *And stop talking to myself.* The door to Clara's room stood open about a foot, a space that granted adequate access for viewing the baby. The small room was big enough for a crib, a dresser, a rocking chair, and a tidy changing table. Opposite the door, Clara rested on her mattress, asleep on her back in her thin cotton sleep sack, tiny arms extended above her head.

"Why do babies always sleep like that?" I tiptoed across the room, taking care not to wake her as I placed two gentle fingers against her tiny sternum, satisfied at the rhythmic movement. In the wee morning hours, I often repeated the same action at home with my three kids.

Content she was safe, I exited Clara's room and placed my feet strategically on the floor as I made my way down the hall—creaking floors and babies never went together. Framed pictures hung in the narrow space, and the glass reflected a few twinkles of the dim hall light. Younger versions of Jackie and Pete in wedding garb, laughing at the base of a tree, stared back at me and brought a smile to my face. The couple looked so tender, so in love; nostalgia rushed through me.

A few steps away, Pete had suspended the new family portrait: Clara sat in a basket between her adoring parents, who both gazed at her with wonder and awe. Tears welled in my eyes, and in my haste to walk away, I skimmed my big toe against the small bucket of nails standing at the base of the wall—items Pete had possibly long forgotten. I bent to retrieve the bucket and the hammer, which I'd so deftly avoided, to find their rightful places.

As I walked toward the kitchen, my thoughts focused on the pictures and babies and weddings and love and...

"Dishes, lady. Right now." Yet another round of talking to myself.

"Dishes? I love doing dishes." The deep voice, familiar to my ears, sounded from the foyer. Soon, the man I'd been thinking about too much came around the corner, his laughing brown eyes crinkling at the corners. My heart stuttered.

"We meet again." Grocery Store Man stood before me, dimple flashing.

"For the love of...you're kidding, right? How? What?"

"Something must be in the cards. Perhaps this time I can get your name?"

Right. Third time meeting this guy and still, no names. "That would be nice." *Or I'll keep calling you Grocery Store Man for the rest of my life.*

He pulled himself forward and extended his hand. I passed the bucket of nails and hammer to my left hand and proffered my right toward him.

He paused when our palms met. "Andrew. Andrew MacKinnon." A tickle of warmth made me want to keep my hand against his longer than normal, but that wouldn't be a wise decision.

"Sadie Rollins-Lan...Sadie Rollins. It's nice to meet you, formally I guess." Keeping calm and forcing my face not to erupt into a smile took more energy than I thought, and I hoped my heart didn't burst through my chest.

"Likewise," he said. "Nice jammies, by the way."

The pilled, gray capri sweatpants and tight, pink University of Michigan T-shirt had seemed like the sensible, practical choice when I put them on, but thank goodness I'd worn my standard camisole under my shirt. My breasts, after six collective years of nursing, probably looked saggy without my sweater to shield them. I snorted and chastised myself for my thoughts.

"Actually, you look like you're still in college. Did you go to Michigan?" he said. I reached up to smooth my straggly ponytail and stepped into the kitchen, hoping to disguise any evidence of having been thrown off-kilter. Andrew placed a key on the counter and draped his light coat over the back of a chair. Beads of rain stood out against the fabric of his jacket and threatened to fall to the floor while my heart still thumped against my chest like a set of Charlie's drums.

"Yeah, I went there, but that seems like a lifetime ago now. So much has happened since then..." The sentiment slipped out, and what I had said invited conversation, but I didn't have any plans to reveal anything to this man. This man I kept running into. How did this happen again?

"So, this might come off as rude, but...what are you doing here?" I asked.

A busy mind and body would benefit me, so I deposited the hammer and nails on the desk in the corner of the kitchen and rounded the island. The warm dishwater welcomed my hands when I plunged them in, my back to this stranger.

"Oh, I don't come over too often, but I live two doors down. Small world and all that, right?"

"Right. Well, if you like dishes so much, Andrew, then grab a towel and start drying. I never do dishes with strange men, so it's good we properly introduced ourselves." Without thinking, I winked at him, a gesture that caught me off guard. Did he interpret my action as flirting? *Oh shit.* Was I?

Andrew strode to the drawer that held the towels and joined me at the sink. He took a piece of the breast pump into his hands without blushing and worked the towel around the flange. *This looks like a good man.*

"And Pete and I have worked together for years," he said. "It's obvious these two need a little help. I offered, and Pete took me up on it. But I guess they double-booked. You all right to share?"

One beat of my heart later, I looked at Andrew out of the corner of my eye as he set the pump apparatus on the counter. Did Pete and Jackie double-book? Or did Jackie have something up her sleeve? There was no way she'd have known Andrew was Grocery Store Man, which meant she didn't have a hand in this. That belief hung on with a tenuous grasp as I passed off the next piece of the pump to Andrew.

"Well..."

This man was a stranger. How would it look for the two of us to stay here, together, overnight? A loud clap of thunder exploded overhead, and the beat of the rain increased in its intensity. No, I wasn't going to head out there in the storm. The plan would remain the same.

"It's not a problem, but there isn't much to do. Clara's sleeping, so I'm going to make tea and settle in on the couch. If you'd like to go home, though, go ahead." I tossed the words out carelessly, unsure of how they would land.

"Trying to get rid of me so soon?" Andrew faced me as he spoke. "Nah, I'm in this for the night. Besides, I called in reinforcements."

"Reinforcements?" His wife mustn't have been at home.

"My parents. They live in town but don't get to spend as much time as they'd like over at my place. They were thrilled to stay." He folded the towel and placed it on the counter as I let the water drain. He leaned against the counter, waiting. For what?

Before the silence became uncomfortable, my inner hostess surfaced. "Would you like tea? Or coffee?"

"I'll have coffee, but I don't mind getting it myself, thank you." Andrew moved toward the cabinets holding the mugs and pulled two down, offering one to me. The coffee pot sat on the counter, but he had to rummage around in the pantry to find the filters and the ground coffee. While he did so, I filled my mug with water, popped it into the microwave, and pushed the START button. Moving the bag of sugar aside and fighting the quivering in my hands, I grabbed a tea bag and a spoon and took them, along with a napkin, out to the living room. By the time I made it back to the kitchen, my water had heated, Andrew's coffee had begun to brew, and my nerves had frazzled.

"You sure you don't want any coffee? I made plenty, and it might be a long night." He folded the coffee bag over itself and placed it back into the cabinet before turning to face me again.

The wonderful aroma of Arabica beans permeated the kitchen, but my nerves were already jangled enough. I glanced at my watch: 9:37 p.m. Andrew might be right about a long night.

"Thanks for the offer. Maybe in a little while. The tea will be perfect for me right now." Desperate for comfort, I clutched the mug between my fingers.

"All right. I'll join you in a few." He flashed a smile and turned to open the refrigerator. My legs trembled like a nervous schoolgirl's as I walked away from the kitchen.

• • • • •

The faint light of Jackie's living room reminded me of my favorite room, which played a huge part in my life. I sat there every evening, book in hand. Theo and I had brought each of the kids home to that living room, where we'd put up a pack-n-play and a temporary changing table. It was the room in which Theo first shared he had PTSD, both of us clutching each other's hand as we leaned toward one another.

"Penny for your thoughts?" Andrew placed a coaster on the coffee table and set his mug upon it. He folded himself onto the chair next to the sofa, which left a space of several feet between us. Grateful for the room, I sipped from my mug, more at peace than I had been in the last few minutes.

"My thoughts would bore you." The drama my life had become might scare the poor guy away and make my life easier, but instead of speaking, I lifted myself from the couch and connected my phone to Jackie's Bluetooth speaker, finding my favorite pop station and setting the volume to low. The music's beat would help reel in my cartwheeling emotions while the two of us chatted.

"I doubt it. We're both parents and could swap a few outlandish stories, I'm sure. Some of the things my kids have done, well, those stories are almost begging to be shared." He laughed out loud, probably at one of those precious memories, and each time he smiled, his dimples seemed to deepen. He cleared his throat as I sat back against the couch again, gripping my mug. "Well, if we're gonna sit here all night, and we don't have a baby to distract us right now, I'll go ahead and tell you a bit about myself if you don't mind."

His no-nonsense approach amused me. I sipped my tea and peeked at him over the edge of my cup.

"So here it goes...let's see...Andrew MacKinnon."

I know this already.

"Lifelong Bloom Market shopper..."

Boring.

"Not allergic to pop music..."

But has a sense of humor.

I smiled in acknowledgment, then looked around the room as he spoke. How long would it be until the room showed hints of a new baby? The single change in the Mills' front room was the hot pink bouncy chair tucked into the corner.

"And friend of Pete Mills..."

Normal, good guy.

"Coffee drinker, any time of the day or night."

Nothing to see here, ladies.

"Love my work and my dog, but I can't live without my kids."

Oh no...

We stared at one another. *Don't say anything else,* I willed him. *Don't say anything else to draw me in.*

"And I'm divorced."

Crap. Crap. Crappity-crap-crap.

Chapter 6: Theo

Staying home alone with my kids on a night when Sadie went out wasn't a luxury I was afforded. It had taken one mistake for Sadie to put her foot down and make her new rule. "When I go out for long periods of time, we either call Brooke to come over, or you all go with me."

The night the rule went into place still haunted me. Charlie's wide eyes, Delia's quivering lips. My shaking hands. When the kids had ripped through the house playing chase, they tore past the coffee table in the living room, causing a pile of books to fall, one after the other. In my world, the books became mortar shells, and the noises turned into the thud of shells landing. To this day, the details of what had happened were blurry, but images still flashed at times: scattered pages, hunched shoulders, frantic movements. And knowing my behavior scared the kids? Shame filled me. Maybe even regret.

But it was hard to come to terms with the idea the mother of your children didn't trust you to keep them safe. Brooke might be a wonderful babysitter—the kids loved her, and frankly, no one better existed—but having someone in my home on a night when I wanted to be with the kids? Difficult. No other word for it.

After dinner, we all helped clean the dishes and the counters and then made our way into the living room. Lexie toddled to her play space and brought out the ocean floor puzzle. Charlie and Delia knew the drill: no television until after Lexie went to bed, so they each got behind that puzzle with an uncharacteristic enthusiasm.

"What about building something?" Charlie asked Lexie as she slipped the last piece of the puzzle into place. In his world, not a day went by he didn't craft something, and he had spoken before about his goal to turn Lexie into the "second best builder in the house."

"I'm game if everyone else is," I said.

"And I'll go check to see if any clothes need folding," Brooke said. "It's the least we can do for your mom."

All three kids knew better than to groan at Brooke's announcement.

Once all clothes had been folded and put away, tickles had been doled out, and buildings had been constructed, Delia glanced at the clock, then at Lexie, then up at me with a smile. "Popcorn?" she said.

Her way of reminding me it would soon be movie time made me laugh. Six months ago, making popcorn wasn't on the list of things easily accomplished. The heat of the air popper and the noise of the popping kernels; everything had been too much at first. But the machine's concreteness—something tangible in front me, touch it if I had to—helped. My mind could be convinced danger didn't exist.

"Extra butter?" I called out to the kids, already knowing their answer.

A quick "Yes, please!" from Delia followed an "Of course!" from Charlie. Sadie allowed extra butter on the weekends—her attempt to stave off clogged arteries and high cholesterol—but even if it hadn't been a weekend, I'd have given in. Too much time spent in hell meant I'd take as much goodness as possible. Goodness might push back against the tension that mounted on some days. Today happened to be one of them. Maybe it *was* appropriate Brooke was here.

I grabbed drinks for the kids, a puffed corn snack for Lexie, and another favorite game, Spot It, and I went back to the living room, serving tray piled high. Charlie and Delia were deep in conversation about something while Lexie spun in a circle. The hushed tones of the kids whispering tunneled into my ears, making me pause, and I stood there, questioning myself and my abilities. *Breathe in, breathe out.* One, two, three.

The whispering turned to chittering, and a clamor inside my chest grew. The tray began to shake, drops of grape juice sloshed over the sides of the cups, and a napkin fell to the floor.

"Theo? Theo? You okay?" Brooke took the tray and set it on the table, then put her hand gently on my wrist. Months before, we'd determined a light touch to my wrist pulled me out of wherever I was. "Take a few deep breaths, okay?" she said and guided me to the chair.

The pounding in my chest subsided, but a ticking in my head took its place. "I'm okay. Sorry about that."

"It's no trouble. Why don't you sit here with Charlie and Delia while I put Lexie to bed? Is that okay?"

"Yes, but let me hold her just a minute, please?" I opened my arms, the universal sign for "give me a hug," and Lexie jumped up on my lap and burrowed her head into my chest as she snuggled against me. Putting her to bed would be my first choice. "Do you think I—"

Brooke held up her hand, palm facing me. "Theo, I'd like to say yes, but I'm going to say no. It's hard to say that to you. But I'm here to help *all* of you. And right now, if you stay out here and relax, that's the best thing for everyone." She checked her watch. "Take all the time you need with her. Okay?"

I leaned forward, kissing the top of Lexie's head before she looked up at me and blinked. "Song?"

I'd never been much of a singer, but with Lexie, it hadn't mattered. A minute into "The Frim-Fram Sauce," and she'd burrowed in so tightly, it took convincing on my part to get her to go to bed once we'd finished. "Honey, I'll carry you to your room, but Brooke needs to put you to bed tonight."

Lexie smiled around the thumb in her mouth and nodded her head. When we reached her room, she flung herself against her small mattress and waved at me. "Night!"

I closed the bedroom door, the ticking keeping time in my head much like a metronome, and then stopped in my room to grab my favorite sweatshirt. Sometimes warming up helped temper the anxiety, but the chair where I'd put the clothing stood empty.

"Charlie, Delia. Where is my sweatshirt?" I asked as I moved through the living room.

"Check the office. And can you hurry? We want to watch a movie!"

"Yes, I'll hurry. But go ahead and set things up. I'll be right there."

And I would have been right there, had a certain slip of paper peeking out of a file folder on Sadie's desk not distracted me. That paper. A letter from me.

The movie's opening credits sounded as I unfolded the paper and turned it over in my hands. Fifteen years ago, life had been so different. So good.

My hands shook as I read the letter, my eyes unable to stay on one word for too long. *Forever. Filled. Home. Immeasurable. Longing. Beauty. Sleep. Image.* And then: *Without you, I can't cope.*

Fuck. A sinkhole formed in my chest and tremors coursed through my legs. It took all my energy to put the letter back where it belonged before emotions pulled me under, forcing me to fall onto the couch. My thoughts ricocheted. Sadie had kept the letter, maybe all the letters I'd written. I'd written those letters in the first place. We were so far from there now. What did it all mean? And the kids. They waited for me, the movie waited for me...

Fear and panic would ensue if I thought about the letter anymore, so I walked back to the kids and tried to watch the movie, fists balled at my sides, my jaw clenched. The time couldn't pass fast enough. Soon, after I'd put Delia to bed with a sloppy kiss to the forehead, I paced while Charlie watched *The Princess Bride* and Brooke watched me, eyebrows raised.

"You okay, Dad?" Charlie asked for at least the fifth time.

"Yeah. I'm just tired."

Fatigue didn't explain the treads I'd worn in the carpet or the hole I'd picked into my jeans. *That damn letter.*

"Brooke, I can get Charlie to bed. It's no trouble. You can head back."

She raised her eyebrows again and narrowed her eyes. "I'm staying, Theo."

"Ah, that's right. Well then, head to bed. Will you be here in the morning?"

"I'll likely leave pretty early, if that's all right with you."

"You know it. And really, I've got this."

"I trust you." Brooke reached over and smoothed Charlie's hair against his head. "Goodnight, kiddo. Goodnight, Theo."

Charlie and I sat for an hour more before I bundled him off to bed, hoping against hope my anxiety would begin to subside.

●　　●　　●　　●　　●

The night vision goggles did nothing to help my view. Out there, in the complete blackness, they lurked: Faces. Eyes. Limbs. Landmines. Everywhere. To the right, to the left, in front, and behind. Flashes of light blinked on and off to my right side, but when I turned my head in that direction, they'd vanished. The flashes picked up to the left, and in anger, I threw my hand out, hoping to hit at least a few, but again, they slipped through my fingers. A blast sounded— one, two, three—with each new step I took, the dust and dirt from the ground flew into the atmosphere, clogging my nose, my lungs. I pulled off my goggles with one hand while trying to hold the gun with the other. A bang thundered against a metal wall, and the blood whooshed through my body. Beat, beat, beat. My heart bumped inside my chest and threatened to detonate.

The steady thrum echoed in my ears. The skin covering my sternum expanded, stretching around the heart as it emerged. Whoosh...whoosh...whoosh. Getting slower, and slower, and...a bell rang—

I woke with a parched mouth and sweat clinging to my brow. For the past several months, my sleep had not been restorative. My dreams had been laced with odd flashes of my past life intertwined with my current life: I'd used night vision goggles in the military, and the prior week, I'd visited the optometrist where my peripheral vision had been tested with flashing lights. Almost all my dreams involved a gun. Me holding it. Me using it to shoot someone. No dreams about me turning it on myself, but it was a matter of time. These dreams scared the shit out of me, but I'd not told Doc about their increase in frequency, the subjects of them, or even the fact I had them. She had to suspect something was off; she told me to "reduce the stress you're carrying around" more than once.

I moved into the bathroom to wash my face, thinking of the stress I'd been carrying. Of course, home life being as it was didn't help much. Sadie had been so busy, almost too busy, like she'd been trying to avoid something—me? And while we still did things as a family—trips to get ice cream or on rainy days the bowling alley—the summer had passed without our annual trip to Walloon Lake.

"Do you think that's the best idea?" Sadie had said when I brought the subject up a few days before. "The kids are so confused about our relationship, and Charlie is enjoying camp. I'm not even sure where you stand, and I'm swamped at work. Honestly, it's all too much. Plus, it would be a bigger drain on the finances. I can't even dream of a vacation right now."

Going by myself had only been a slight possibility—Sadie had been adamant about not letting me drive alone. So instead of Walloon Lake, I spent more time at the gym: lifting weights, running on the treadmill, trying all the equipment I used to loathe. Thinking about all that now, it was clear the one thing keeping me grounded was my job. The routine, the people, even the grind. A few weeks earlier, I'd articulated that thought aloud.

"It's good to be needed somewhere," I said to my coworker one morning, just after I'd logged into the system. The coworker, a college student with too much on her plate, scrunched up her face at my statement.

"Yeah. You don't get it. Someday, you might."

"I believe you. In the meantime, here comes the rush." She smiled and fiddled with the lanyard around her neck, ready for the onslaught of morning questions that always came our way. She hadn't heard much about my past and neither did the rest of my coworkers, and they respected my boundaries. Everyone was too busy with their own lives to care about anyone else's.

A creak behind me brought me back to the present, but it was only the house settling into the night. As I turned out the bathroom light, my mind roamed to my job again, to all the people I saw daily, those patrons who had wheedled their way into my life one exercise session at a time. The mom with the twins who came in every Tuesday and Thursday for her hot yoga class always stopped at the desk with a cheery hello. The elderly gentleman who walked the track for an hour each morning had a quick wink for me. One of the aquatics students often placed a piece of chocolate on my keyboard before I got in. And Andrew MacKinnon, the man I'd chatted with about the Browns and beer, liked to stop and ask once a week, "Want to work on web development?"

The first time he asked back in July I'd said, "No." But each week after, I'd listened a bit longer to what he had to say. And soon, we'd chatted about his project needs, met for coffee, and lifted weights together.

In one of our sessions, Doc asked, "Would you call him a friend?"

"Sure. He reminds me of my college roommate, a lot." Liam had seen me through four years of college before shipping off for his tour of duty, and he'd managed to live eight years before having been blown to bits. Andrew's humor—snarky but rarely disrespectful—echoed Liam's.

"Then I'm glad you're spending time with him. If you're going to go through with this divorce, you need a support system. Sadie can't, and won't, serve as support if you're no longer married."

"But I—"

"But nothing. You two get along, yes, but is it fair of you to ask her for something she shouldn't have to give?"

That comment stuck with me every day as summer marched on, as the kids went back to school, as tension came and went in my spine, as the crackle of firecrackers reminded me of bullets, as Sadie and I still managed to exist separately, yet slightly together, as I watched her move on with her life, including friends and the kids. The comment hit me again as I moved into the office, back to the letter I'd found. I pushed it into the envelope and then under a stack of papers. The same divorce papers she'd asked me to sign, again, the day before. Why hadn't I? What was I holding on to?

Chapter 7: Sadie

Andrew was divorced. *Of course he was.*

"I'm so sorry," I said to Andrew. "I'm sorry about the divorce." What other words were there? *You're a fine-looking man, Andrew. You'll find someone, if that's what you want. And by the way, let me tell you the effect you have on me.* None of those statements were quite appropriate to say as we sat in the dark waiting for Clara to wake.

But in the split second before he expected my answer, a bubble of recognition emerged at the surface of my mind. Andrew represented a taste of something I didn't possess: *freedom.* The freedom to pursue what he wanted, when he wanted it, anywhere he wanted it. He didn't have to sit and watch a former love fall apart, nor did he have to witness three lovely children deal with the drawn-out drama of their father's and mother's failures. The stress of my life brought tears to my eyes. I wanted to be *free* too. Of my obligations, my job, my kids, my situation. Free of my life. My napkin served a wonderful purpose—to blot at my tears under the weak lighting that hopefully shielded my emotions.

Andrew waved his hand, as if trying to push away the past, and took a sip of his coffee. "Thanks. The thing is, and yes, I realize how unimaginative this sounds, we got married too fast. My ex and I harbor no ill-will and try to keep everything running smoothly for the kids. The little guy will be starting second grade. And he's at an age where he's noticing *everything*, especially when it comes to his mom and dad." Andrew placed his mug on the end table. "His vulnerability reminds me every day to keep the relationship with my ex-wife as amicable as possible."

The man had his head on the right way. The more I learned about him, the worse off I'd be.

"Did it get bad at all?" Theo and I hadn't legally parted ways yet, and with him still living in the house, the burden of divorce was still an unknown to me. What if Theo and I did divorce? What would our lives be like then?

"Thank goodness, no. Both of us had the wisdom to see we'd grown apart. While we tried to figure out a way to make it work, it just wasn't going to happen. We agreed divorce was the right option for us." His movements—leaning forward to place his napkin on the coffee table and then settling back against the couch cushions—stirred the air, bringing with it the clean scent of laundry detergent.

The music crooned in the background, and my thoughts roamed to my situation. What would Andrew say if he knew about my life? A woman living with a man she used to love. Some might say I was an enabler, but Theo needed help and was seeking it out with therapy. Our situation served as a bandage of sorts.

"Heavy stuff here, Andrew, and I just met you." A few stray tears clouded my vision, and I blinked them away, ever grateful for Pete and Jackie's lighting.

"Well, technically this is the third time we've met, so it's okay." His heart-stopping smile beamed across the room, setting my discomfort on edge.

A cry came over the monitor and both of us froze, looking at each other in surprise.

"Let's wait and see what happens," I whispered.

"But we don't want her to wake Pete and Jackie up."

"True, but they're sleeping downstairs anyway, so let's give her a minute. Sometimes, they go back to sleep—"

A burst of crying blared over the monitor, and I clutched my hand to my chest. It had been so long since I'd heard wailing like that.

"And sometimes, they don't." Andrew flew from the chair. "I'll get the baby, and you get the milk."

Thank goodness I'd had the foresight to keep a bottle standing on the counter because a quick rinse under the hot tap water had the milk ready when Andrew walked into the kitchen. Still fumbling with the kitchen towel, I started at the sight of such a large man with a petite baby in his arms. Clara looked snug and cozy, protected within the confines of Andrew's embrace. Her tiny mouth, however, hung wide open.

"Shh, shh, shh," I said and handed Andrew the bottle. "Do you mind trying first?"

"Not at all. Let's go back to the living room so the noise doesn't carry as easily." A stack of diapers on the counter caught my eye, and I grabbed a few, along with a burp cloth, and followed Andrew to the living room, where he sat on the sofa this time.

"Go ahead and get settled in, and if you need something..." I handed him the burp cloth. With ease, he positioned the still-crying Clara into the crook of his left arm, placed the burp cloth under her delicate chin, and popped the bottle into her mouth. She took three sucks with her tiny mouth and spit the bottle out.

"Uh-oh. This does not bode well," he said and looked up at me with trepidation in his eyes.

"Let's be positive. Go ahead and try again." Hoping for the best but expecting the worst, I held my breath and scrunched up my shoulders, ready to fall to my knees and ask the universe to help us. Clara's heart-wrenching cries went right through me. "What about a walk?" I said and moved toward the foyer to get my flip-flops. Andrew had gotten up off the couch and was standing with his feet wide, rocking the baby back and forth. She hiccupped but seemed to be settling. "Or maybe not. Which is a good thing because I forgot about the rain."

"Will I have to stand like this all night?" A certain fear suffused his face.

"Can you? Just kidding. Let's hope not. Do they have a swing? We used to prop up the kids' heads if we needed to use the swing before they were old enough to do so. Let me go check."

Trying to be as quiet as possible, I surveyed the living room, then peeked into the foyer closet and made my way to Clara's room, but there was no swing in sight. By the time I made it back to Andrew, Clara was fast asleep in his arms, and he'd managed to sit. He leaned over the baby's hair and took a gentle sniff.

"There's something about the smell of babies, isn't there?" I said.

A huge smile spread across his face as he nodded, stopping me in my tracks.

The faint lyrics to "I Want You to Want Me" streamed out of the speaker as Andrew sat there, a picture of complete contentment. Shit. My soul couldn't take much more of this. My heart felt like a lead weight in my chest.

Had I any common sense, I would have simply braved the rain and left. Or, I would have told Andrew I felt a virus coming on or any number of things that would let me escape and get away from him and my attraction. At that point, an artificial excuse should have been so easy to produce. Instead, in a strategic attempt to keep the conversation away from me and my life, I settled into the chair and suggested we should get a little sleep.

"I'm not sure if I can sleep while I'm holding someone else's baby. What if I drop her? Pete and Jackie would kill me." Concern flared in Andrew's eyes, and I laughed.

"Really? You have two kids. You're afraid you'll drop her?" I swallowed my laughter.

"Uh, yeah. I might look big and strong, but inside, I'm a tender lamb. I can't stand hurting anyone." He lifted a large hand to the top of Clara's head and smoothed the fuzz she passed off as hair.

An afghan off the side of the couch would be enough to prop his arm, so I stuffed it under his elbow, making sure his arm was sturdy, then tossed a few large pillows on the ground in front of the sofa, in the event the sweet little bundle rolled.

"There," I said, "that should do it. I doubt you'll drop her."

"I don't know, Sadie. I should stay awake. Anyway, while she's quiet, why don't you take a nap? I'll wake you when I need you."

"Are you sure?"

Andrew had given me a pathway out of the conversation, and there I was, not taking it. I held my breath.

"Yes."

I released the air I was holding in. "Thanks. I'm not a deep sleeper though. I'll hear you if you need something."

"All right then. Sweet dreams, Sadie."

• • • • •

Sleep claimed me, and the talk about family sent me back in time, to a younger Theo and me. The summer we met, I had just turned nineteen and had been spending my time babysitting and doing laundry for a local couple, putting money away for my second year of college. In the evenings, I'd sneak off to the outdoor sand volleyball court. Many of those hours were spent vying against the tall guy with the messy hair. He was loud—truly obnoxious at times—but he possessed a wicked serve I came to appreciate.

One sultry night I rode my bike to the courts, expecting a leisurely ride home after an invigorating game. But after the game, my bike's tire was flat. The walk home would be long.

"Hey, looks like you have a flat there." Messy Hair Guy had snuck up behind me. "I live right over the bridge, *and* I have a repair kit. Do you want help?"

Spatters of green threaded throughout his brown irises. He smelled of sweat and grass and spearmint, and the crooked smile he gave as he pulled his hand through his mussed hair tugged a little on my heart, surprising me.

"I guess help would be nice," I admitted, hesitancy feathering my voice.

"The name is Theo. There, now you have my name. I promise, I'm not a madman." His bright white teeth sparkled under the parking lot lights as he held out his hand.

I laughed as we connected. He'd read my mind. "I'm Sadie," I said with a quick handshake. "And thanks."

That evening, after removing the nail from my tire and repairing the tire's rubber, we sat on the front porch of his rental home, ice water in hand, talking into the early hours of the morning.

He told me about his home life as a child, riddled with strife and worry, as his father battled severe depression. He spoke of the issue as one would talk about a black sheep cousin: someone who showed up from out of the blue and caused trouble, and when you'd gotten used to the behavior and hoped for a reprieve, came back with a vengeance. His mother was all alone, after the death of his father a few years before from a self-inflicted gunshot wound. Theo had plans to work with computers but sometimes wished he had an interest in medicine. He wanted to find a better treatment for the illness that had wrecked his family.

"I'd like to make someone else's life a little better than mine." He sat that night with a far-off look on his face, condensation from the glass of water dripping over his fingers and his arm, hitting the wood floor of the porch with a soft plink. His face, lit in the reflective moonlight, transformed as a certain resolve snuck into his deep, hazel eyes. I'd only spent a few hours with him, but if anyone could shed a better light on severe depression, it would be Theo.

"But what about you?" Theo asked once he shook off his reverie. "And by the way, would you like more water? I'm sorry I don't have anything else."

"That's okay," I said. "Water is perfect. Although if we stay up any later, we'll need to have some coffee." My watch read 3:43 a.m. Where had the time gone? "And what would you like to know?"

"Anything. What brought you here? To school, I mean. What do you want to do with your life? And how do you manage to make an underhand serve so demonic?"

I laughed out loud. "That serve is embarrassing. I never had the strength as a kid to get an overhand serve over the net, so I perfected the art of the underhand serve. It isn't that lethal. It's just disarming."

"Interesting choice of words, Sadie. The same word applies to you." The ice clinked in his glass as he glanced my way. The heat of embarrassment washed over me, and I was thankful for the darkness that still lingered even underneath the light of the porch lamp. Did he mean what I thought he meant? Theo must have sensed my discomfort, for he looked away and moved his legs out in front of him. The muscles of his thighs rippled in the moonlight, making me think it was completely understandable how well this guy jumped on the volleyball court; he had legs of pliant steel.

"I'm here to study I haven't decided what yet. I thought economics would be a good idea, but that's a major my parents thought would be good. I don't say this to many people, but what I'd like to be is a writer."

"Why don't you say it?"

"Because most people would say I won't be able to support myself. As if a writer is grouped into the starving artist category. Which I guess it is. But then, I have this penchant for science too. I might try to combine the two." I shook my head. "I'm only nineteen. I have time, don't I?"

"Yes, you do. I wish my dad had had the time."

This guy was still hurting. What to do? Despite my inexperience with boys and a heartbeat that thumped as I moved my hand, I curled my fingers over his and squeezed gently. My gesture was meant to say the impossible. That even though I didn't know this boy sitting next to me, I understood the pain of losing someone; I'd experienced the same with the passing of my beloved grandmother. Difficult, but with time, he'd achieve peace, although he'd never forget.

"I guess I should go." I moved my hand away from his. "First, a nap and then I need to get myself over to work for a few hours. Thanks for everything. It was great to meet you." I placed my glass on the small outdoor table.

"I can't let you go by yourself. Let me get my bike, and I'll ride home with you."

On the way back to my apartment, the cool summer air rushed through my hair and against my flushed face. I felt light, happy, and cleansed. Despite my fatigue, an unusual energy thrummed throughout my body. Theo and I didn't say anything until we pulled up next to each other in the driveway of my apartment.

"Thanks again, Theo. Be careful on your way back, okay?" The early birds had begun to tweet in the damp darkness. On other days, the noise annoyed me, but at that moment, their song gratified me.

"I will. You have a nice nap."

A moment of silence stretched between us as we gazed at one another. I started to dismount my bike, but Theo leaned in, the delicious smell of summer and grass and sweat and boy preceding him. He placed a gentle and brief kiss across my surprised yet waiting lips.

"Sweet dreams, Sadie."

• • • • •

The sound of Velcro startled me, and I turned my head toward Andrew, who knelt on the ground, fastening a new diaper onto Clara.

"Do you need help? Why didn't you wake me?" I blinked away the sleepy grit that had accumulated underneath my eyelids and rolled my shoulder blades. My body had acclimated to the length of the couch, but its small size had affected me.

"Oh, take my word for it. If this had been a huge delivery, I would *not* have hesitated." The corners of Andrew's eyes crinkled unexpectedly. Was this man always so happy?

"Okay. Well, now that I'm up, what can I do?"

"Would you believe she took the whole bottle? Right after you fell asleep, she fussed for a minute, and I slipped the bottle in, just at the right moment, I guess. She drank the entire six ounces and, well, this happened." He'd finished putting Clara's clothes back together and held the dirty diaper in his hand. "Mind keeping an eye on her while I go wash up?"

"Not at all. How long did I sleep?" I crouched on the floor next to the baby.

"About an hour. How do you feel?"

What words would suffice? I dreamed about Theo, a former version of him, and my spirit had plummeted further than I thought possible. But Andrew didn't need to know any of that. Andrew didn't need to know anything.

Chapter 8: Theo

The morning after I found that love letter, I sat in the dining room with a proposal Andrew had asked me to look at. When Sadie shuffled into the kitchen through the door from the garage, I glanced up. The fatigued look on her face meant her night with the baby might have been on the long side. Her view didn't include me: the angle of my chair in the dining room compared to where she stood in the kitchen kept me out of her gaze. On the periphery seemed to be my preference these days.

Charlie sat hunched at the breakfast bar. He held a book in one hand and a spoon in the other as he ate cereal. We'd skipped Saturday morning waffles for the first time in a long time: patience and I didn't always make nice. A drop of milk spilled from the spoon and landed back in that favorite glass bowl of his as he flipped the pages of the book.

"Hey, Mom," Charlie said, without looking up. "How's Clara?"

"She's good, honey. She's good." Sadie hung her sweater on the metal hook next to the door and pushed off her flip-flops. Had she eaten breakfast? Should I get up and help her? She hadn't seen me yet but eavesdropping never led to anything good. Everyone knew that.

"She's not a miserable vomitous mass?" A slight smirk crossed Charlie's face and humor danced in his eyes." Oh, shit. Leave it to the kid to out me. I rose from the chair and moved to the doorway between the dining room and the kitchen. I'd have to defend myself.

"All right, wise guy. Who's been letting you watch that movie?" Sadie's tone held me back from revealing myself. "As much as I adore it, it's not appropriate for you kids. Your father should—"

"It's okay, Mom. We didn't let Delia or Lexie watch it. It was just me and Dad sitting on the bean bags, eating popcorn. He had a rough night. He seemed more tired than he has been."

Rough night? Is that what Charlie called it? The angst. The pacing. I'd done a good enough job hiding them from him. But it seemed like no matter what I did these days—more exercise, less screen time, more meditation, meds—none of it helped the symptoms. My skin still felt too small and the tiniest of agitations triggered me. Of course, that damn letter and divorce papers didn't help.

My problem wasn't realizing I had a problem it was—

The crash of a bowl against the wood floor sounded, and I peeked my head around the corner. Charlie stood frozen, wide-eyed, and shaken, surrounded by the remnants of his favorite bowl. How had that happened?

"That's, that's..."

"Shh, sweetie. It's your favorite bowl. But it was an accident." Sadie took two steps toward the pantry and pulled the broom and dustpan from their respective hooks. She'd need to sweep up the large chunks of glass first and then press duct tape against the floor and vacuum to get the finer pieces. It was a routine she rarely remembered, but it worked the best. "Don't move, not yet," she said to Charlie. "Let me get those large shards of glass before anyone else comes in the room."

"No, Mom. You can't." Charlie reached and began to place glass chunks into his shirt, which he'd fashioned into a makeshift bag. "I need to get what I can. I have some glue. I can glue these back together." His voice shook, and tears tumbled down his ruddy cheeks. Still, I stood and said nothing to alert them to my presence.

Sadie touched Charlie's forearm and moved the broom to her shoulder. "Honey. You loved this bowl, *really* loved this bowl, but it won't be safe, and gluing it isn't the best idea. We need to get rid of the pieces. Charlie, I promise I'll get you a new bowl."

"No." More tears dropped onto his cheeks, and he hugged his full shirt to his chest, turning away from my view. "You can't get me a new bowl. This bowl came from Dad...I use it every morning...it's...it's..."

"Sweetie, please, you have to throw the pieces away."

"No, Mom, I need them. I *need* him."

Shit. My hands shook as my son collapsed against the breakfast bar. I'd given Charlie the beloved bowl when life was still good, whole. Even in my fucked-up state I knew the bowl represented everything kind and healthy about me. About our family. And breaking that bowl...Charlie clutched the bulge of glass pieces closer to his body, making it possible he might cut himself. An itch rose within me: getting my son out of the dangerous position of holding sharp glass moved to the front of my brain. But with patient movements, Sadie reached out to Charlie, lifting him up and placing her hands against the full shirt.

"There's no point in holding onto those pieces, Charlie. They're broken." Finality laced her voice as she pried the pieces from Charlie, who stood there in a daze. A certain guilt overcame me: for listening in on a conversation that wasn't meant for me to hear, for lurking in the other room when I should have announced my presence. But then: anger. At Sadie's words, at her inability to see what Charlie needed, at her in general. *That glass.* Sharp, razor-edged. She should have taken those damn glass pieces from Charlie right from the start. And those words...

Breathe in, breathe out. One, two, three. He hadn't gotten hurt. At least not physically.

Still hanging back, I said nothing. Sadie swept up the remaining glass fragments and put them in a grocery bag, then headed to the utility room, probably to grab the vacuum. Apparently, my method *had* gotten through to her. I moved into the kitchen, waiting with folded arms over my chest. Sadie opened her eyes wide when she came back into the room, duct tape in one hand, vacuum in the other.

"I heard what you said." My low voice barely rang in the air. "About the pieces of the bowl. Is that how you view me? Is there no point to holding on to me?"

Sadie had an answer for everything. This time, there was no point in sticking around to find out what the answer might be.

Chapter 9: Sadie

"Bless me, Father, for I have sinned."

The smell of the leather chair in Kate's office hit my nose as I slid onto it. Kate wasn't my therapist, but she was *a* therapist, and one who kept Saturday hours. I'd called her after having been made frantic by Theo's words, which had rankled me to my deepest emotion. It had been a long time since I'd stepped foot into a confessional, but Kate would appreciate my humor.

"Too funny, my friend, too funny. I'm glad you came in. You sounded so frazzled over the phone." Her kind voice sent a calming presence throughout my body.

"It's good to see you too..." A slight uneasiness settled into me. Only the air-conditioning whirred in the silence stretching between us.

"Well. How long has it been since your last confession?" Kate winked.

"Too long. Can we leave it at that?"

"Sure can. And clearly, I'm not suited for that job. Now what can I do for you? What *happened?*"

The chair's leather back embraced my body, lending me confidence. "Theo said something that got to me. After a small accident—Charlie's favorite bowl broke, and I got a bit upset—I convinced Theo I was throwing him away, throwing our relationship away. And based on everything that's happened in the last couple of months, I'm...I never thought I'd be one of these people." I contorted my fingers on my lap, resisting the urge to haul my body out of Kate's office and run all the way home. That wouldn't solve a thing.

"One of what people, hon?"

A silent shiver traveled along my spine at the addition of the endearment. Kate would be able to understand me, but would I understand myself? "The type who seems to invite drama. The type to be having impure thoughts."

"Impure?"

The tone of her voice was a good sign she'd taken me seriously, and I pulled in a deep breath, filling my lungs with the cool, cleansing air. "I haven't acted upon them. But..."

At least a few moments went by before Kate spoke again. "Ah, this must be about Grocery Store Man, right?"

"Yes."

"And why is he a problem?"

"Well, for one, I'm contemplating having an affair." I gasped. "Did I just say that?"

This time, Kate's laughter reverberated against the office walls. "Yes, you did, and it isn't the first time I've heard someone use those words, so don't be embarrassed. We're all human. Please understand I'm not laughing at you. But the look of shock on your face..."

"Oh no worries. At all." I shook my head, unable to go on.

Kate leaned closer. "Do I need to remind you that you and Theo aren't a thing anymore? If you're interested in this new guy, is it time to follow that interest?"

"I've thought of that—not being with Theo but being with Theo. But if I give in to the rush and pursue this guy, everything might change. Guilt would do me in."

"Why guilt? I'm not sure your thoughts are as impure as you think. They seem normal to me."

"Normal." I sighed. "That's such a relative term, isn't it?" My life hadn't been normal for some time, or at least it felt like it hadn't. What it needed was a change, but—

"And what do you mean by 'change everything'?" Kate asked.

"My life. The kids' lives. Theo's life for sure. Would he try to take the kids away from me? How would he handle the PTSD and the kids, by himself, in a house alone? I can't leave him alone with the kids anyway. And I—"

Kate held up her hands. "Whoa. Slow down. You're getting way ahead of yourself here, aren't you?"

"Maybe?"

"No maybes about it. Listen. You like this guy. You're not married to Theo—"

"I'm not divorced from him yet either—" Theo still hadn't signed the papers.

"But you *want* to be, divorced from him I mean. That's the most important thing to remember. And you have *plans* to be divorced; you're allowing Theo to progress at his own pace. So, explore the situation, get to know this guy a little. If things go well, you worry about the future then."

Kate had the knack for being sensible and often allowed me to see the things hiding behind my clouds of judgment. But something still seemed not right. "What about Theo?"

"What about Theo? I'm sorry, Sadie. You're my friend, and I'm on your side more than I am his." Kate gripped her fingers against mine and held on tight. "Yes, I want to see him recover fully. Yes, I want to see him whole and lead a productive life. But I want to see *you* happy too. And these last few years—you haven't been happy. That's partly why you both decided on the divorce in the first place."

"You're not telling me anything I'm not aware of. It's just..."

"It's what?"

"Change is hard. Even considering divorce took so much of my time and energy, took so much life out of me. I'm not sure how much I have left. To give myself or to give anyone else."

Kate's face softened. "Honey, I understand—you still care for Theo and his well-being. He's still, in many ways, the man you married. But he can't—or doesn't want to—get the help he needs to come back to you. Is that what you're waiting for?"

Another good point. Was I holding out hope Theo would come back? Is that why I had agreed to our living situation?

Kate didn't wait for me to answer, just shook my hands once against my lap. "Here's the thing you need to remember. Life doesn't always go as planned, right? You know this *all* too well. But also—when we think life is going along as we want it to, it's because we've manipulated the situation, whether we recognize it or not.

"Placed in the 10K race? I bet you trained for it. Got the promotion? Didn't you put in twelve-hour days for weeks? You force the hand, so to speak. Stop thinking of Theo or the family or anyone else who might play a role in your life right now and rewrite the stars, Sadie. What is good for *you*? You can shape that narrative, as you book editors like to say." Kate let go of my hands and leaned back in her chair, a soft, kind smile filling her face.

A snort escaped from my body. "Are you kidding? It's not that simple!"

"Yeah, I might be a little bit optimistic, but you love me." With a quick wink and a smirk, Kate patted my hand.

Before I left Kate's office, she suggested sitting and having a heart-to-heart conversation with Theo. "It will be tough," she said, "But I'm speaking as your friend and as a therapist, and it would be the best thing to do."

She was right: going through with the divorce would effectively "throw him away," at least in his eyes, so a conversation was the least I owed Theo. But on the way home from Kate's office, the idea I'd failed my son with respect to his bowl came crashing down on me. Of course he wanted to hold on to it, to hold onto his father. It wasn't just *any* bowl, but I'd treated it as such. Who should I go to first: Theo or Charlie?

The traffic light switched to green, and my mind accelerated with the car. I might be able to fix the bowl—find an epoxy or something to glue the pieces together. Charlie couldn't eat from it then, but he'd be able to use it for something. *Fix bowl* landed at the top of my mental to-do list as I opened the door to our house.

Theo was nowhere to be seen but wouldn't have gone far. He rarely pushed back against my preference for "no driving alone," and his car was in the garage; I exhaled a large, relieved breath. Like it or not, Theo would have to wait and so would any discussion of my prior "bad parenting" moment. I would fashion a good excuse for my unacceptable behavior during my slight reprieve. Before I asked where Theo was, Charlie barreled toward me.

"Mom! I have that camp project to work on, and I want to be able to show the leader what I'm doing sometime this week. Can you help?" Concern flooded Charlie's eyes as he handed me Lexie's sippy cup, covered with stuck-on cereal bits and melted cheese. I worked to pry off the cheese, but there was no hope, so I tossed the cup into the sink for washing later.

"Yes, the project. I guess Dad can't help with it, can he?" The habit of passing off work to Theo wasn't something I engaged in, but if he handled part of the task, then I could prepare lunch for the five of us—a job Theo wouldn't try to take on since some activities took too much patience.

"Well, no...but...come to think of it, I guess I don't need actual help. I need to use the computer and printer," said Charlie. "And Lexie can be with me. She can help me choose pictures."

A huge smile passed across Lexie's face as she reached out a chubby hand to her beloved brother. I leaned to pat Lexie's bum, checking the diaper contents, and then straightened back up, smiling at my youngest daughter and marveling at her admiration for Charlie.

"Yes, of course you can use the computer. Go ahead and get my laptop but take it in the dining room. When you're ready to print, I can help you." Turning over the lunch possibilities in my mind, I strode to the kitchen. A trip to the grocery store needed to happen soon, but the thought of going to the store set my mind on edge. Instead? The babysitter. A note on the kitchen wall whiteboard would remind me to speak with Brooke later.

"Thanks, Mom. And by the way, the hospital called." Charlie's voice and face were devoid of worry, but the word *hospital* always caused a toothache. I turned around, my back to the kitchen sink.

"The hospital? Or the therapist? Did they tell you why? Did they leave a message?" What did they want? Despite his fatigue, Theo's overall mental health seemed balanced. At least I thought so.

"I'm not sure, Mom. She gave me her name and number, and I guess I thought it was the hospital. I left the paper by the phone. She said to tell you she wanted to talk to you, and she'd be there until eleven thirty today."

Charlie always got most the details right. I checked the watch on my wrist and exhaled a heavy breath. Practitioners normally called my cell phone. "Did you see if your dad was around?"

Charlie tipped his head back, looking at me sheepishly. "Well...he was asleep."

Annoyance coursed through me, and I slammed my hands against the surface of the countertop. "Asleep?"

Charlie shrugged. "Yeah."

"The whole time I was gone?" My irritation grew with each beat of my heart.

"Um, yes."

"If he was asleep, *who* was watching Lexie and Delia?" Fury replaced irritation. I didn't mind hiring Brooke when necessary—and in this case, asking her to come back—but Theo had to tell me when we needed her or to call her himself. He. Knew. That. Theo had said he'd be fine for sixty minutes. And I had been gone for fifty-eight.

"It's okay, Mom. I—"

"Don't argue with me, please."

Charlie held up his small hand. "But you have to listen. Dad needed the sleep, really. So, I had the girls work on a craft in the basement, and I helped them. It wasn't too hard for them and actually, we had a great time."

With a sigh, I pulled Charlie into my arms and pushed my face into his hair. He was still young enough to embrace me back, his strong but wiry arms stretching around my middle. "Taking care of the girls isn't *your* responsibility, Charlie. I'm so thankful you were an awesome big brother but looking after your sisters is my job or Dad's or Brooke's. Next time, call me."

Charlie pulled away from me, his eyes big and round. "I did, Mom," he whispered. "I called, but there was no answer."

Bless me, Father, for I have sinned. Again. This time, I didn't find the phrase funny.

Chapter 10: Theo

Monday morning came too soon. Fire raced underneath my skin, and my muscles coiled, ready for action. Once Brooke had left to take Lexie for a walk and Charlie and Delia had gone on to camp, Sadie and I were the only two left in the house. One thing I learned from Doc was the power of clearing the air. Now was the time. A clink and clank of dishes being put away meant Sadie was in the kitchen. As I entered the room, she stood at the counter, preparing her coffee for the road. I pulled a mug from the cabinet, poured myself coffee, and reached for the milk. With shaking hands, I splashed milk onto the countertop and knocked a stray water glass as I reached for the paper towels. In two steps, Sadie had the dishrag in her hand and sighed at the spreading puddle.

Sighs had always annoyed me, especially from Sadie, and my mind pushed back at the inclination to say something snarky. *Breathe in, breathe out.* One, two, three. "I can get that spill. You go ahead to work. You're running a little late."

Being helpful *or* thoughtful hadn't been my M.O. as of late—Doc had been quick to point that out to me—and I still grimaced when I thought of Charlie's bowl and our discussion from two days before. Or lack of discussion, rather. Sadie and I had an argument without having one: she'd walked away from the conversation, and I'd gone about my own business. Maybe my helpfulness now served as a subconscious way of trying to make amends.

She looked at me with kind eyes. While there was no way to know what was going on in her mind, the softness in her face made me consider if she was reflecting on how we used to be, on those days when we had time for one another. The nights when I'd be home for weeks on end, before the nightmares in the middle of the night forced me to the bathroom, up against the cool wall tile, trying to talk myself down from the ledge. What would she do if she knew I had another one of those episodes the night before? Would she care? I'd changed, but so had she. Where was the girl I fell in love with?

"I'm good, Theo. I'm the mom, and it's what I do—clean up the spills. But yeah, I should go. I have a couple phone meetings with other editors I can't push off." She pressed the lid of her travel mug—*snap!* A noise that set my jaw clenching. Between the sound and that she had no time for me, my ire rose.

"Are we going to talk about it at all?" The question hung in the air—so palpable it was almost visible—and I waited for an answer. Did she get what I was talking about? A ticking inside my head counted off the seconds. *One, two, three, four...*

Sadie's face blanched before her usual mask of calm slid into place. "About what?" She refused to meet my gaze as she fumbled around in her purse, most likely to find her keys. Her lack of organization skills with respect to those keys had always surprised me. With everything else in her life, things seemed to fall in line. But not with those damn keys. Hell, right after our wedding, I'd even bought her a key tree. It stood empty on the counter right now.

"About what you said...me being broken. About us."

She set her full mug on the kitchen table and pulled her phone out of her bag. Somehow, her phone was always easy to locate. "I didn't say *you* were broken, Theo." A touch of the screen and she started to text. "Hold on a minute. We can talk now, but I need to let Jackie know not to expect me until later."

Of course. The curse of the phone. "Yeah, Sadie, it's always that phone. Can't you leave it alone?"

My words dripped with contempt, and I shook my head. *Breathe in, Breathe out.*

Sadie looked up at me, twin spots of red on her cheeks. "What are you talking about, Theo? What would you do, and what would you want your colleagues to do? The right thing to do is inform a coworker I'm going to stay and speak with you." She punched at her phone and then put it back in her bag. "If you want to talk now, then we'll talk. But I'm going to be late, and work needs to hear about it. That's called *common courtesy*."

A few choice words slipped back down my throat, and I gripped the counter, hoping they didn't choke me. "Well, you don't choose to use common courtesy when it comes to me now, do you?" I threw the words at her, turned my back, and walked toward the bedroom. My anger seized me from within, and I slammed the bedroom door shut, the quake of the force shaking the doorframe itself.

What was wrong with me? Fuck that. So much was wrong with me. But uncharacteristic heat still coursed through my system when I thought about the hole I'd blasted through Sadie with my behavior. Stupid, petulant behavior. Doc would have told me to go back and apologize. "Apologies are necessary for any relationship," she'd have said. "Even those on the verge of rupture, especially if you want to keep that relationship from dissolving." I forced myself to return to the kitchen.

"I'm sorry. That's all I can say." I beelined for the garage, hoping to keep any more anger at bay until she left the house.

A few moments later, Sadie put her hand on my shoulder. Recoiling internally, I tried not to flinch externally.

"Do you need a ride?" she said.

"No."

"So you're not going in to work today?"

"Nope."

Just like Doc, Sadie possessed an aversion to one-word answers, but something kept me from speaking more.

"Okay," she said. "Then do you want to talk about my statement or how you're doing this morning? Going from kind to unkind in sixty seconds seems to be par for the course these days." She paused. "This is difficult. Life, the PTSD, the lack of control, the divorce papers, all of it. But you seem a little off today..."

I turned to her and hoped to keep my face unreadable. A long time ago, she'd been able to read my emotions with a simple glance, whether I was angry, tired, confused. This time, all three might have been part of the equation. "Leave it. I'm done here." I averted my eyes. Conversation over.

●　　　●　　　●　　　●　　　●

Twenty minutes passed. I wore a path in the carpet of my family room as thoughts about Sadie and who we were to each other bombarded me, followed by resentment at her "no driving for Theo rule." The wall became a punching bag for both my left and right fists.

Punch. *Fuck the service. And Afghanistan. And PTSD.*

Punch. *Fuck this life, Doc. All of it.*

Punch. *Fuck Sadie. She can't tell me what to do.*

On the fourth punch, the wall had had enough, and sweat beaded on my brow. I found a framed picture in my bedroom and covered the evidence of my meltdown before remembering I was due into work. My boss depended on me to be on-site and do my job, and the clients also expected me to show up. A cool shower and an ice pack and bandages for my knuckles were in order, and then— well, I'd take myself to work, Sadie's rules be damned.

The chances of her finding out about a solo driving journey were slim, as I was due home before she was. Would the kids tell if they knew? Revealing that secret wasn't in the plans, so I decided to risk it.

It was a short drive, and when I arrived, I felt more like myself despite the throbbing knuckles. I logged into the system, saying a quick hello to the usual folks who walked back and forth in front of the reception desk. A sticky note on the side of the computer had my name on it. "Andrew M. called for you. Says you'll know what he needs."

He probably wanted to get my answer on another work project he'd proposed. I'd left the papers at home on the table because the argument with Sadie had distracted me. But I'd seen enough, and what he wanted me to do was interesting. What about the screen time, the possible increase in stress? Would taking on that project help or hurt me?

Being up front with Andrew might be warranted. Up until now, I'd not told him about my background, and he'd been polite enough not to pry. Family and past lives had been off-limits in our conversations. And despite our rapport, even calling him a friend—or at least an acquaintance—I didn't know much about him.

Personal information didn't matter when it came to doing work for him though. Decision made, I placed the call.

Andrew picked up on the first ring. "Hey, Theo. Thanks for calling me back."

"No worries. Is this about the proposal you had me looking at?"

"It is. Just wondered about your level of interest."

"I'll be honest. The details are amazing, and I'd love to look at it..."

Andrew laughed on the other end of the line. "But. I hear a 'but' coming. Those are always easy to infer."

"I'm not sure I have the time." I glanced out the front window, trying to figure out how to phrase what I wanted to say. The bright sun bolstered me, blasted my misgivings away. "Things at home are...up in the air right now."

"Everything okay?"

"Yeah. It's that..."

"Hey, I get it. Why don't we agree you'll pass on this proposal, but I'll ask again on the next one. I'm sure something will come up in the next week or so. And then, we can head out for a burger or something. The kids will be gone over the weekend."

A bit of information from the guy who didn't say much. He could say the same of me though.

"Sounds good. But—" Tonight might be a good time to meet with him. A few hours away from home..."Any interest in grabbing that burger tonight? Only if you have time."

"I can make that happen. Does six at the Kennedy Grill work?"

The perfect spot. Close enough to drop the car off at home after work and walk to dinner. "Sure."

"All right. See you then."

Chapter 11: Sadie

The minutes spent in my car allowed me time to contemplate Theo's dismissal—which stung—and my life, which for the most part, was good, great even. Blessed as a wife and mother, only Theo's PTSD and the hot mess of my (sometimes) guilt caused me issues, but it took every ounce of my energy to fight back, stand tall, and move forward each day. The realization our lives were going to be different whether I stuck with Theo or not was too much for my wounded self to take on a Monday morning.

Jackie whistled in her office as I rounded the corner to mine. Apparently, a good night's sleep did wonders for her. The same could not be said for me.

I opened the door to my office and stopped. There, at the foot of my desk, stood Andrew. As unexpected as it was to see him, I'd have been a liar if I said he wasn't a sight for sore eyes.

Willing the puffy-eyed look to vanish, I moved deeper into my office. "Hey, there, Andrew. I didn't expect to see you here." I hung my jacket on its designated hook.

"I was in to check on Jackie, and she said you'd be in soon. I thought I'd see how you were. Did the late night get to you?"

"Nope. I was okay yesterday, although I have to say I did hit the hay a little early last night. I'm not cut out for all-nighters anymore." Keeping the smile out of my voice proved difficult. I wasn't ready to be frank with Andrew, and he was only there for small talk anyway. Averting my gaze might help.

"Well, thanks for letting me sleep away most of the night. I'm sorry about that. I dropped the ball on that task, didn't I? If we do this again, I'll let you get the shut-eye next time," Andrew said.

My insides stuttered, and I was glad my head was down as I examined the pages of my desk calendar. Next time? Would there be a next time?

"You're welcome—" The phone cut off my words and gave me a natural out, allowing me to avoid the place the conversation might lead. Where did I *want* it to lead? "Would you please excuse me?" The phone trilled again.

"Certainly. Have a great week. I'm sure I'll see you soon." Andrew smiled a sweet, slow smile, saluted me, and crossed over the threshold. Boy, did his pants fit nicely to his backside. Gah.

"Get a grip," I mumbled to myself. "Get a grip on reality and answer the damn phone."

As I picked up the receiver, sweat beaded on my palms and my fingers shook, remnants of both my argument with Theo and the effect Andrew seemed to have on me. I barely remembered being so discombobulated about Theo when I was younger. Had I been?

"Good morning, Sadie Rollins speaking."

"Hi Sadie. It's Mom."

Oh shit. Not a week went by I didn't phone my mother, who lived one town over. Except for yesterday. Shocked she hadn't already called to find out why I hadn't spoken to her, I resigned myself to an early conversation with her instead of Andrew.

"Oh hi, Mom." I fell into my chair, already exhausted by my morning.

"Don't 'Oh hi, Mom', me, Sadie Rollins, or Lancaster, or Rollins-Lancaster, whatever you go by now. How are you? How are the kids? I didn't hear from you yesterday. I thought something had happened to you." Mom always asked how the kids were doing. The conversation concerning the kids and their little lives could take at least fifteen minutes. And she always jumped to dire conclusions. Why would she think something had happened to me, a healthy woman in her late thirties? Would she ask about Theo? If anything critical were going to happen, wouldn't it most likely occur to him?

"Everyone's good, Mom. Charlie has a project, and the outline for it is due sometime soon...this week...and he seems to be handling it all himself. And Delia starts ballet on Tuesday night. She has her tutu hanging up on her bedpost and her slippers ready to go. Lexie is with the babysitter during the day, which of course, is a dream for both." I tapped my fingers against the edge of the desk. How to tell my mother I had a mountain of work to do and needed to end the call?

"Well good. Say, should Charlie be handling that project by himself? Does he need help? Did you ask him if he wanted help?"

The vein at the top of my forehead started to thump, and I pressed my left index finger against it. "Mom, he's set up in the dining room, and I told him to ask for help if he needs it. I can't be a helicopter parent. Charlie wants to do it himself, so I'm going to let him. There's only so much I can handle." The conversation needed to finish, before I allowed my mother to ruin my day.

"All right. I guess I should trust you." *Yes, you should.* No reply from me meant she continued. "Well about that weather? We've been having a lot of rain, right? So much rain the weeds are almost as tall as the sunflowers. I should try to get out there and do that weeding, but I have so much to do inside. Never ends, does it?"

Those same words had filled my ears for years. "All right now, well, I need to get going, Mom. I got in a bit late because Theo—"

"Oh. Well when are you and the kids coming over?"

Was Mom crazy? Did she not hear me when I said the name *Theo,* or did she simply choose to ignore the mention of his name? Could she dance any more around the subject of someone who used to own my soul? She avoided Theo because she didn't want to see how he was doing, because she couldn't stand I might need a little help from her. Because if she knew we needed extra hands around the house from time to time, then she might be morally obligated to head over once a week, and Mom didn't want to do that. Mom didn't ask me how Theo was doing because if she didn't have the details then she wouldn't, no couldn't, accrue guilt. It was always about her, when really, this time it wasn't, and it hadn't been for a long time.

My thumb clicked the END button on the phone, and for the first time in my life, I hung up on my mother. Crossing my arms over my chest, I leaned back in my chair and smiled.

•   •   •   •   •

The first day we realized Theo needed help was one of those frigid December mornings that unexpectedly energizes the world. I'd risen to go for a pre-dawn run, before the bustle of day care and work began. Tiptoeing out of the still-sleeping house, I ran the two blocks to Brighton Avenue and reveled in the dots of ice and snow hanging hazy under the streetlamps. The road was empty, save for a few cars, and the crunch of my footsteps on the pavement rang out as the miles added up. My lungs ached from the frosty air and my nose grew numb, but when I meandered back to the driveway, a sense of vigor permeated my being, and I was ready to begin my day.

So as not to wake my still-slumbering house, I slipped my key into the lock and then tiptoed to the kitchen, listening for signs of life; the only sounds were the purr of the ancient refrigerator and the whisper of the furnace. A creak on the staircase alerted me someone had interrupted the near silence. There in the foyer stood a sleep-rumpled Theo, his eyes expanded by an emotion that looked like concern.

"I can't do it," he said, his posture a sign of defeat.

Words refused to form as confusion filled me. "Do what?" I asked as I began to peel off the multiple layers of winter running garb.

"I can't do it." Theo stood rooted in his spot, although his body seemed to sag more with every word he spoke. He'd been moody lately, volatile almost, but I'd been so busy I hadn't taken the time to find out what the problem was.

"Honey." I moved toward him and gripped his shoulders, which caused Theo to flinch under my touch. "Are you actually awake?" Theo had been known to sleepwalk and talk before. The last time he'd done it he'd ambled right out the front door and all the way to the neighbor's house before waking up on his own.

"Yes, I'm awake." Irritation infused his voice. "And I can't do it. I can't live like this anymore."

"Live like what?" I asked.

"Have you *not* noticed?"

"Not noticed what? I'm sorry...but...what do you mean?" What was Theo trying to tell me? It was too early for my brain to be working on all cylinders.

"It's...it's..." He dropped his head toward his chest.

"O-kay." My damp running socks stuck to my feet as I worked to slip them off, then the chill of the ceramic tile floor shocked my toes on the walk back into the kitchen. Why was he talking about this—whatever this was—at 5:53 in the morning? Why not wait until later? Making coffee rose to the top of the priority list. If I waited any longer to get caffeine into my body, my day would turn from delightful to deadly.

"You don't understand, Sadie." Theo had followed me into the kitchen and slumped into a chair. "Charlie called out while you were running. He was scared. I went into his room to bring him into ours. But when I went to pick him up, it was like my arms wouldn't work. His thrashing—something about it...I panicked." Theo paused, his face haggard in the low lighting. "It isn't that Charlie's too heavy. It's that I can't get through...the screaming, the flailing...it brought me back. I can't help him."

My body felt drained of all blood as I glanced then at my husband. At the man who still played volleyball on the weekends and coded websites well into the night. The man who carried me over the threshold on the night of our wedding and tugged the children in the little red wagon with the wheel that squealed like a banshee. The slouch of his shoulders and curve of his spine indicated a true problem, and the fingers of his right hand tapped against his thigh, as if to remind him at least one part of him still worked properly. I pulled his fingers against mine and looked into his eyes, studying them. They were the same, but different—Theo, but not. Slightly muted, not as strong as they once had been, like old decals that had faded in the sun.

I've rarely been struck speechless, but that day, not even one single appropriate word came to my mind. The quiet of the kitchen surrounded me as I thought about what it meant to Theo and me if he had issues to work through. Up until that time, Theo had always been the robust one in our household. But on that wintry December morning, the entire universe as we knew it shifted without warning, and now, my veneer had started to crack.

I pressed my back against my office chair, daring it to ground me in the here and now. Where did Theo and I stand? What did our argument that morning mean? Holding the kids together, the family together, mainly for the sake of his health and happiness, was becoming too much. Simply caring about Theo wasn't difficult, but we'd made our choice, hadn't we? All signs pointed to the fact I needed to let go. Scorching tears ran down my cheeks, and I clawed at my chest, hoping to keep it from caving in as I thought about what to do about Theo and our situation.

• • • • •

After my cathartic cry, the scene outside the enormous plate glass window of my office held my interest for a long time. Thoughts of everything that had happened over the last twenty years hovered in my mind. Speaking to my mother did that sort of thing to me, brought memories and emotions to the surface that had no business being there. Here I was, a thirty-eight-year-old woman and mom of three, and my mother had managed to push the exact buttons she knew would bother me. Somehow, she always had.

Putting off work just a bit longer, I reached into the lower drawer of my desk and pulled out the small, leather photo album hidden there. Recent technology made photo albums almost obsolete, but having physical proof of my life, something tangible to hold in my hands, made it easier to wade through the muck and focus on all the wonderful treasures scattered throughout my current existence.

The plastic pages stuck together at the front of the album where a few photos of my early life lay, gummy but dried adhesive peeking from the corners. Three pictures of me with Mom and Dad. Judging by the fashion in the photos, I must have been about six. My long hair was pulled into pigtails, and Dad's huge yet artificial grin consumed his face. Mom, well, she looked like she always did— the proverbial deer caught in a car's headlights. As if she was afraid the person manipulating the camera would somehow, in the act of taking the picture, also capture the reality that loomed behind the lens. What was that reality then? Was she happy?

Moving onto a later photo of the family showed nothing had changed: Mom's face held that same expression. I hadn't recognized it when I was younger, but with the wisdom of time and photographic evidence, it was clear my mother might never have been happy in her marriage to my father. That she might have needed to change, or at least be flexible, and because she hadn't, happiness had been intangible. Dad had tried to make Mom happy: coming home early to help make dinner and taking care of me on the weekends. He told Mom to go out, get a job or go to school, whatever she wanted, to "do something for you, Marjorie," and she never did. She'd conjure a plethora of excuses for why her life was the way it was, but none of the reasons made sense. Mom was the master of placing responsibility on another person's shoulders: it was always someone else's fault. And the fact that she wasn't happy? That specific problem she had attributed to my dad.

A trap like that was a place I didn't want to fall into. If my life was screwed up, it was my fault and only my fault. After all, I'd agreed to our living situation. But shaking the anger toward Theo that had ignited from our morning argument seemed almost impossible.

A couple of pages forward in the album brought me to a more recent photo of Dad and me. Charlie and Delia peeked out from behind my back, while Dad's hand rested on my newly pregnant belly. It had been taken before Dad cut the ties to my mother for good. He made sure Mom was financially stable and she received the house in the settlement, his final selfless acts in taking care of a woman who thought of him as selfish. Dad looked restful and happy in the picture, full of warmth and love, pride shining from his eyes. "I wish you were here, Dad," I whispered to myself. He'd died the year before, right after Lexie had been born.

While it had taken Dad a long time, in the end, he'd admitted the truth: *his* personal happiness was important, and something he had to think about. Unfortunately, that meant leaving Mom. Would I have to do the same thing? Would I be able to place *my* personal happiness above all else? Dad's situation was so different from mine, wasn't it?

The hum of the copier across the hall and the trill of the secretary's phone interrupted my thoughts and prompted me to move to the next pages in line— a few pictures of Theo and me. Both of us on the volleyball court, our faces flushed from having played one another in one-hundred-degree heat and humidity. On the swing of his front porch, our legs extended in front of us, beers in hand. We'd been dating over a year by the point those pictures had been taken, and the vivid memories from that night stood out. That evening, I'd decided Theo Lancaster was the boy I was going to marry; I was sure of it.

That thought amused me now. The certainty and depth of my love. What about Theo had made me so secure in my feelings for him? Something about him had made me believe we'd make it. *Forever.* What had happened to make my love waver?

My intercom buzzed and broke me out of my reverie, ushering me back to the present and the urgency of work. The intercom button yielded against the tip of my finger.

"Hi, Sadie," said Jackie. "How are *you* this morning?"

If she only knew. "I'm great. Something you need?"

"I wanted to say thank you again for this weekend. I can't tell you how much we appreciated your help. I hope it wasn't awkward with Andrew there."

Jackie hadn't heard yet that Andrew and Grocery Store Man were one and the same. How would Jackie react to the news? The admission would shock her.

"That's what friends are for. If you need me to do it again, don't hesitate to ask. But I might like to be on baby duty myself next time." Flying solo would be easier on my heart.

"Oh. Did something happen? Pete spends more time with Andrew than I do, but he seems like he's a great person. We hadn't planned on having two people there, but it was late when Pete told me he'd asked Andrew too. Was Andrew difficult to talk to? Didn't he help you?"

"Oh no, nothing like that." The burden squatting on my shoulders needed to be released. Jackie was my friend and would do anything to help me. "I thought you might want to know that Andrew..." Under the desk, I wiggled my foot, nervous about my next words.

"Yes?" Jackie's impatience boomed over the intercom. "He's what? Boring? Rude? A real piece of work? I would bet that." Jackie's throaty laugh echoed over the speaker. "Several of the characters Pete hangs out with, well, they can be quite a handful—"

"No. Andrew MacKinnon is Grocery Store Man, Jackie."

The clang of an object, like something dropping onto Jackie's desk, sounded.

"Shit. Stay put. You hear me?" she said. "I'm heading over."

Chapter 12: Sadie

Jackie walked into my office with such swiftness I thought she'd trip over herself in the process of trying to get through the narrow doorway.

"Oh. My. God." Her face painted a picture full of shock and delight all rolled into one. "Andrew MacKinnon? Are you serious?" She shut the door behind her before stepping toward my desk. Jackie's entire person sparkled with intense interest under the fluorescent lighting of my office.

"Yep. And why don't you sit?" I gestured toward the chair.

"Why don't I, indeed? This could take a while." Jackie smoothed her skirt over her knees after she sat and then leaned back in the chair. "Do tell, girl, do tell." A mischievous smile leapt across Jackie's face, which deepened her dimples. "Andrew MacKinnon?" Jackie asked again. "*Andrew?*"

Suddenly, my office felt too warm, but Jackie deserved the truth, starting with my morning argument with Theo. My friend listened, her emotions flickering across her face, until she interrupted me with a question.

"Is Theo okay? How's he doing?"

"He's pretty closed up about everything, and if I don't go with him to the doctor, if Brooke takes him, he doesn't tell me all that much."

"So...what about this argument? Where did it come from?"

Theo and I weren't the type of couple who normally quarreled, but since the realization of his symptoms and the increase in chronic stress, we spent more time at war with one another than in the past. At one of Theo's visits I had attended, the doctor said something about Theo's behavior that stuck with me.

"Remember," she said. "Sometimes the PTSD will do all the talking." The phrase hadn't made sense at the time. "Everything he perceives is real to him,"

69

she had continued. "Theo's hurting, and he doesn't comprehend what to do with that hurt. His life is uncertain right now, and that's a tough issue to come to terms with."

Tough issues? No shit—we all had those. Then and now.

A response to Jackie soon surfaced, and I revealed to her the details surrounding my situation with Andrew: being torn in two, how I'd spoken to Kate, and the overwhelming thought I was floundering. And as that last thought spent time in my mind, it morphed into a new realization: maybe Theo floundered as well, in a place he knew he'd never find purchase. The doctor had said it: Theo's life was chock full of uncertainty, and by default, uncertainty affected me. Meeting Andrew added more chaos to the mix, and if I reacted to it, Theo would, also by default, be affected. The push and pull, the interconnectedness we shared. Were we both at fault for the increase in arguments?

"So, you're in over your head? Well go ahead. I'm no professional, but I *am* an excellent listener." Jackie's warm smile melted my heart. She was a dear friend, someone to confide in, someone to accept help from. Now was the time.

"Jackie, I'm not sure where to start." My office window beckoned to me. Concentrating on the beauty of the day outside the glass might help everything on the inside of that window fall into place. It wouldn't—it couldn't—but I could hope.

"Well then, let me see if I have this right. You like Andrew? And he seems to like you."

She was right, and she knew as much. *I* knew as much. My response to him was apparent: the butterflies, the energy, the impulsive flirting.

"Hear me out, dear friend, when I say you don't need to jump off the deep end on this one," she said.

I swiveled my chair back to face Jackie.

"You can be attracted to someone and not act on it. You can be attracted to someone while you're living with your soon-to-be ex-husband, although you need to make that decision soon. Sever the ties or don't, but you need to get out of this state of limbo."

Jackie was right. The thought of spending time in a whirlwind of confusion didn't appeal to me.

She went on. "Cut yourself some slack here. You have a lot on your plate, girl. Kids, work, Theo. Maybe consider Andrew a new...acquaintance?"

"Or not," I said.

"Or not?"

A hum began in my ears at the thought of Andrew. "I don't know if I can." My admission hung between us, but Jackie held enough emotional intelligence to read between the lines. At least the courage to admit one of my weaknesses had arisen, although it was probably written all over my face.

"Oh...okay. But one more question."

"Yeah?"

"Do you love Theo?"

What a simple—and at the same time complex—question, and one I'd already answered when I filed for divorce. Filling Jackie in on that painful detail was easy, talking about being *in love* versus *loving* someone. Even the thought made tears imminent, and I reached for the tissue holder on my desk.

"It's all so complicated."

"That it is, my friend," Jackie whispered. She leaned toward me and patted my hand. It was a gesture I would only accept from someone like her. "It's okay."

Despite everything *I* was going through at that moment, I had a friend like Jackie. A thought that made me ask, what or who did Theo have? He couldn't even count on one of the supposedly dependable people in his life—me. Being more sympathetic toward Theo and what he was experiencing should take a higher spot on my priority list.

"No, it's not, Jackie. It's not okay, and I need to figure out how to make it all okay. If I want to pursue Andrew, then I need to be up-front with Theo, and he needs to sign those papers. But I need to find the Sadie I once knew too. I need to clean my life up, to clean up *me*."

Heat flared on my face and neck, and I placed my head in my hands, embarrassed at the melodramatic revelation. How had my life gotten like this? Prior to this conundrum, I'd taken things in stride, adjusting to what was thrown at me and making decisions based on what was right. And somehow, things changed without my realizing it.

"And Andrew?" Jackie said as she leaned in over the desk.

"What about him?"

"Does he factor into this at all?" Jackie's voice was so quiet, I almost didn't hear her.

Her question hit me hard. "I don't know," I said. "I'll figure that out as I go along."

"And I'll be here to support you." Jackie stood up, walked around the desk, and wrapped her arms around me. She held tight, as if she was trying to transfer positive energy to me. What gifts—her warmth, friendship, and love?

"You should be a therapist, Jackie," I said as I wiped the tears from my lashes with my overused tissue.

A huge grin broke out across her face as she pulled away from me. "The bill will be in tomorrow's mail." Jackie moved toward the door before turning back. "By the way—and I wasn't going to tell you this, but I'd like to be honest with you—Andrew left his card for you on his way out earlier. I haven't said anything about you and your situation, but he told me to tell you his cell number is on the bottom of the card. 'Feel free to contact him,' he said."

Jackie winked and walked out of my office.

Chapter 13: Sadie

Once Jackie left my office, I had plenty of time to contemplate my life. My mind first jumped to the idea of Andrew's business card, complete with cell phone number, but it didn't stay there. Thoughts of Theo and the PTSD that had so changed our lives gripped me by the shoulders and wouldn't let go.

Theo before PTSD and Theo after PTSD were antitheses of one another. He'd always been driven—at work and at play—but once he'd been diagnosed, the smiling, chipper, hands-on dad we knew and loved melted away like the spring snow. Gone were the days of impromptu hikes at Cranberry Hill and time spent wrapped in each other's arms. He no longer sat in the recliner, child in lap and book in hand, nor did he sneak up on me while I was cooking, whisper sweet nothings in my ear, and trail his hand down my spine. Instead, we'd become intent on figuring out our individual lives, not our collective one.

"PTSD can manifest differently for each person," the doctor had said when we'd spoken about what life would be like. "Yes, you'll feel different, and you'll be frustrated a lot, and you might have an anger like you've never experienced before, but you can't let this beat you. Not yet. You've got a lot of life left to live."

During the days following the diagnosis, Theo and I did all the things we thought we should. We researched everything about living with PTSD. We hired Brooke to sit with Charlie and Delia, who were eight and five at the time, so we'd be able to head to appointments sans children. We sat through lectures, videos, and chats with counselors, all to understand the intricacies of PTSD. Of course, Theo knew and understood more of the details of it, having been in the military, but it was something he never thought he'd experience.

"It's all too much!" he said after he'd read yet another statistics-filled report. "Give me something I can work with!" he yelled. "I don't want data!"

With a vengeance, I set about trying to find *something* he wanted, something useful. For several days, and with Kate and Jackie's remote help, I spent time in my office, looking into online information from respected veterans' clinics and psychiatric journals; culling lists of what the professionals suggested someone with PTSD should do; and comparing lists of what someone living with a person with PTSD should do. Enormous amounts of coffee accompanied me as I scrambled to get work done between journal articles. Jackie covered for me when naps trumped everything else, and I brought more work and journal articles home, hoping I'd find something, anything, Theo found helpful.

The doctor had other ideas.

"You need a personal connection, and I have just the couple. You'll love them. They have bright personalities and are generous with their time. They're both busy, but I'd bet my last dollar they'd be willing to speak with you and Theo."

"I'm not sure," Theo had said, passing a hand in front of his face, the hand that would cover up the doubt in his eyes.

"We should try. What is your day-to-day life going to be like? How long will you be living like this? Does it kick you in the gut, every day, or is there a way to live happily? And what about the kids?"

"Call them, Sadie, Theo. Call these people." The look on the doctor's face urged me to make the right choice. "And if you can't do that right now, then watch this video," the doctor said. "Their community has rallied around them, and you'll get a good sense of who Rick and Laura are. More importantly, you'll understand the sort of people you and Theo could be."

Up until that moment, the information I'd gotten regarding Rick and Laura Sullivan didn't help me much with anything on the PTSD front, so I was hoping the video would paint a picture of who they were. Time seemed to stand still as the opening scenes of the video burst forth. In front of my laptop computer, I sat, mesmerized by the voice of a man living with what my love had.

Rick and Laura had been high school sweethearts who had gotten engaged and married while in college. They both went on to become successful lawyers with three handsome sons and a life to envy. But Rick had served three tours, and when he'd been discharged, Laura knew something had happened. Instead of letting PTSD own him, Rick had taken the diagnosis in stride and sought help.

It had taken time and patience—something Theo was short on—but eventually, Rick healed. Part of that healing resulted in a program he'd started for veterans.

The Sullivans were malleable and optimistic, encouraging, and enthusiastic, characteristics I hoped we'd emulate. On the video, Rick said that before his tour of duty, he'd been living the life he wanted. But since the emergence of his PTSD symptoms, everything had changed. He had to adjust, go forward in life while grappling with the condition.

Inspired and frankly, enamored, by these people, a flood of relief hit me when their voices rang out on the other end of the phone one afternoon. After an introduction, I told them why I was calling. Rick had said they would either speak with us over the phone or meet up with the both of us. I chose the latter.

"Of course," Laura said. "Send us a list of dates and we can figure something out."

And Laura stood behind her words. Within a day, I had sent them dates and we coordinated a time to make the 200-mile trek to their home. Brooke agreed to take care of the children for the day, and Theo and I hopped into the car and set out for the highway. The miles clicked by, and as we approached their subdivision, a sense of warmth and longing overtook my thoughts. The tree-lined street reminded me of our place in Kettering, and when we pulled up to the colonial style home, complete with a six-panel door and dried flower arrangement adorning the front, I bit back my laughter.

"You have to admit, this is a little odd," I said to Theo as he peered at their house, so similar to ours. "If they have gold-leaf paisley wallpaper in their powder room, we're leaving."

He tipped his head back and laughed as he reached for my hand.

That visit with Rick and Laura kicked off a hopeful time for me. They had welcomed us into their home and shared their coping strategies, describing how to create a safe environment and a safety plan and tips on recognizing triggers. Their infectious laughter and obvious love for one another, their lives, their children, and their home made me walk away from the meeting with a new sense of purpose and vigor.

And here I was, reminiscing about all that happiness—that which we didn't have.

The picture of Theo gracing my desk caught my eye, and I leaned back in my office chair, thinking about all I had learned since then, all the phases Theo had gone through, most of them predictable, some of them not. But if there was one thing I was certain of, it was that PTSD could be tricky. Some days, Theo seemed fine; others, he did not. Some days his anger barely simmered; other days, it boiled. And then there were days where he looked as though his tether to life had thinned, desperately.

Despite having Rick Sullivan as a good role model, Theo hadn't risen to the challenge placed before him as well as Rick had. The Theo I left that morning, the one who barely lived—he wasn't the same anymore. Sure, he still had good days when his humorous and gentle side surfaced, like we'd seen on Father's Day. But other times, he seemed far more depressed than I would have expected. He didn't hold a consistent positive attitude, like Rick. What I'd seen in his eyes sometimes in the evening—I knew what it was. Theo was losing the fight. Taking up the battle wasn't in his makeup, or there was something he detected in me— that floundering perhaps. If he found out about me and my fascination with Andrew...what would happen to him or to us?

Chapter 14: Theo

The burgers at the Kennedy Grill used to be my favorite until I came back from Afghanistan. At that point, the thought of eating meat was too much, most likely because the charred flesh once possessed a true life, a potential that hadn't been realized, unless sitting on a plate waiting to be devoured counted as potential. Sadie would have said plants have souls too. No surprise here: I didn't buy it.

But the smell of the place made my mouth water in a way it hadn't in a long time—the aroma of peppers, garlic, and cumin hung in the air. I glanced around the place, my gaze landing first on the metal salt and pepper shakers, then the silverware against the white napkins. Location never mattered: targeting anything metal seemed to be my new superpower. Soft music—something unidentifiable but appealing to Sadie—filtered through the speakers.

My phone buzzed in my pocket with a text.

Found a booth in the back.

I wound around the bar and down two stairs where Andrew waited. He tipped his head back in a manner I was beginning to view as "Andrew style." Doc would be glad I'd noticed something that made him stand out from all the other people I encountered during my day. "Means you're not always focused inwardly," she'd say.

Hesitation made me pause, a slight worry the blinking neon sign affixed to the ceiling at the edge of the bar would trigger something in me, so I chose a seat with my back to the sign. It put me right across from Andrew, who, in the darker lighting of the bar, recalled Liam, the friend I'd lost. I'd been around Doc enough to understand maybe I was holding onto Andrew as a way not to forget Liam. If that was true, why was I holding onto Sadie?

Andrew didn't know about Sadie though, and he had no reason to. I pulled a menu toward me, hoping he said nothing about the bandages on my hands. Doc's voice rang in my ears: "You can get away with a hell of a lot if you keep those manners intact." If anyone had told me I'd be seeing a therapist who placed so much emphasis on manners, I'd have called them crazy. Of course, I never thought I'd end up seeing a therapist either. Sometimes, life was cruel.

"Did you already look at the menu?" I held one out to him.

His gaze flicked to the bandages and then back to my face. "As sad as this sounds, I get the same thing every time I come here."

"Why is that sad?" The plastic edge of the laminated menu grated against my fingertips.

"Makes me remember how old I am, how set in my ways. You'd think I would live a little from time to time, but not when it comes to my burger."

"Ha! There's a T-shirt for you," I said. "Never come between a man and his burger?"

"Did someone actually say that? That Guy guy, right? The one on television, goes and eats a lot, and his hair...Guy Ferrari! He'd say something like that."

"You mean Fieri. I used to have a friend who loved that show." *Liam.* Somehow, thoughts of him came up every time Andrew was around. "So, I haven't been here in a while. Any thoughts about what else might be worthwhile? I'm not eating too much red meat these days."

"Any reason why not? You look as healthy as a horse."

If Andrew knew the state of my brain, he wouldn't be saying that. But my body did look healthy—with the exception of my hands. "Nah, no reason, other than I enjoy chicken and fish better."

"Then go with the fish and chips. They are good, if you're not afraid of a little grease."

"Sounds good." I placed the menu on the table. "So where are the kids tonight?"

"At Grandma's house. Yes, it's a weeknight, but the kids love my ex's mom and go to bed fine for her. I'll get them in the morning and take them to school. Works out well for me to get a break."

"A break. Do the kids live with you full-time?"

The more information I had, the better prepared I would be if I signed those damn papers and moved out. Part of my reasoning for delaying involved the kids. I hadn't done much right in my life, but those three...

"Yes and no. They split time between two houses, but we live less than a mile apart, and we have two sets of everything. A bit of an expense, but it works for us. Makes the best of a shitty situation."

Andrew had no idea what he'd touched on with his "shitty situation" comment. While I once believed living together but not being together would be easy, our situation *had* turned not only shitty but also fucked-up. Sadie wanted little to do with me, and I'd become confused about my future, our future.

"Yep, I get it."

After placing our orders with the server, Andrew shrugged off his jacket and draped it over the chair. "What about you? Kids? Wife?"

How much to tell? "Yes to the kids, and it's complicated to the wife. We're at a point that, well, we're fine, but fine isn't what either of us want."

"Fair enough. Moving on?"

I nodded my head. "Moving on."

Andrew and I chatted and whittled away the time. We spoke about the responsibilities of owning a business, the monotony of jobs in general, and the antics of our kids, though I was careful not to name mine. Somehow, being a dad changed my outlook. I never would have thought I'd be exchanging stories like I'd heard moms do, but there we were, swapping memories like we were showing off scars or tattoos. Against the backdrop of laughter and a news program, we covered a lot of ground, and I made sure to stay on this side of vague. He didn't need details about the PTSD or my trips to see Doc.

"So how long have you been divorced?" I asked.

"Going on three years."

"And how is that? I mean, I never thought I'd get married much less divorced, and now—well, how is it?"

Andrew didn't pry; he answered the question between bites of his burger, which, I had to say, looked all right. The fish and chips were tasty; almost as good as Sadie's.

"It was difficult at first—my kids mean the world to me," he said. "But owning my company helps—when I need to take time off, I can. And my relationship with my ex-wife is as amicable as it can be. Now, I haven't dated anyone yet, but I'm sure that would change things."

Dating was a topic I had no intention of touching with Andrew. This wasn't some Hallmark movie. But the redness of his face told me something. Like there was someone he was interested in. And that thought had me picturing Sadie and her smile and the way I used to be the luckiest man alive, and the spiral swirled from there: my incessant fury at the station I held in life, my inability to do the job I had trained long and hard to do, the extreme probability my home life would be changing sooner rather than later. It was all too much.

"Andrew, you know what? I'm not feeling great right now, so I'm going to head out." I grabbed my check and left a tip on the table. "But let's chat if another project comes up, if that's good for you."

"Sure thing. Hope you're all right." Once more, his gaze darted to my hands.

The din of the silverware against the plates and the incessant chattering of the diners chipped away at my nerves. "I will be. Lots of long days lately. Thanks for meeting up with me."

Andrew tipped his chin up. "Anytime. I'm sure you'll be okay soon."

I would be okay; deep inside my brain I trusted that. But what would make everything else okay? And, I wanted more than the word "okay" to describe my life.

Chapter 15: Sadie

Talking to Theo that evening took top priority on my to-do list, after washing the dishes and putting the kids to bed. Usually, we had a couple hours to sit with each other. When we were still together, we'd watch a movie, read poetry to each other, or even play card games until we knew the kids were asleep, and then we'd sneak up the stairs, giggling like young lovers, barely making it to the bedroom before we removed each other's clothing and became lost in one another.

Times had changed. I crept toward the back room, expecting to encounter Theo in the recliner, watching one sport or another, but instead, he sprawled on the couch, fast asleep, bandages on his hands. He hadn't been home at dinnertime; I had no idea how his day had gone or what he'd done to drain his energy, but those bandages...they spoke volumes.

After turning off the television, I sat next to him, taking care not to wake him, and looked at him in his moment of peace. When he slept, he resembled a child, like the Theo I first met. The dark shadows under his eyes and the light stubble on his chin weren't as apparent in the muted lighting of the family room, and his eyes shifted underneath his eyelids. Was he dreaming, and if so, about what? Did he envision images of his former self? Or was he dreaming of what was to come? Pleasant dreams would be better than nightmares, but I wasn't sure he'd tell me if I asked him.

I reached for Theo's hand and placed my cool fingers into his lukewarm ones. His grip tightened reflexively against mine, and for a moment, a connection tethered us. Tears formed at the back of my eyes, and I clenched my eyelids shut, willing the tears away, uttering a silent wish that the strength to do what was right might infuse me. Amid my murmurs to myself, Theo woke up and blinked his eyes.

"Hey," he whispered, attempting to grip my hand even tighter.

"Hey," I said back to him. "We need to talk about what happened this morning, don't you think? And this?" I lifted his hand between us.

"Yeah." Theo shifted against the couch, straining to move himself into a sitting position, never letting go of my hand. He pulled me close to his body, my head up against his shoulder, and his thumb traced circles against my palm. We sat like that for a minute before he nudged me and said, "I'm sorry, Sadie."

"For what exactly?" I asked.

"For everything, really, but especially my attitude this morning. I know what you have on your plate. I see what you do around here for the kids, for me. And it breaks my heart I'm not helping more. I didn't sign up for this, and you certainly didn't, either."

Sitting so close to his shoulder provided a whiff of the laundry detergent scent still clinging to his shirt. The aroma did nothing to soothe my somewhat frayed nerves as flashes of Andrew flared before my eyes.

"You're forgiven. This is difficult for you...you want to do what you used to do and can't sometimes." I turned toward him and caught his chin in my free hand. "But you and I both have to stop looking at you as broken. You aren't what you once were, that's true. There are plenty of other things you can be though. Have you thought of that? How can you make the best of this situation? How can *we* make the best of it? Think of Rick and Laura, please. You need to stop looking at what's going on as a life sentence and start living with it. If not for me, then for Charlie, Delia, and Lexie."

Throwing out the child card might be unfair, but the topic would hit home. Theo had always wanted a gaggle of children. His PTSD and our impending divorce had put a stop to that plan.

"It's hard, Sadie. More difficult than I can articulate. I saw what depression did to my dad, and here I am going through something similar." He clenched a bandaged fist against his thigh. "I should have learned how to accept this state by now. I've read the literature. Shouldn't I have known?" He placed his head into his hands and soon, his shoulders heaved, and his breath stuttered.

His predicament sat front and center in my mind as I embraced him with the singular hope a simple gesture would help ease some of the pain. But as I lay my head against his and touched his tender fingers, my predicament pushed his away from the front of the line: caught between a love that might be and a love that wasn't anymore. Had I ignored what was coming? Shouldn't *I* have known?

• • • • •

Theo rarely showed his vulnerable side. Almost never, in fact. Which gave me a lot to think about over the ensuing weeks and reaffirmed I had an issue on my hands. Theo still needed help, and if I could, I would give it to him. And that meant anything with Andrew would have to wait. Yet, I still pulled out Andrew's number, entered it into my contact list, and sent a quick text.

As August's blanket of humidity led into a cooler September climate, two things happened: one, Theo put forth his best effort in being dad and housemate; and two, I did *my best* to avoid Andrew. At least in person.

Early fall barbecues at Jackie's did not become a part of my schedule, and Brooke took over most of the weekly grocery shopping. When Kate and I met briefly for coffee, usually at her or my house, my focus stuck to the buzz of school news and inane stories about her job. But that didn't mean Andrew was far from my mind. Thoughts about him emerged at the most unexpected times: when I was running, cleaning the toilet, changing the sheets. That last task always brought my thoughts to Andrew. Go figure. And that phone of mine Theo hated so much? It tethered Andrew and me. Daily texts became the norm.

But somehow, despite my great attempts to avoid him around town, we ran into each other all over the metro area. We exchanged brief hellos at Breaking Bread (time to find a new coffee shop), in the checkout line at Grocer Jim's (what was it with the grocery stores?), and in the lobby of the Dominion Theatre (a place we rarely visited) on a sunny, pleasant, Sunday afternoon, among other places.

Each encounter made me recall my conversation with Kate, and her voice resonated throughout my thoughts as I conducted my daily business: *Stop thinking of Theo or the family or anyone else who might play a role in your life at this moment and rewrite the stars, Sadie. What is good for you?*

Fighting a war against myself and my feelings for Andrew and scrabbling to find something to hold on to took center stage at times. And why? Hadn't Theo and I decided to divorce? What was binding me to him? Fear? Guilt?

As of that moment, Theo knew nothing about what had happened on Father's Day at Bloom Market. And even though I'd spent little alone time with

Andrew, getting the scoop on who he was and what he wanted out of life, an entity of him grew in my head. My body yearned for the man I'd built up based on text conversations, but what information did I have about him? What side of the bed did he sleep on or what brand of toothpaste did he use? Did he wear boxers or briefs? (My thought: boxer briefs, the topic had never arisen, sadly.) Which way did he lean politically, how did he feel about social justice issues, and what sort of role did science play, or not, in his life?

These were all things I wanted to find out, and why shouldn't I?

But what about those things I *did* know? His life as a business associate, his relationship with his ex-wife and kids, his willingness to volunteer for the parks and rec department at a moment's notice. And our random chats sometimes turned into marathon talk sessions, where one of us looked at the clock and begged off, saying we had things to do and "really should go." Those sessions had revealed a lot about Andrew. A lot about what I liked about him. A lot about who he was. A lot about where *we* could go.

That consideration came at me full force one afternoon toward mid-September when I ducked out of work early to get Lexie to the pediatrician's office.

"What are the chances our children would be sick at the same time?" Andrew's voice echoed behind me as I stood in front of the receptionist. "And in September? December, I can understand. But summertime just ended…it's fate." Turning to face him, I hoped the heat flooding my cheeks wasn't noticeable.

"Perhaps it is, Andrew." I couldn't hold back a smile at his flirtatious style.

The kids congregated in the play area and moved the child-sized chairs back and forth into rows. When they were finished, the space looked more like a private movie theater than the waiting area, sans the movie of course. Which apparently, the kids didn't need.

"You'd never guess a few of them are sick, would you?" Andrew asked.

Nodding my head in agreement, I sat. "I'm pretty sure Lexie's got an ear infection. She never cleared her cold, and she's been waking up screaming in the middle of the night. They try not to medicate here, but today, I'm here for the antibiotic. I think they'll give her one. In fact, if Lexie doesn't have fluid on that eardrum of hers, I'll owe you a coffee."

My words surprised me. Practically inviting Andrew out for coffee. When did my conscience make that decision?

"Three kids and you can diagnose, right Doctor Mom?" Andrew's words didn't scoff me; they stated the facts. And it was true. After three kids and countless trips to the pediatrician, I'd learned a lot.

"Yeah, what about you? Sydney looks a little worse for wear. Lexie shouldn't be tiring her out."

"It's my kid who shouldn't be with yours because she might have strep." Andrew leaned forward, as though he might pop out of his seat any minute to grab his daughter.

A quick shake of my head stopped him. "Oh, sorry to hear it. But it's okay. For some strange reason, my kids don't usually pick up strep. That's one sickness I'm not versed in."

"You're lucky. It can be a pain, literally. I'm surprised she's playing as much as she is. Sydney's got everything: bright red throat, fever, stomach issues. I even felt the glands in her throat. Textbook case. If you ask me."

"You're very thorough."

"I am when it comes to those I love."

Andrew kept his gaze on the little ones as they played. But something in his chosen words registered with me, and an ache sliced through my gut. Then, he leaned in, over my armrest, so his lips were inches from my ear. His breath tickled the nape of my neck, which sent shivers down my spine.

"Jackie doesn't gossip, you know that, but between what she's said and what I've gathered, how's life?"

As much as I wanted to turn toward him, to breathe him in, infuse myself with his essence, I was careful to move in the opposite direction from Andrew because he was still so close I smelled the soap he'd used that morning. I blinked away a few tears. Each day—keeping the facade intact, moving on with my oddly structured world—was so demanding, and here I was, in the doctor's office with a man who showed sincerity. Thoughts twirled in my head and confusion mounted: what to reveal or what *should* I reveal? Keeping my answer simple and superficial seemed best. For my sake.

"We're doing all right. Most days, we try to pretend everything is normal, but really, it's not, and it hasn't been for a while."

"I can't imagine it's easy to be living in a situation like yours."

He didn't state specifics, probably because he didn't have them. Even though we'd chatted and learned so much about one another—Andrew's favorite color was blue, and he preferred no sugar in his strong coffee; he yearned to see social injustices rectified and hoped to retire by the time he was sixty-seven—I'd never offered too many details about Theo and me. Always referring to my "soon-to-be ex" seemed like a way to preserve the distance, helping me sever my heart from where it once had been.

"It's an interesting one, and something I thought I'd handle. Now, I'm not so sure."

"Everything okay?"

"Yeah. For the most part we're good: food on the table, cars in the garage, therapy appointments that aren't always being canceled. But I wonder at times, if the kids shouldn't also be seeing a therapist. I mean, how fucked-up—sorry for my mouth—is it that they see their parents living together but not?"

Andrew didn't speak at first, a habit that meant he was thinking. "No family situation is exactly like the next one. Some are pretty, special, to say the least. And kids are resilient. But I'd listen to your gut on this one. We'll be sending our kids to therapists for one thing or another, but if you don't want it to be because of this and your—ex...ish?—then do something about it now."

In the confines of the pediatrician's office, my sick child's laughter pulled at my heart. How long would the laughter last? Would my children be pulled into the darkness because of what we were doing? How was Theo's behavior affecting them, and what would the repercussions be? Would there be any at all?

Andrew patted my knee, escorting me back to the conversation. "I'm sure it's hard for your—"

"It is. It is. He's still doing okay, for the most part, and he's found a job that suits him. It's just, he's volatile, and some days, he's an enigma. We'd decided on divorce for a reason, and I thought I'd experience some closure. There's none involved when you still live together though. And I wonder about his psyche, his ability to hold it all together. I might not want to be married to him, but I still worry. About him, about the kids." Swallowing back a lump in my throat, the floor became my focus.

"All of you will live long and happy lives. It might take a while to get there, but you *have* to have hope. It's all we have sometimes." Andrew covered my hand with one of his in a gesture meant to impart comfort, but one which, because of my heightened state, did anything but comfort me.

Thankfully, we didn't have much more time to sit and chat. The nurse entered the reception area, and my hand fell away, torn from another universe in which Andrew and I sat as a couple, not friends. The nurse called Lexie's name, and she ran to me as I stood up and grabbed my purse and jacket. Andrew's eyes sparkled, full of genuine concern mixed with hope for me. Saying he was a good man would be an understatement. My entire being sensed it.

A shudder passed through me, forceful enough to make me stumble against the chair, as if long arms had pushed me, over the precipice and into an abyss. The battle within me ended as I toppled into that metaphorical void, a place it would be hard to come back from. I clutched Lexie to my chest, hoping to hold onto something concrete, positive, and innocent. My gaze held steady with Andrew's.

Chapter 16: Theo

Doc had been right: having an acquaintance was useful. I told her as much at my next therapy appointment, recounting most of the details of my dinner with Andrew. She didn't verbally say a word, but her smug smile was all the answer I needed. Looking back on that night, I hadn't given any details to Andrew, but I felt a bit uplifted by our camaraderie. That wasn't a phrase from my vocabulary, but Doc seemed to use it often. And it made sense now. I'd been doing a lot of thinking about my situation, and something needed to change, but what? Some days, I still looked at Sadie and wondered what the hell had prompted me to agree to divorce. Actually, make that most days. She was and always would be the one who got away. Had I any balls, I'd have done something about it. But I didn't. I barely took care of myself, much less anyone else.

So, how the fuck would I take on a project the size of what Andrew proposed? Though I'd turned him down, I still carried it around with me in a folder everywhere I went, maybe as a desensitization technique. That afternoon, while I was at the kitchen table perusing the details for the hundredth time, my phone rang: Sadie's name popped up on the screen.

"Hello?"

"Hey. I need to talk to you about something."

"Okay, what is it?" It had to be close to time for her to be home. Why not wait until she got here?

"Can you come out here? I'm outside in the driveway. I'll meet you on the porch."

Inside my head, I laughed at her, but to do so outwardly might cause trouble. She wanted to chat about something and didn't want the kids to interrupt. "Sure. I'll be right there."

I pushed my papers to the side, put the pen on top, and walked to the front porch. We'd put the porch on after we bought the house, a little space for Sadie to have her quiet time in the mornings. Those mornings were more important now that we were no longer together. She'd never said as much, but I sensed it. And now, she sat, staring forward at the neighbor's house.

"What do you need, Sadie?" I reached for the wooden swing and tumbled into it. The paint on the arms of the swing curled up in spots, and beneath the seat sat the remains of Charlie's bowl—still waiting to be fixed or repurposed. Hadn't Sadie said she was going to do something with it? Would she ever get around to it?

"I don't need anything, Theo. I want to talk about something."

"Okay. This sounds serious." What thoughts crossed through her mind? We'd already discussed divorce and were on track for that. Sort of. Was she going to pressure me to sign the papers? I needed to—

"I guess it could be Theo. I've been thinking about getting the kids into therapy."

Visions of the kids lined up on a couch, their faces long, swam in my head. "Therapy? Really?"

"Well, we're a bit stressed here these days, and I wonder if, I wonder if they're handling everything the way they should. Like maybe this is all too much for them."

Trying to hold back a smirk, I pursed my lips. How could she tell if they were handling things or not? She worked. A lot. Now, Brooke? Asking her if the kids were okay made sense. That malignant thought worked its way through my head, and a benign one came on its tail: she worked to keep life going the way it had in the past. But knowing it and believing it, with addled emotions, were two different things. The ups and downs of this condition continued to shock me, at least when I recognized them.

"I don't know," my voice sounded tired, a bit annoyed.

Delia wandered onto the porch, moving her head as if she were searching for something.

"What are you looking for, honey?" Sadie said.

"My snail. I can't find her anywhere." Delia sniffed.

"Did you ask your brother and sister?" My tactic always involved Charlie and Delia. Those two would find the proverbial needle in a haystack if given enough time.

"Yes. They can't find it. Brooke can't either." Delia crossed her arms over her chest, and a tiny scowl marred her features.

"Listen, we'll be right in to help you look. Give me a couple of minutes to speak with your dad, okay?" Sadie's sweet voice cut to my gut.

Much like I would have done, Delia narrowed her eyes and cocked her head before speaking. "Okay. Just a couple minutes?"

"I promise." Sadie patted Delia's back.

She made her way back into the house, poking into each crevice she encountered along the way. That snail—her favorite—ended up everywhere. I was tempted to call her back to us: a little interruption like that diffused the tension, at least a bit. It still hung in the air though.

"Well," Sadie said. "What should we do? I'm at a loss, Theo. A true loss."

"That's a first. I swear you always know what to do, Sadie."

Sadie's face blanched, and she blinked her eyes. I scanned her face for a reason behind those actions but saw nothing. She'd always been the voice of reason, the beacon of common sense, the person to find the solution to many of our problems. Why not this time? I still trusted her, or I wouldn't be living in the same house.

She shook her head. "This time, I don't. I can keep an eye on them all, talk with them, see how they're doing but—" A quick lift of her eyebrows and then nothing.

What did "but" mean? Did she want me to do more? Could I do more? Doc had been pleased with my involvement with the kids. Even with my episodes, I always had time for them. I had my own "but" though. That "but" roared to life.

"But what? It's hard on you? It is, I get it. Because it's all hard on me too. Fun fact: sometimes I wonder about all this, my life, you, the kids. Sometimes, I wish I hadn't signed up for the service." Bits of paint on the swing crumbled away as I gripped the arm with tight fingers. "I wonder about my dad and his propensity for depression and whether I should have gone to Afghanistan. Sometimes, I'd like to go back in time and redo everything. And I mean everything. As much as I love—," I almost said "you" but pulled the word back, "the kids, I'm not sure I'd help you with that flat tire."

A fire exploded in my chest. Those words had been unplanned. Did I mean them? The shock, the hurt that crossed Sadie's face, pained me.

"Mom! I need you!" Delia's screechy whine filtered through the cracked window. Any more conversation regarding this topic had to wait. Tentatively, I stretched out my hand to Sadie's and squeezed her fingers before she jerked them away. If I'd learned one thing from Doc, it was I had to try and be present for my family. "This partnership," Doc had said, "regardless of what it looks like at the present, needs everything you can give to it." Even if it kills me? I'd thought. On some days, it felt like it might.

Chapter 17: Sadie

When I was young, I wouldn't have won any awards for Most Observant Child. In fact, my mother used to yell at me, "Get your head out from under the pillow, Sadie! What are you, an ostrich? Look what's right in front of you!" She said it loudly, and often, and even though she had messed up the idiom so completely, her meaning was clear. By the time my college years rolled around, Mom had spoken those same words to me so regularly, I always looked twice at everything, and oftentimes second-guessed myself.

Had I placed my head underneath the pillow once again? How had I not even considered how Theo might feel?

After a long day of work and far too much thinking, I considered texting Andrew and asking him to meet for coffee. The idea of a gentle friend to sit and listen to me, someone nonjudgmental, brought warmth to my soul. But I didn't have the courage to do so; plus, if I did contact Andrew, my motives would be more spurred on by selfishness than anything else. Instead, I needed to do one of two things: be honest about Andrew or walk away and move forward with my life.

But Theo's words had shaken me. In his heart, Theo would never trade in Charlie, Lexie, or Delia, or even our love that was; he'd been speaking from a bruised body and soul. No matter how much what he said had hurt me, I understood his stance. His words haunted me, though, as October gave way to November. We filled our lives with maintaining the necessities, both of us avoiding the topic of that conversation or possible therapy for the kids. We'd bring the subject up eventually, but Theo and I each went back to "putting our heads under the pillow," as Mom would say. What Andrew would do if he were in the same situation niggled the back of my brain, but we hadn't seen one another for a few weeks, and our texts to each other had dropped, mercifully, to simple hellos from time to time.

But one day in mid-November, I arranged to meet them—Andrew and his two kids—at the small creek that wound through the local arboretum. When they saw us, the three of them raised their arms in unison, hands undulating back and forth, almost as if meeting up occurred every week.

Andrew was a refreshing sight: tall and lean, a broad smile pasted to his face, a look that welcomed me forward to say "good afternoon." He exuded calm and unfettered joy at the same time, putting me at ease in a way I wasn't used to. Perhaps Andrew was right, and fate's hand had brought us together.

Brooke volunteered to take the kids, my three and his two, to the butterfly house. Because it was fall, the house would be closed, but the kids had always enjoyed walking around outside the enclosed space, peering in through the windows and looking at the leftover foliage that had survived the caterpillars' wrath. And the butterfly house was adjacent to the colossal Steepled Tree, an observation tower rising forty-six feet above a large cluster of conifer trees and one of the kids' favorite places to visit while at the arboretum.

The children ran off in the direction of the butterfly house, feet scampering, dust and gravel flying, the side of Charlie's face visible enough to witness an enormous smile break out when Brooke challenged him to a race. Basking in the moment, I reveled in the sound of my children's laughter and then suggested to Andrew we head in a different direction, to the newly installed Midwest Maze: a simplified form of the classic configuration of hedges one might find at an English estate. It resembled the kids' bush maze that dated further back than I remembered. However, the adult version was far more challenging. If you made it through the maze, you'd, of course, get to the other side. But finding your way took time.

Andrew and I walked for several minutes without speaking. I tilted my face toward the sun, looking for strength, hoping the rays' weakened warmth would give me courage, but right then, a cloud passed over, darkening the landscape. Was the shadow an omen?

A few steps farther, and the maze came into view. Crinkles formed at the corner of Andrew's eyes as he bet he'd get through to the center first.

"See you soon, maybe." Andrew took off without looking back.

Something about this meeting made me want to speak my honest mind to Andrew, but I wasn't quite sure what I wished to say to my Grocery Store Man. Hanging back, I let my mind wander as the arboretum's surroundings enveloped me. The desiccated sycamore leaves tossed by the November wind distracted me, and I bent and grabbed one, allowing the air currents to twirl the leaf between my fingers. If I gave Andrew enough time, he'd make it to the center of the maze well before I would. Because I wanted to speak with him before the children returned, I took the shortcut a park ranger had shown me on our last visit.

Creeping out the front of the center hedge, I traveled along the east side, found the thin space between two large arbor vitae, and glided in toward the center where a circle of wooden benches stood. There, Andrew stretched out on one of the smaller benches, hands behind his head, waiting for me to exit the maze. He opened his eyes wide when he saw where I came from and threw his head back in laughter.

"I should have known you might not have the patience for that maze. You're a practical woman with no time for trifles." He wiped a single tear from beneath his eye as he patted the spot next to him on the bench. Such small bits of life made this man laugh to the point of crying. Being able to let yourself go, no matter the time, the place, the situation, was a characteristic I admired.

"You're right. I figured the shortcut was the way to go. Another time I'll follow the rules." My voice sounded tired and preoccupied, even to me. Did he notice? I folded myself onto the cool bench, as leaves still attached to the nearest maple tree fluttered in the wind. A few dry ones fell off, floated to the ground, and landed at our feet, where they'd be stepped on by numerous strange shoes and boots. Those leaves had lost their tether to life, and this time, a tear formed in *my* eye when I thought of Theo and us. Did he ever consider himself like these leaves? They described me sometimes, except...except when I was with Andrew.

I looked his way then, to the shadows of the tree limbs dancing across his smiling face. He was close—close enough for me to smell the scent of his shampoo in the wisps of wind sailing by. His proximity unnerved yet calmed me, all at the same time. Again, the word *free* formed in my mind, and I knew I had to release that word from my vocabulary.

"I could sit here for hours, pretending my life back home didn't exist. Do you know that?" I still didn't tell him exactly what that life consisted of; I had no plans to reveal any more of those details.

"Yes, I do." His gaze held mine. "It's completely normal for you to want to sit and have peace. To not have to think about anything for a while—"

I didn't let Andrew finish his thought. "Kate says the best thing to do is to be honest, to do what's right for me. And she has a point." The words slipped out easily, no stutter or stammer in sight; a confidence had grown within me that hadn't been there before.

A line creased his brow, and he squinted with confusion. "Be honest about what?"

A slight hesitation occurred then, only for a moment, because so much about life can turn on a dime. And what I was about to do, to say, could change things in unfathomable ways. The impact my words would have and the impact I wanted them to have encompassed the unknown. I teetered on another precipice of which I was aware, but what lay beneath? I had no idea. And yet, I recklessly swallowed my fear and plunged ahead.

"That I look forward to your texts. That our random meetings make my day. That I asked you here because I want to learn more about you and...that I have feelings for you." The words hadn't gotten stuck in my throat like I thought they would. They poured forth *freely*. Shit, that word, again. I turned my head away from Andrew, this time before he glimpsed what lay inside me. There was no way I wanted to look into his eyes, as the bold confidence I had previously possessed fled. The swallows chirped, and the breeze danced as one moment went by and then another. How long could two people sit in awkward silence? And then Andrew moved a few inches, positioning himself so his entire being faced me. With a steady hand, he placed his fingers against my cheek and turned my chin toward his. So much emotion shimmered in his eyes I almost started to weep, for me, for him, for whatever *might* be but never *would* be.

"That admission had to be distressing and exhausting...for you to say those words...And I want to be honest with you because you deserve it. You need to know how difficult it is for me to say this." He paused, and I dropped my head toward my lap, which caused a few strands of hair to slip in front of my face, effectively shielding my eyes from Andrew.

A burning stung my palms, and my stomach felt as if it had folded in on itself. What was he going to say? That he didn't feel anything for me? As much as that admission might hurt, it would be the better option, the easiest thing for us both. If Andrew didn't, I'd go on with my life, and he'd go on with his. Story over and no harm done.

"Sadie." His calming voice encouraged me to lift my chin. With a free hand, he brushed the hair away from my face as I scanned his, trying to find something unidentifiable. Again, Andrew paused, as if he was scripting the words before the wrong ones spilled out.

"Yes?" Our faces were still so close. Had I leaned in a couple inches I'd taste the lips that hovered so near to mine. As it was, his cool breath fanned against my cheeks and tickled my insides. Andrew moved forward by mere centimeters and then stopped, as if he was troubled about what his next course of action would be or should be.

"I'm going to do the right thing here. And I don't want you to view me as a saint, because I'm far from it. But this isn't right. This...this...you and me. It could be right, but it's not right...right now." He held my face for a moment longer and then placed his hand back onto his lap. Andrew broke any visual connection we had, squared his shoulders, and looked off into the distance.

A sagging weight engulfed me, but I continued to stare at him, his touch lingering almost everywhere, even though he'd only had my chin in his grasp. Telling him the truth was easier to do than I thought, listening to Andrew let me down, telling me what I was doing was wrong, that in one word, I was again, being selfish. That's what he meant when he said it wasn't right, whether or not he used those words.

And then he spoke one more time: "But I'm not going to lie to you. I feel something for you too."

Andrew continued to gaze ahead, saying nothing further. He blinked a couple times, and while I wanted to stay and see if tears welled in his eyes or if he'd reach for me or if any other endearing gesture would be forthcoming, it wasn't the time. In the interest of self-preservation, I rose from the bench, pulled my coat around me, and walked away from him, from us, from a possible future. It might not have been the best response to his words, but it was the only one that seemed appropriate.

As my steps beat a quick pace on the gravel, my curiosity got the better of me, and I glanced back over my shoulder, just once. He again sat with his legs stretched out, hands behind his head. His graceful and leisurely posture—did it belie what he was feeling inside? Due to the distance I'd placed between us, his face wasn't clear. Could he make out the stain of tears littering mine?

With a rumpled tissue that had seen better days, I swiped away my tears and forced myself to walk beyond the maze to find Brooke and the kids. Lexie and Delia ran up the path and charged me, each of them grabbing a leg.

"Mommy! We saw a stick insect and a green worm!" Delia's words rushed out while Lexie smiled up at me. Charlie sauntered behind, with Brooke and Andrew's kids, but the brightness he exuded told me he was having fun. Seeing my children happy was something that made my heart burst every single time.

"That's great! What else did you see?"

Before anyone responded, my phone rang, and despite my intention not to answer it, when Brooke offered to take the children again, I let her. A quick goodbye and a quiet whispering of "Andrew is that way," in the event she wanted to return the children to him, and they were off once again.

Brooke had been with us a long time. How observant was she? Who would she blame? Thankfully, those questions would remain unanswered because Brooke remained loyal to both her charges and to me.

Without looking at the screen, and thinking the call might be Theo, I accepted the call.

"Hello?"

"Sadie, it's me." Kate's voice met my ear and an irritation washed over me. Kate always had impeccable timing. She seemed to make a phone call at a time when I didn't want to talk to anyone, usually when she needed me. I loved Kate and our history together, but at times, the relationship drained me more than it should.

"Hey, Kate," I said and mentally kicked myself for not checking who was calling. "Now's not a great time. Can I call you back?" A mottled stink bug attempted to climb a thin stick balanced between a limb and a tree trunk. The poor insect tried in vain to cling to the stick, but it kept falling backward, onto the gravel, only to repeat the same, feeble action. Cocking my head, I leaned down to get a better look at the bug.

"Uh, I guess so. Seems like it's hard for us to catch up these days," Kate said. The reserved tone of her voice indicated she wasn't happy with me, but she'd pulled the same tactic on me before. We both had lives to lead; she and I knew it. And sometimes, those lives got in the way of catching up with friends.

"I appreciate that. I'm in the middle of something right now." I tried to lend sweetness to my voice that wouldn't tip her off to anything. We'd been friends for so long, she read into my voice like no one else, but I had no plans to inform her I'd made no progress on the suggestion she'd made many Saturdays ago.

"Yeah, well, sure. Call me back when you have a chance."

The phone dimmed, and I placed it onto my lap, surprised Kate had let our conversation, or lack thereof, go so easily. Kate had never let anything go so simply, ever, and despite my first thought, my mind wondered if she had an ulterior motive in not drawing out the conversation. What was she trying to tell me? Was she still annoyed about the last time we'd seen each other?

That had been a month ago, long after she'd given me advice and at a time when she'd tried to push Theo into seeing a new therapist. Kate was into homeopathic means of relief and sometimes shunned traditional Western medicine. She felt if Theo admitted to a negative mindset, he'd be better able to resolve his issues. I'd often brushed aside what she had to say when it came to medical issues, but the day Kate told me of her negative mindset theory, I had exploded at her and questioned her credibility. We'd exchanged daggers—I'd accused her of making everything about her, and she'd done the same of me—and since that day, our closeness had waned.

Her phone call reminded me to check in with Theo, who would be home from work already.

You home? All okay? I texted.

All good. Thanks. He replied.

With the kids at the arboretum. Will be home soon.

Have fun.

I texted back a thumbs up.

Between the tree limbs, the rays of afternoon sun streamed onto my shoulders, warming them, and the smell of the loamy soil filled my nose as I ambled along the empty path to find Brooke and the kids. November in the arboretum was lovely, thankfully, and the beauty and simplicity of the natural surroundings soothed my mind, which ached with unanswered questions about Andrew, about Theo. About me.

But with the thought of Andrew, a giddiness erupted within me, my heart raced, and tingles broke out all over. *All over.* And while I was sure now, after his admission, we would go nowhere, the whole scenario was too much to deal with. The muscles of my back and shoulders tightened, and I twisted my fingers into the fabric of my skirt as I cursed myself for being in the same place I was back on Father's Day. How was I in the exact mental place?

If things had only been different, I thought, and stomped my foot against the damp earth. If Theo hadn't gone to Afghanistan, then we'd be fine. If Theo didn't have PTSD, then I wouldn't be in the middle of what was supposed to be a divorce, and I'd never have noticed Andrew at the grocery store. If I cared about Theo, then I'd be doing more to help him get better. *If, if, if.* That's all I focused on these days. I couldn't live my life inside a bunch of *if-then* statements; I'd never been good with them anyway.

The tap of a woodpecker narrowed my focus as I wound around a copse of pine trees. A fallen log had formed a nice stopping point, a place where the kids and I liked to rest our weary legs. I sat hard, too hard in fact, and the usual tears pricked against my eyelids, which caused the torrent to begin. The droplets fell to the ground, splashing onto the debris, displacing dust. With nothing left in my heart, I left my head fall forward into my hands, and I sobbed.

A quick beep from my phone alerted me to a text.

Nothing urgent! A message from Kate, which included a smiley face.

I should have asked her if she needed something. I should have apologized for my outburst about the "negative mindset." Had she been right that day months ago—that I thought it was all about me? Another stink bug caught my eye. Had the one I'd seen earlier crossed from the stick to tree trunk? Was he successful in his quest?

Having no way to know, I imagined he succeeded and crossed into his desired territory. If he could do it, so could I.

Chapter 18: Theo

I had always trusted Sadie to make the right choices, but when she surprised the entire family with her getaway idea, doubts plagued me. Big doubts.

"All right, kids, we're going on vacation!" Time seemed to stop in the kitchen as Sadie strode in with her arms wide open and cheeks bunched up from smiling.

"What? What do you mean, Mom?" Charlie asked. He hurtled from his seat at the breakfast bar and planted his body in front of his mother. "What about school? Film club? Piano? I'm going to miss a lot..." He looked like I felt sometimes: defeated, his small shoulders slumping, almost imperceptibly. He'd been having fun with school and with everything after school—so I'd been told. It was possible the activity took his mind off everything happening at home.

"Don't worry, Charlie. Part of this vacation spans Thanksgiving break, so you won't be missing as much school. If you don't want to go, we won't. But you're a great student, and you'll be fine." She put away the few items she had picked up from the grocery store and opened the window an inch. The cool fall breeze slipped in and brought dampness with it. A second later, Sadie cranked the window shut again. Rejected the harshness. To be able to crank my life closed at times.

The last few weeks had been ugly. In the morning, when it was time to get the kids moving and out the door, my usual "Let's move it, kids! What's wrong with you?" resulted in a resounding cringe from the kids and a "Really, Theo? It's more than just your tone!" from Sadie.

She tried to remind me whenever my "tone" was off, which happened most often when it was time for bed or if one of the kids needed help with their homework. My mood changes frustrated me, but I didn't always control them. I should tell Doc about that fact.

"If you're angry, be angry with me," Sadie would say. "Be angry with the PTSD. With the doctor. With yourself. But not the kids. And what about a change in meds? What are your thoughts?"

"It's hard," I'd reply, answering only half her question. "It's so damn hard."

And it was. Our situation exasperated me, and while I "turned inward"— again, thank you, Doc—much like Sadie would, it meant I spent too much time thinking about me, about us. The more I did, the more I had reservations about signing those papers. A simple signature would dismantle two decades of memories. Was I ready to be finished with all things Sadie? Doc's lips would twitch if I shared my thoughts, and I might get a "nice touch, being more self-aware" comment too. Maybe Sadie was right about this vacation. It would be a good idea. But where—

"And...we're going to...Walloon Lake!" Sadie announced.

"Yesssssss!" Delia and Charlie cheered in unison and fist-bumped each other. The enormous smiles on their faces said far more than words: they were ecstatic to be heading to our haven, and school could wait. For Delia, who normally didn't say much, a fist bump to her brother was a big deal, and she looked over at me and Sadie, sheepishly, as if we'd caught her taking a cookie from the cabinet without asking. Sadie smiled at the two of them.

"When do we leave?" Charlie asked and then spun around on his toes to grab Delia in a hug. "We need to bring the sand toys and our swimsuits and the raft and markers and the pool bag and sunscreen—"

Charlie's enthusiasm spread throughout the room: Delia twirled around the kitchen, continuing to list the items we'd need to cram into the minivan.

"Whoa, hold up, kids. It's fall, and the weather's pretty cold. They might have had snow already. Not sure about the pool bag or the swimsuits." My words might have deflated other kids. But ours? Not a chance.

Charlie slapped his forehead, a smile dimpling his face. "Oh right. But we should bring the toys to make sandcastles. We can build a snow family and a snow fort and what about the lake, will it be iced over yet?" Charlie's squint indicated he'd already started construction of the fort—complete with intricate, elaborate details—inside his head.

"We'll see," Sadie said. "I've never been to the lake in any other season than summer, so this'll be a new experience for us all. But I've heard good things, really good things about this time of the year up there. The trees, the leaves, the snow if there is any. It's supposed to be gorgeous."

A huge grin, much like the sort she'd sported when I first met her and she'd serve an ace, spread across her face. That face. If I concentrated on it, I'd fall down a rabbit hole again. Getting away from this place might be a good thing.

"A few more arrangements need to be made, but then we're good to go." Sadie flung her hands back and forth in front of her, trying to forge her way through two dancing children to the phone desk. She picked up her calendar, which reminded me that even with a vacation in mind, work still called, for both of us.

I turned my chair, the legs scraping against the tile, as I beat my fingers against the tabletop. "What about your work?"

"I've triple-checked with everyone there already, and we're good. Jackie can handle in-house items, and I can do some tasks from the cottage. It should be fine."

"What about Wi-Fi?"

"Really, it's fine, Theo. The library has great hours, and if the owners have caved and gotten it at the cottage..."

Of course, Sadie had a ready answer. She always did.

She was right, though. We'd been staying at a private cottage for several years, and much of the reason we both enjoyed our time at Walloon Lake was because of our ability to unplug. No land lines and weeks without Facebook and Twitter. No email, even, if that's what you wanted. That time away from technology used to be sacred, and any Walloon Lake vacation was deemed "blissful" by Sadie's standards. On the other hand, having Wi-Fi access would make the trip much easier this time. However, my job—I'd need to take vacation days, those I might not even have.

"But what about me?" I continued the drumbeat on the tabletop and realized the act helped me, kept me in the present with my family; maybe it even tamped down the "mercurial swings in mood" Doc and I had discussed.

"You, Theo? Did you think I was going to leave you here?"

Sadie's tone of voice teased me, yet at the back of my mind I had to question her motivation: did she have a notion that time away from me, from us, would be a good thing?

"Do I have a choice?"

"Actually, you do. If you want to stay here, so be it. If you want to come, the offer is open."

"But what about the kids when you're trying to work? Is Brooke coming?"

Comprehension seemed to wash over her, and she stretched out a hand to cover my fingers, stopping their movement. "Oh, no. She couldn't this time, but thankfully, I found someone who would be more than happy to earn a couple extra bucks by helping out when I'm out of the house."

Sadie—always prepared for come what may—would have a current itinerary of a typical day drawn up in no time, including all emergency numbers and applicable medications. Her ability to multitask, well, it was admirable at times. She "got shit done," as Liam used to say.

"Well, it's clear you've thought of everything, haven't you?"

With a quick nod she said, "I hope so. Which means I should get our belongings together and find all the extra things we need and contact the teachers and principal with a few more questions, and we'll be good to go! Let me know what you decide!" Sadie turned on her heels and headed toward the stairs. Her form retreated and her footsteps faded. A new thought came to mind: enabler. That's what Sadie was; that's the role she played in our story. Doc would be so proud of me for recognizing it.

●   ●   ●   ●   ●

The decision was easy: as much as Kettering was a great place to live, Walloon was a great place to visit. And work had no issue with me taking time off. Again, the byproduct of working for someone who pretty much gave you a job.

"One thing you can do for us, Theo," the boss said. "Scope out the area. See what the fitness centers are like up there and how many they have."

"Can do, Boss."

Walloon had never been a place I looked to for a workout, so I had no idea what was available, but I'd have time to investigate. And as usual, being busy would be good for me. Not that I didn't have plans to spend time with the kids, but the boss's mission would give structure to my day. Doc and I had both determined my best days were those where I'd planned my activities—fewer changes, less unpredictability.

While I was entering my vacation time into the computer log, Andrew stopped by the desk.

"You okay?"

I hadn't spoken much to him after I left him at the bar. No reason; just busy, and I didn't want to discuss the possibility of dating again. He might be ready, but I wasn't. In fact, I was still hung up on the woman I legally called my wife. *Shit*. Thankfully, my knuckles had healed and another interaction with the wall hadn't occurred.

"I'm fine. I'm not sure what that was the other night."

"Working too hard perhaps?"

"It's happened before."

Andrew patted the counter. "Haven't we all? Glad you're okay. See you later." He turned toward the locker rooms.

"Hey, I'll be gone for a few weeks. Headed on vacation with the family for a bit."

Andrew stopped and furrowed his brow. "Might I say it's an odd time to go on vacation?"

I laughed. "You're right. But I need it. I'm pretty sure we all need it."

He didn't ask more. "Enough said. Then I'll see you when you get back. And maybe we can talk more about future projects?"

Andrew's projects. What I'd read had lured me in. If I was to keep making forward progress, I might need a better distraction. "Sure. I'll text you."

After work, I stopped by Doc's office. The receptionist told me I was lucky: Doc's latest appointment had been canceled, and she had a few moments to chat.

"The mood swings—they keep coming—but a vacation might help," I told her.

"Really? Is it a means of escape for Sadie?"

"Well if it is, then I can place the blame on her, right? Her idea and all."

"You know what I'm going to say."

My thoughts coalesced in the silence of Doc's office, and it didn't take long. Yes, I'd blamed Sadie. I could have said no to the idea of a vacation. Staying home by myself would be a "staycation" as they said, time to myself if the rest of the family was gone.

"I do, and you're right. No was an option. But Walloon Lake—"

Doc held up her index finger. "From what I hear, it's tough to stay away from. Someday, I'd like to go there," she said.

"You should. I'll give you the contact information for the place we rent."

"Let's not get distracted. Is this about Walloon or Sadie? Going on vacation together," and Doc used her fingers to put air quotes about the word, "might not be the best way to get over your wife—soon to be ex-wife—is it? Your feelings for her, unresolved as they may be, are getting in the way. It might be..."

Doc's true thoughts didn't interest me, but I knew better than to be rude about it. I held up my hand, and she graciously paused. "Yes. I'm waffling on my feelings for my wife."

"So, you admit it..."

Yes, I'd admitted it. I wasn't sure what it was about the last few months, but one thing had become clear: I wasn't ready to cut the cord. However, she was.

And Sadie was the type of woman you didn't force into anything. Plus, who wants to be with someone who doesn't want you back? The question was: did a way to get her back exist?

"Theo." Doc leaned in, her voice almost a low whisper. "I understand what makes you tick. Deep down, you're a good guy. You *want* to get better—for yourself and for your family. And I don't doubt you still love Sadie. But I have to wonder if we shouldn't consider something more, change your medications, look at other CBT therapies than we're using...an inpatient program for you. This waffling...it might be indicative of something else."

"Like what?"

"Well, have your episodes been increasing? We haven't talked much about your anger lately or whether you've still been having nightmares. And I wonder if you aren't actually in denial."

"About what?"

Doc sighed. "About Sadie. About her perspective. I don't want to upset you, but the two of you had decided to divorce. For a time, Sadie was encouraging you to sign the papers—"

"But she hasn't in a while!"

"Okay, she hasn't in a while. But have you spoken to her? You said yourself a few months ago, in the summer," she looked at her notes, "she seemed different, distracted. Did you talk about it? If she wanted to get back together, wouldn't she have come talk to you?"

Breathe in, breathe out. Doc's words rebounded off the walls of my brain. I tried to shut them out but couldn't. The arms of the plush chair dimpled under the crushing weight of my fingers as I gripped them, and I took a final, deep breath in through my nose once again.

"Don't say anything. Not yet. I mentioned this before a while ago, and I'll admit...I even called Sadie to talk about in-patient possibilities—"

"You did what?" I rose, ready to punch not Doc, but the wall, the door, the chair, whatever I found in my path.

"Hey!" Doc got up from her chair, palms facing me. "Hold up. I didn't speak to her. She never returned my call, and I admit, I dropped the ball. But now, I need to speak with her."

"Not yet. Let me talk to her first."

Doc tapped her chin with her finger. "Okay, I'll give you until after you return from vacation. Is that fair? We can hold a virtual session or two while you're gone, but check in with me when you return, and if you haven't spoken to her about your feelings, and even if you have, if you'd be best in hospital, that's where we're going."

My vacation plans had veered in a direction I didn't want them to go. Such was the state of my life.

Chapter 19: Sadie

Kettering sat about fifty miles north of the Ohio-Kentucky border, while Walloon Lake was nestled almost the same distance south of the tip of Michigan's Lower Peninsula. With three kids and a front-seat passenger who might need to take frequent breaks, I wasn't sure how much time the journey *would* take or how many hours it would *feel* like it took.

The strum of the tires against the pavement lulled me into a false sense of security. Inside the car, with the radio on low and Theo and the kids asleep, it was easy to imagine this vacation would be like any other Walloon vacation we'd taken in the past. Lexie would point out the taxidermy on the walls of the gas stations where we stopped, and Delia would clamor for snacks from Ann Arbor to Elmira. Nonstop talking from Charlie—about the merits of Petoskey stones—would begin about the time we turned onto Evergreen Road. While Theo had proven beyond measure that Walloon Lake vacations agreed with him, this time, based on the reason for booking this vacation, my confidence waned.

After our third stop in five hours, discontent engulfed me. Little things jumped to my attention: the dust covering the dashboard; the large amount of paper receipts left in the console; Theo's snoring drowning out my beloved alternative music. I pushed away at the minor annoyances and tried to concentrate on the passing landscape—barren, the skeletal trees projected foreboding—but even there, the poor driving skills of the truck to the right of me drew my attention.

With a quick shake of my head and a roll of my neck, I gripped the steering wheel until my knuckles turned white. When had I become so focused on the negative?

A slight shuffle from the passenger seat alerted me Theo was awake, with sleep still trying to hold his eyelids shut. Dragging my gaze back to the road, I waited for him to speak.

"Hey," he whispered.

"Yeah?"

"Traffic okay?" Theo shimmied his shoulders against the back of the car seat—an attempt to get more comfortable.

"Yeah. You need anything?" While the snack bag and drinks sat nearer to his feet, I was used to asking that question. As for the seat belt and the lack of circulation he was sure to be experiencing—something that might tip his irritation off—there was nothing to do.

"No, I'm good. Thanks."

The angle of the road shifted enough, and the muted afternoon sun sliced into my eyes. One more little aggravation that took on monumental proportions the longer I sat in the car. Envisioning the quaint houses lining the streets surrounding Walloon Lake helped my ire dissipate. "Remember when we looked at the cottage on East Street? The one with the three bedrooms and front porch?"

We'd considered purchasing a piece of property near the foot of the lake, but once Theo's symptoms set in, we pulled back on any extra expenditures in case we lost insurance coverage or another emergency emerged. A short vacation once or twice a year was no trouble; purchasing a second home constituted a grandiose dream that had to be shelved, at least for the interim. And now with an impending divorce....

"I do. It would be nice to have that house right now though. We'd come up here whenever and however often we wanted to." Theo's voice sounded wistful, as if he longed to be somewhere else in his life, and I imagined he did. What would he say if he knew I did too?

"Sure, but what about your treatment? Another doctor might not want to take you on." Pausing, I pursed my lips because of my mangled words, somewhat annoyed Theo had woken, and he had started this conversation in the first place. "You know what I mean...I didn't mean it the way it sounded. It's just that, you'd miss Doc." The dust motes on the dashboard caught my attention once again.

Theo chuckled, and the vestiges of his old self rang out loud and clear. "We've been together long enough. I knew what you meant and didn't take it any other way." He awkwardly patted my knee once, a sign that he stood behind his words. But how long had it been since Theo had performed such a gesture? And how did I feel about it? Truth be told, I felt nothing beneath his touch, and that realization—

"Charlie! You can't do that!" In the few moments Theo and I had been speaking, Charlie must have woken and erected a mountain of pillows that blocked my view out the back window.

"Sorry, Mom."

I tried to catch his gaze in the rearview mirror. "It's okay. I need to see out the back. Just keep the pillows down, all right?"

"Okay." He lifted his arms above his head and cracked his back, a motion I'd always loathed. "Are we there yet?"

"Hush! If you say it loud enough, Lexie will wake, and that's all we'll hear for the rest of the trip."

Charlie nodded once and grabbed his most recent acquisition from the library—the next book in the *Percy Jackson* series—and within minutes, he'd been transported elsewhere.

Lexie and Delia stayed quiet, and while no one else demanded my time, I glanced again into the rearview mirror to spy on the girls, whose slender necks were stretched back, their heads resting on the car seat head rests, mouths hanging open and eyes closed.

"You sounded a bit harsh there, to Charlie I mean." Theo said.

"I what?"

"You didn't need to yell at him is all."

"I didn't—"

"To me it sounded like you did."

Arguments were never fun, especially in tight surroundings when the kids were within earshot. "I'm...sorry. I didn't intend to sound that way. It's been a long trip. We can talk about this another time. Little ears and all."

Theo nodded in understanding. "Well, I'm sorry too. Maybe I misheard. I've had a tough few weeks. And months. Actually, it's been rough for a couple years. You know that."

Yes, and I sympathized with him, what his life was like, and where he was headed in the future. If he knew all I was going through, he'd have no sympathy for me. There was no way I wanted to reveal anything to him on a car ride up the interstate. He deserved more than a shoddy conversation.

A safer conversation topic would allow Theo and me to speak quietly while at the same time let me release some of my frustration. "So, I planned out this vacation with the idea we'd run it like we have any other year."

"Which means?"

"Well...I'll need to get to the store for groceries pretty much right away, but I want to meet the babysitter first." Before we'd left Kettering, I'd called a few people we knew at Walloon, who suggested contacting a local church for babysitters. Not that I didn't trust Theo, but he needed this vacation in a way I didn't, and stress from the kids—which came at any time—meant we should keep a babysitter handy for those times when I needed to work.

As luck would have it, a family we knew had a cousin, a woman in her early thirties named Lena, who was between jobs and would be happy to help. "After such a long car ride you won't want to go to the store, will you? You can chat with her and see if she'll work out."

"You're right. I won't want to get back in the car. But we can get a few things from the general store tonight and then go in the morning. What do you say?"

The grocery store bag between us stood three-quarters full, and I mentally checked everything I had loaded into it and the small travel cooler. We'd be fine with what we had and a gallon of milk from the small general store at the heart of the village. "Let's see what time we get there, and then we'll make a decision."

"Sounds good." Theo clumsily reached for my right hand and took it in his. His long fingers, which used to be so warm, now brought a chill to me, and they seemed to cling to mine, as if to gather heat and...what else? "You always know what to do, Sadie. How do you do it?"

That was the second time in as many months Theo had spoken those words. I swallowed a large lump in my throat and forced a stiff smile onto my face— the best I could do to cover up the lie spreading between us like a blood stain. *If you only knew, Theo. If you only knew.*

Chapter 20: Sadie

Because I didn't have time off from work (or life), I left for the Walloon branch of the Crooked Tree Library at the first available opportunity, which was 4:00 p.m. on the Monday after we arrived. I stepped up the library's wide, wooden stairs and opened the heavy, oak door, the rush of the warm air blasting against my body. Michigan was having an exceptionally warm November, but that term, warm, was so relative. Fifty-two degrees, in my mind, didn't even touch lukewarm. Now seventy-five degrees and sunny—I'd take it.

Once I'd nodded a quick hello to the library volunteer at the front desk, I settled into a cozy chair in the corner of the magazine section. The wall opposite the magazine racks housed floor-to-ceiling windows backing up to a chorus line of magnificent pine trees, making the room feel as though you were in the middle of a forest. Plugging in my laptop, I switched my phone to vibrate and placed it on the desk, then opened the lid of my computer. A few projects required my attention, and the details of the book covers were logged into an excel spreadsheet. The necessary accompanying site online loaded as my computer dinged, indicating a new email message.

from: Jackie Mills <Jackie.R.Mills@percolettiwinn.com>
to: Sadie Rollins <Sadie.M.Rollins@percolettiwinn.com>
date: Mon, Nov 12, 2018 at 4:13 PM
subject: Vacation

Hi, Sadie! I hope you made it to Walloon Lake safely. How was the trip? As long as usual? Keep me posted on whether you made it there, and I won't bother you too much! xo Jackie

I should have expected as much from Jackie and was shocked she hadn't contacted me earlier. She knew the first few days at Walloon Lake would be full of energy and chaos. I had planned on emailing Jackie anyway—and phone service here was often spotty—so I keyed in a quick reply.

from: Sadie Rollins <Sadie.M.Rollins@percolettiwinn.com>
to: Jackie Mills <Jackie.R.Mills@percolettiwinn.com>
date: Mon, Nov 12, 2018 at 4:15 PM
subject: Let's hope it is a vacation

Hi, Jackie. Thanks for your message. We made it, and because the kids are older, we didn't have to stop too much (only six times!). Theo didn't mind the trek, either. In fact, the worst part was Lexie's request for the Unicorn Song thirty times. Theo decided the whole CD should be burned. I had to literally rip it out of his hands before he threw the CD and case out the window. Good times. Talk to you soon. Sadie.

I kept the email tab open and clicked on the file icon I needed. The client was a big one, a company that had requested our services a few years back and had been surprised at our efficiency and thoroughness. Based on our past history, they trusted me to do a phenomenal job, even from a seat inside the Crooked Tree Library. The problem was, with all the turbulence in my personal life, the project might overwhelm me, and a good brainstorming session could be in order. *I should ask Jackie if she has time to help.* I clicked on the window that exposed my email and allowed my fingers to fly over the keyboard.

from: Sadie Rollins <Sadie.M.Rollins@percolettiwinn.com>
to: Jackie Mills <Jackie.R.Mills@percolettiwinn.com>
date: Mon, Nov 12, 2018 at 4:18 PM
subject: Help!

Hi, Jackie. Me again (obviously). I opened my file and realized a brainstorming session is badly needed before I can move forward. Any time for a call soon? I'd prefer that over an email discussion, if you have the time. Thanks. Sadie.

from: Jackie Mills <Jackie.R.Mills@percolettiwinn.com>
to: Sadie Rollins <Sadie.M.Rollins@percolettiwinn.com>
date: Mon, Nov 12, 2018 at 4:19 PM
subject: Oh, I can help...

Hi, Sadie. Sure, I can schedule a call, but it might not be a good time right now. I have someone here, and I need to speak with him. He just left to take a call of his own. And he says hi, by the way. xo and ;-) Jackie

from: Sadie Rollins <Sadie.M.Rollins@percolettiwinn.com>
to: Jackie Mills <Jackie.R.Mills@percolettiwinn.com>
date: Mon, Nov 12, 2018 at 4:20 PM
subject: No!

Really? It's Andrew isn't it? Why did you tell me that? Remember why I went on this vacation? Didn't I tell you? Yes, I'm sure I did. What kind of friend are you anyway? :P Sadie

from: Jackie Mills <Jackie.R.Mills@percolettiwinn.com>
to: Sadie Rollins <Sadie.M.Rollins@percolettiwinn.com>
date: Mon, Nov 12, 2018 at 4:21 PM
subject: Yes!

It's Andrew, and I guess I wasn't thinking. Can I blame it on the hormones? I'm STILL not back to my pre-baby self, in mind or body. Will I ever get there? And you ARE a great friend, one who I would NEVER intentionally do anything bad to. You know that, right? Sorrysorrysorrysorrysorrysorrysorrysorrysorrysorry. xo Jackie

from: Sadie Rollins <Sadie.M.Rollins@percolettiwinn.com>
to: Jackie Mills <Jackie.R.Mills@percolettiwinn.com>
date: Mon, Nov 12, 2018 at 4:23 PM
subject: Yes, and you'll get there

You're lucky I'm one of your GREATEST friends because yes, I can forgive you. And I get what you mean about mind and body. It takes a long time, but you will get back to some semblance of who you were before you had Clara. Of course, it won't ever be the same, and you might have to tape a few body parts up, but that, my friend, is way too much for me to delve into in this email. I guess I'll be polite, and you can say hi to Andrew for me. But that's all. You don't need to say where I am. And now, you owe me. So call me tomorrow at 9:30 a.m. We can brainstorm for a bit, and then I can come back here to the library. They open at 10 a.m. Thanks. Sadie.

from: Jackie Mills <Jackie.R.Mills@percolettiwinn.com>
to: Sadie Rollins <Sadie.M.Rollins@percolettiwinn.com>
date: Mon, Nov 12, 2018 at 4:25 PM
subject: Okay

I'll give your best to Andrew and I'll call you tomorrow at 9:30. I wrote you in on the desk calendar, IN PEN. How about that? Now let's hope the connection goes through (if you don't hear from me by 9:35, give me a call). But please don't work the entire two weeks while you're up there. You have a lot of memories from that place, and memories can work *magic* sometimes. Remember, your family needs you. You need you. xo Jackie

from: Sadie Rollins <Sadie.M.Rollins@percolettiwinn.com>
to: Jackie Mills <Jackie.R.Mills@percolettiwinn.com>
date: Mon, Nov 12, 2018 at 4:26 PM
subject: Payment

Your check is in the mail.

After making progress on a smaller but as important project, I packed up my belongings and made my way out of the library. The walk home would be short, no more than five to seven minutes, and the anticipation of extending the quiet that had ensconced me at the library energized me. I pulled my wool coat around my waist, tightening the belt, and thought back to what Jackie had written to me. She was right: Theo and I had years and years of memories embedded in this place. From time at the beach to the hours spent at the playground, moments in each other's arms on the front porch and in the back bedroom. In fact, I was certain Delia had been conceived in this place. And this was my time to get away from the life that had started to spin out of control at Kettering Plaza. If I connected with the memories and remembered how invested we had once been—in each other and in us—winding myself back on the right path, the path toward a more authentic me might be possible,

When I stepped around the corner at Lake Street, I almost walked into a little old lady and her beagle. Even in the dark, the woman's houndstooth coat and plaid scarf stood out, and a huge smile splayed across her face. A flower clip sprang from her ashen hair, and her blue eyes sparkled as she lifted a gloved hand to wave. Year-rounders liked to stop and chat, check in on all of life's comings and goings, so I hesitated, but with a wink and another smile, she kept on her way. Taking my cue from her, I waved back and continued my walk toward the cottage.

Something pushed me to turn back and watch the lady as she progressed up the street while keeping up a conversation with someone invisible. She had to have been talking to her pet—an amusing thought—as she shuffled away, straightening her skirt from time to time and stopping to pick up rocks from along the road. Her short, jaunty movements emitted joy, and the small encounter with her produced a warmth within my chest.

I pulled my phone from my pocket and sent a short, quick text to Andrew: *Away but you're on my mind anyway.*

His reply arrived within an instant: *Me as well. Enjoy your time away.*

A smile graced my face as I ambled around to the front porch at a little after eight in the evening and placed my feet upon the sagging, cedar steps. Lexie and Delia, possibly even Charlie, would be in bed if the afternoon had been full of outdoor activity. The wood squeaked under my shoes as I touched the edge of the red, painted door and peeked through the side lights.

The end table lamp illuminated the living room area. Lena and Theo sat on the pin-striped sofa, watching a sitcom of some sort, the glow of the television highlighting their grins. My curiosity got the best of me as I looked at the two of them, both so close on the furniture, as if they'd known each other for longer than a day. A slight pang of—what, jealousy?—murmured within me, an emotion that shocked me for two reasons. One, I might be seeing something that wasn't there. And two, my feelings for Theo had been extinguished long ago, as evidenced by my encouragement for him to sign the divorce papers.

I opened the screen with a light hand and turned the brass doorknob, entering the living room. The dry heat from the electric heaters brought tears to my eyes, blurring my vision. Even with my sudden presence, Lena didn't jump back from Theo. Instead, she pushed the button on the remote control and placed it on the coffee table before giving me her undivided attention. Theo followed her lead and moved to catch my gaze. My glance danced back and forth between the two of them. Was I being unreasonable and seeing something? Was my mind preoccupied by my own flaws and projecting? What did Theo think about a young woman like Lena, a stranger, sitting so close to him?

"How was the library?" A trace of fatigue laced Theo's voice as he pushed his hands through his hair and pinched the bridge of his nose, both telltale signs he was annoyed. By my arrival or by my going to the library in the first place?

My work bag slid off my shoulder to the floor, where I scooted it with my foot into the corner so the children wouldn't disrupt it in the morning. "Not as productive as I had hoped, but I finished enough for now. I do need to go back tomorrow..."

"But you promise not to be there the whole day." Theo finished the sentence for me as his eyebrows rose to his hairline.

Lena must have sensed discord for she rose from the couch to gather up the water glasses and headed to the kitchen, her footsteps so light they barely registered in my ears.

"Yes, I promise." I pulled off my gloves and stuffed them into the coat pocket before shrugging the garment from my shoulders. "And I mean it. I have a call with Jackie at nine thirty, and I'll go to the library at ten, which means I should be done with the first installment by noon."

Theo quirked his eyebrows, a silent notice of his disbelief. The sound of dishes in the sink indicated Lena must be cleaning up the kitchen, something I'd have to remember to thank her for before she left for the night.

"Hey, I mean it, Theo. I love this cottage, this place." My gaze darted around the room, taking in the familiar furniture, photo collages, and books before it landed on Theo again. *This place...but not you.* Why was I still questioning myself?

"Yes, but you also love your job." He looked at me as he spoke that simple truth, as if daring me to deny it. His posture—tight shoulders, straight neck—told me he expected my rebuttal, something I'd give to him to avoid the answer to the question I'd asked myself.

"I do. But this job is keeping us afloat right now. Without this job, our budget would be tighter. You're only working part-time, and that's to be expected. But we wouldn't be here, at the cottage, if it weren't for *my job*." Utter irritation clawed at me as my voice fought to stay low and not wake up the kids. Theo had probably meant to start an argument, but I didn't want to rise to the bait. What he said was the truth—my job sometimes came before family time—but right now, what *I* said was also the truth. We needed my job.

A simple shuffling of feet behind me forced me to turn and acknowledge Lena, who held her thin coat and purse in her hand. She placed the purse on the floor as she slid her slim shoulders into the arms of the fleeced denim jacket.

"Well," she said, "It was a pleasure to meet you all, but I should get going. I've got a few projects of my own to do at home." As she adjusted her collar, she inclined her head toward Theo. "Do you need me tomorrow? I'd be more than happy to come for part of the day. I'm not sure I'm needed here the whole time: the kids were great, and Theo seemed fine today."

Theo would prefer I not go back to the library and spend time on my work commitments, but in my mind, the outcome was a given. He nodded slightly, and I knew I'd won the battle. When had our life gotten so competitive? Our situation—on many levels—needed to change soon.

"Sure. Can you come by about nine fifteen or so? You may have overheard—I have a call at nine thirty. I'll aim to be back by noon. If you can get lunch ready, I'll be here to help set the table, and of course, you're welcome to stay and eat with us." I looked at Theo before I continued. "We appreciate what you're doing for us, so always plan on staying to eat if you want."

"Thank you. I had a good time today with the kids, and I hope I was helpful." Lena turned toward Theo and addressed him. "See you tomorrow, Theo. You too, Sadie."

Her face held no hint of anything that might make me pull away from her, anything that said she had found Theo attractive and by having her here, I'd be doing more harm to our family. Nothing in her soulful eyes and genuine smile gave me pause, but my belly still roiled with unease.

"Thanks for doing the dishes. And we appreciate you being available on such short notice."

She paused at the door before pushing the screen open and heading out onto the porch. "You're welcome. I'll see you in the morning. Have a great night."

"You too."

Lena's thin form meandered up the street. I closed the door and locked the deadbolt, then closed the blinds and adjusted the thermostat. Theo had tilted his head back against the couch cushion, but he followed my movements. The exhausted look on his face worried me.

"Long day?" The couch still radiated heat from Lena's body. I snuggled in against the fabric—anything to chase away the coldness that had overtaken me the last few minutes.

"Yes, but it was good. Lena didn't say it, but she might have been uncomfortable at first. I'm not sure why. Because I was around? But the kids enjoyed playing at the beach, despite the cooler temps. You should have seen the castle they built. They even dipped their feet into the water." He chuckled, probably at the memory of the kids in the water. "Actually, so did I, and it wasn't too bad. I was concentrating so hard on the cold water and anything else that might be wrong with me fell to the wayside." Again, a smile passed across his face.

I leaned my head against the back of the couch but kept my sight on Theo. "Huh. I hope the weather holds then. I'm going to assume the kids are all asleep?" Theo nodded his head in affirmation. Later, I'd be sure to stop in and smooch the sweet darlings, in case Lena and Theo forgot anything, like the perpetual water glass by Charlie's bedside or the extra stuffed animal standing guard on the dresser next to Delia.

The thought of the kids tucked into their small beds made me consider my sleep habits. Despite the early hour, the stress of the long drive on Saturday mixed with a full Sunday and too much jolting of my heart that morning had made me exhausted.

"Are you heading up?" I asked Theo. Visions of fluffy pillows, a warm comforter, and a good book danced in my mind.

"No, not yet," Theo said and laid his hand on mine. The look in his eyes seemed full of questions, ones I didn't want to know about and didn't care to answer. If I shut my eyes, I could pretend I was more exhausted than I was. "It's just, we're supposed to be divorcing, but..."

A trace of nostalgia echoed in Theo's voice, so I opened my eyes and peeked at him. His tired face, full of a sadness I understood, irritated me. We were here, at Walloon Lake, our "happy place." Talking about an impending divorce seemed so tasteless, something I wanted to avoid. We'd covered all the "buts" already, many times over. And despite the odd circumstances, he had a good life. A safe life. His face should have shown some positivity, at least contentment. Did he even recognize something was off?

The energy within me didn't exist to draw out whatever was on his mind. Everything surrounding our conversation radiated "awkward," sitting with my soon-to-be ex in a place that held such fond memories for me, but knowing my life was riddled with unrest, that the memories made from this year forward would be different, for both of us. My hand fell away from his in the process of standing up.

"Holler if you need something. I'll be reading for a while." Smoothing the hair on Theo's head with my fingers felt right and for a moment, he leaned into my palm.

"All right, Sadie. Sweet dreams."

I turned away before Theo caught the teardrops perched on my lower lids.

Chapter 21: Theo

"Any thoughts about having a fitness center in the area? As in, right in the village?" I asked Mike, the owner of the general store. Tuesday morning and I wanted to get a jump on things. Leaving the kids with Lena for an hour—Sadie would be heading to the library, again—I'd walked up to the village area to gauge the interest of the year-rounders. Walloon Lake Village had a lot to offer its visitors and residents by way of food, drink, and entertainment—both indoor and outdoor—but a fitness center didn't round out the list.

"Here? In town? You know there's one up in Petoskey, right? And that...that thing. A spa or whatever the ladies like to go to? It's up on Michigan Street, I think, plus there's the salon next door."

I jotted down the three places he mentioned on my data collection clipboard. "Yes, here. In the village. My boss is scoping out new sites, and he wondered if a fitness center might do well in this area."

"If you can get to it in the winter." Mike smiled.

"Yeah, there's that. But people get *here* in the winter, don't they?" A blast of cool air pushed against my back as a customer entered the store.

"Touché. But in the summer, well, there's the lake. The trails. We're all so used to driving over to Petoskey or Charlevoix when we want something a little bigger. Sometimes it's pretty clear we're not so good about change here."

Change? Who *was* good about it? Wasn't that part of my inherent problem?

"And yet, five years ago, you might not have used the word 'touché' in everyday conversation, right?" Mike shook his head at my words and tapped a roll of quarters against the counter as I continued. "You've had a lot of change here. The new restaurants, the hotel, the pop-up shops. I'll keep asking around, but thanks for giving me your opinion."

"You're welcome. I'm not sure it was the one you wanted."

"It's fine." I clicked the end of my pen twice before stopping myself. There was no reason to be irritated with Mike. "And I wouldn't say it if I didn't mean it. So, one last question: *if* a fitness center went in up the street, not blocking the view mind you, but something that fit in nicely with the area, would you use it?"

Mike patted his belly and then flexed his right arm. "Well, I have no reason to use it, obviously." His deep laugh rang across the store, and a few customers glanced at him. "All kidding aside, yeah, I'd go. Having one close would force me to stop procrastinating."

Procrastinating? Is that what he liked to call it? Since we'd been coming up to the lake, Mike had been telling me how he had big plans for an exercise regimen. I had yet to see it happen. "All right. That's useful data. I'll see you later—when the kids want ice cream." I tapped the counter with my pen and backed toward the door.

"I bet I can predict what flavors they'll get this afternoon," Mike said. "Wouldn't it be great to have their metabolisms?"

"My point exactly, my friend." As the door closed behind me, a smile spread across my face. It felt good.

•   •   •   •   •

The next on my list? The hotel. It had a twenty-four-hour fitness room for the guests, but what about the employees? How would they feel about a place, as close to on-site as possible without being on-site, to work out after a long day on the job? Turns out, they'd feel just fine about it: all the employees I surveyed gave me an enthusiastic thumbs up.

After the hotel, I popped my head into the always-busy restaurant, the antique store, and the post office. The pop-up shops that sold seasonal clothing, accessories, and tattoos had closed months before, but we could always send them a survey via email or snail mail. I noted the thought on the clipboard, along with a few store names and descriptions.

My phone buzzed in my pocket. A text from Lena. *Kids are fine. Just checking in with you. All okay?*

Had Sadie set her up to do this? The day before with Lena had been comfortable. The kids took to her like they would Brooke, and she had been helpful but not smothering. The situation felt less like she was babysitting me than I thought it would.

Yep. Still making my rounds. Kids okay?

Yes. We're outside in the yard. Thank goodness for this weather.

We'd been lucky. While we needed jackets and long pants, I had originally thought we'd be dealing with snow and ice. Most of the country was experiencing a warm spell, and Walloon was no exception. When I was finished with this task, I'd like to come back to the lake and have the kids dip their feet in. The water would be frigid again, but we'd have fun. Lena could get them ready.

Do the kids want to dip their feet in the lake this morning?

All three say yes. To today and tomorrow!

Ha! Can you get them ready? I'll be back soon.

Sure can.

Thanks.

The next text that came through showed a lineup of emojis: a unicorn, a star, a heart, a birthday cake, and four smiley faces. *Lexie.*

And then a new text from Lena: *Sorry. Lexie grabbed the phone!*

Not a problem. See you in a few.

Lexie confiscated phones often, which is why Brooke always put hers on top of the countertop microwave and set the ringer to the highest setting so she'd hear it no matter which room of the house she was in. Lena would learn, quickly, how to deal with the little imp. The thought of Lexie, Charlie, and Delia—

Someone up ahead drew my attention as I rounded the corner of the post office. From the back, the man looked like Andrew, but that didn't make any sense. His company was back in Kettering. The man ducked into the general store, and I shook my head. That project of Andrew's had been on my mind so much lately I was seeing things. He wasn't here, was he?

The thing about a veteran with PTSD is this: when in the throes of recovery, we can still be paranoid. And the thought of Andrew MacKinnon, a man I didn't know too much about, being in a place I was? That sounded just too convenient. My pulse slammed against my skull, and my breathing staggered. How had the thought of him triggered me? I had to find out if it was him or not and what he was doing here.

I could send a text, but I had to be cool about it.

Hey. Just tossing the idea of future proposals around in my head. Leaning toward a yes. You busy?

His text came back in an instant. *Yes, I'm working on a couple things right now. Aren't you out-of-state anyway? Shouldn't you be relaxing?*

I am out-of-state, but my mind doesn't stop. And I thought I just saw you.

Way to be direct, Theo. My foot tapped a steady rhythm against the concrete, and my hands shook as I waited for his reply. What did I expect him to say? Why in God's name would he be here, at Walloon Lake? Instead of an affirmative or negative reply, an undeliverable message popped up. Damn! The service here had often been spotty in the past and now here again. As I contemplated heading to the coffee shop, my phone vibrated with a text—another from Lena. What was so special about what she had to say that her texts were all deemed deliverable and some of mine weren't?

Kids almost ready. Do you want us to meet you at the beach?

I looked up at the sky—part blue, part white, with the sun cresting right above me—and closed my eyes. Lena's texts concerned the kids, so any message she sent *should* come through. *Breathe in, breathe out.* One, two, three.

A reply jumped to my mind.

Just humor me, Lena. Tell me I'm not crazy. And yes, just meet me there, if you would.

You're not crazy. See you in ten minutes.

On the walk to the beach, I glanced in the windows of the coffee shop but didn't see Andrew. Trick of the mind? Stranger things had happened to me before. But the thought of him stuck with me until the sight of the kids and Lena—beach towels tucked under their arms, wide smiles on their faces—broke my concentration. And for the next forty minutes, nothing but beach, laughter, and cold water occupied my thoughts. We all waded in—if you called it that—up to our ankles, standing there until our teeth chattered and our lips turned blue. And then we brushed off the cold sand, dried our feet, and put our socks and shoes back on before ambling over to the general store for hot cocoa. I'd been so busy having fun with the kids and Lena I didn't think about Andrew until our walk back to the cottage, when Charlie brought up his project.

"Dad, I have this project."

"Okay, what is it?"

Charlie had always had trouble walking and talking at the same time. I expected him to tell me to wait until we got back to the house, but he surprised me. "Well, I don't want to tell you the details, but it involves Dads."

"Huh." Lexie's movement next to me drew my attention, and I grabbed her by the waist, hauling her onto my shoulders. Her position above would amuse her to great lengths, and she'd be safer up there—the lake was directly to our left. She stuck her fingers into my hair and kissed the top of my head.

"Dads? That's it? How vague. Do you need help with the project?"

"Well not really. But I wanted to ask you a question. Did you always want to be a dad?"

Talk about a question only Charlie would come up with. Delia would have asked me what I liked about being a dad.

"That's a complicated question, Charlie. But the short answer is no. When I was young, I didn't even consider it."

"At all?"

I turned toward him, catching his gaze. "Do you think about it?"

"I guess not. But then, what changed?"

"Well, I met your mom, and who knows? But when she took the pregnancy tests, I was happy. Surprised but excited. Why? What's this all about?"

Charlie didn't answer right away. He bent to pick up a pebble and threw it into the lake, then turned to me with a smile on his face.

"Did you see how far I threw that?"

"I did! That's quite an arm. But let's go back to what you said. Is something wrong?"

"No, it's just that I have a friend who asked his Dad the same question, and he said he'd always wanted kids. I'm not sure if it matters but..."

I stopped in my tracks and put a hand on Charlie's shoulder, urging him to look at me all while holding onto Lexie. "Want to hear what I think?"

"Yes."

"If you asked a dozen people, you'd get a different response from each dad. I bet there are dads who always wanted kids but don't have them. I bet there are dads who always wanted kids and now, they're not so sure. I didn't imagine having kids when I was young, but from the moment I thought about you—when your mom stood in front of me, tears of happiness in her eyes and a pregnancy test in her hand—my world changed. For the better. And when you were born? I cried. Did you know that?"

Charlie's eyes grew wide. "You did?"

"I did. And, I'm not ashamed to admit it."

Charlie scuffed his shoe against the street, dipped his head, and then looked back at me again. "Do your military buddies know about you crying?"

A glint of amusement shimmered in Charlie's eyes, and then he took off, running ahead on the gravel road with his arms spread out, hair flopping in the breeze, a complete picture of happiness. Left in his wake, I deflated and clutched Lexie against my shoulders, grounding myself in the present. A present that included ushering the kids home safely. My gaze darted from Charlie to Delia to Lena and to the road ahead as a cloud passed over the sun, which sent a chill down my spine. Something was off. With me. Maybe even with Charlie, who had so nicely deflected any of my questions about the project.

Chapter 22: Sadie

After a phone call with Jackie that was interrupted twice by the neighbor's dog next door—something about the backyard called to him and his digging—I gathered up my laptop, phone, and water bottle and rushed out the front door. Five minutes later, I stood on the wide, wooden porch spanning the front of the Crooked Tree Library, waiting for someone to unlock the door. It was already three minutes past the hour, and while I considered knocking on the sidelight of the library, I chose instead to adjust the strap of my shoulder bag and check for messages one more time. The morning breeze caressed my ears and reminded me Walloon time was different than Kettering time, and relaxation and family were supposed to be the focus of our week. So far, that plan wasn't—

A click sounded, and the door opened.

To my surprise, the little, gray-haired lady I'd seen walking her dog the evening before peered at me from behind round glasses that did nothing to disguise the deep blue of her eyes. In the daylight, the gray streaks in her hair fought for control over the fading blond highlights, and she had affixed, once again, a flower clip to her side-swept bangs.

"Well I guess you'd be waiting for me to open now, wouldn't you?" The lady pushed the door toward me with one arm and ushered me forward with a wave of her other hand. "Sorry for the wait," she continued. "I'm getting up there these days. It takes a little longer for me to do about everything now. Someday you'll understand what I mean." Crinkles fanned out from the corners of her eyes, and she smiled, her mouth turning upward into a huge U. "Come on in, sweetie."

With little time for chitchat, I spat out a short, "Thank you, ma'am." The door handle required a fierce grip, and I bore the brunt of the weight since this woman couldn't have weighed much more than one hundred pounds. My time here was precious, but rudeness never got anyone anywhere, so while my gaze darted toward the large clock hanging on the wall above the circulation desk, I said nothing.

"Oh honey, don't call me ma'am," the woman said. "Call me Pickles. Pickles Martin."

By the look on her face, she caught my surprise, despite my attempt to hide how much her first name shocked me. What an endearing, yet odd, name. Her parents didn't really—

"Yes. Pickles *is* my rightful name. It says so on my birth certificate. My folks always said my mom ate so many pickles when she was carrying me it would have been a crime not to call the baby Pickles. Of course, if I'd been a boy, they would have gone with Dill. They felt that would have been more suitable for a male."

Despite my annoyance I hadn't yet begun my work, I laughed out loud, and Pickles' face erupted into another smile. "I'm not laughing at you, Pickles. I *love* the name. But somehow, the thought of baby Dill cracks me up." The slight echo of my laughter reminded me I stood in a library, a place meant for quiet, and I shook my head and looked around, searching for other patrons.

"Not to worry. You aren't the first to laugh at that name, and there's a difference between laughing like yours and laughing that does harm." Pickles moved her hands to her skirt, where she shifted the material to the left and patted her hips. "Now, is there anything I can help you with this morning?" Then, she adjusted her glasses and looked up expectantly at me.

"Why thank you, but no. The tables near the magazine rack will be perfect for what I need to do, and I should get started soon." Without hesitation, I turned to leave the desk but then thought better of my lack of manners. "If I need something, though, I'll be sure to come find you."

Pickles nodded her head and opened the drawer of her desk, about to start her day. I thought about her dog, possibly all alone at home. But at the back of my mind, the clock ticked on my allotted work time. My computer powered up, and I attacked my project.

About ninety minutes later, the presence of someone nearby, right behind my elbow, distracted me. Slowly, I pulled my earbuds out of my ears and looked to the right, where Pickles hovered close. A little too close, considering I'd just met her.

"I'm about to take a quick break for tea. Would you care to join me?"

My digital wristwatch read 11:35 a.m. If I stopped working, I would be leaving details unfinished since I needed to be back at the cottage by noon. On the other hand, Pickles stood next to me with bright, eager eyes.

"Sure. Let me close this up, and I'll join you. Thank you for asking."

"Great." Pickles extended her hand and pointed to a hallway tucked behind the circulation desk and flanked by two enormous bookshelves. "The break room is right through the doorway at the end of the hall. I'll have a cup of tea and scones waiting for you. Cream or sugar?"

Who could resist tea and scones? "Just cream, please. And thank you again." My annoyance at having been disturbed dissipated as I closed the lid to my laptop and slid it into its case, making sure to secure the zipper and lock. One mishap a few years prior with a runaway laptop had taught me a lesson I had no intention of learning again.

As I pushed my earbuds into the side pocket of the bag, Pickles sauntered toward the break room with the same nonchalant gait she used yesterday. Halfway down the hallway, she leaned over and spoke to the air, her head bobbing back and forth as she gesticulated wildly, as if the person she was speaking to had argued a valid point. Had her beagle snuck into the library? A quick glance to the ground proved no one was there, and I chuckled to myself. *That might be you in thirty years.*

By the time I entered the break room, Pickles had poured two cups of what smelled like peppermint tea and plated up a tray of scones. The bench against the wall served as a perfect place for my bag and purse, and I approached the small break table, stomach rumbling from hunger. In the center of the table sat a thin vase with fake, pink roses inside. Not a spot of dust stood out on the petals, which were as soft as Lexie's skin to the touch.

"How do you keep those roses so clean? Artificial flowers and plants are lovely, but my ability to keep away the dust is as good as my ability to use a map. What's your secret?"

The older woman sat across from me, took the lace napkin off the table, and placed it into her lap before speaking. "It's not hard. You need to find the time to do it each week...Oh heavens, I didn't even get your name!" She pursed her lips, blew across the teacup, and sipped the beverage. Within an instant, the tiny china vessel was empty. She must have had a stomach of steel; my cup was still too hot to touch.

"It's Sadie. Sadie Rollins. We're from Ohio, and we're only visiting for a few weeks." The smell of the tea wafted up to my nostrils, filling my head with memories of my grandmother's house. Thoughts of Grandma and her afternoon etiquette lessons served as my reminder to remove my napkin from the table and place it onto my lap.

"Oh, we get so many visitors from Ohio. And my son lives there. Have you been here before?" Pickles' blue eyes sparkled under the fluorescent lighting of the break room as she poured herself another cup of tea. The whir of the small refrigerator and the click of the radiator muffled her words, and I had to lean in to catch what she was saying.

"Actually, yes. We've been coming up here for quite a few years now, and I used to come when I was a child. That's how we found this place originally."

"It's quite the place, isn't it?" A smile danced across her lined face, and a fleeting image of her as a young lady crossed my mind. Had she always been this content?

"You can say that again. Do you live here year-round?" In all the time I'd been visiting Walloon Lake, I'd never seen Pickles Martin. My family was on great terms with the workers at the general store, and we knew the owners of the marina. Even some of the people in Petoskey, like the proprietors of the fudge shop, knew June meant our family planned to visit. I wondered then, if anyone had missed us that summer.

"I do now." Pickles dabbed the corners of her upturned mouth with her napkin much like I would do to Lexie or Delia. "I am so pleased to meet you. It used to be Henry and I, that was my second husband, traveled here only during the summers. We then retired to our little bungalow on East Street and after he passed on, God bless his soul, I chose to stay. The place is in my blood now. I can't imagine living anywhere else." She smoothed the napkin across her knees against her blue cotton skirt and then nibbled a tiny bite of a cinnamon scone.

"I hear that from many people," I said. "That they can't imagine living anywhere else. What is it about this place that makes people want to stay?"

I knew why I'd like to stay. The idea of finding a sliver of happiness amongst a lifetime of confusion and angst. The gorgeous mirror of a lake, the splendid sand, the shade of the imperial pine trees. Mix into that the easy-going attitude that tagged along with summertime and even autumn, as I was finding out, and

I'd move here in a heartbeat. That sort of mindset would be beneficial every moment of every day during every season.

"It's a little bit magic, if you ask me. Or a lot of magic. Henry always said I believed in fairies, and yes, I do. But since I can't prove otherwise, I'm sticking with that theory." Pickles' cheeks crinkled with a full-blown smile. Theo would have rolled his eyes at her statement, calling himself too much of a realist to even consider the idea of something that couldn't be proven. But I couldn't help grinning myself. To think I'd been annoyed by her initial intrusion into my space.

The older woman made a valid point, though. There had to be something, whether we possessed the ability to name it or prove it or not, that led people to Walloon Lake and then convinced them to stay there. With cooler summer temperatures and mountains of snow, the winter season often brought with it something else that lured people there. If it wasn't magic that kept people in a place so cold, then what was it?

I put my hand to my heart and closed my eyes, taking a moment to pause, enjoy the silence, and hope the place lent even a little bit of its magic to me.

Pickles grabbed my attention again with the tap of her fingernails against the laminate of the table. "Many people tell me I'm nuts. But the lives I've seen over the years, the number of broken people who come up here to this idyllic place, who stay for merely a few days or several months and end up being repaired." Pickles punctuated her words with a nod of her head and a bob of her gray-blond curls.

My dampened mood perked up at the words *broken* and *repair*. Our marriage, my life, my psyche. They had so much defective in them, and I considered whether anything could be reconditioned, much like the ancient and rusty mountain bike Theo had placed by the curb this past summer. The only facet of my life that seemed mostly unchanged over the last couple of years was my relationship with Charlie, Delia, and Lexie.

For the most part, I put forth an extreme effort to be a decent mother, and I thought the kids were having an adequate childhood. But the words *decent* and *adequate* didn't seem enough to give to my wonderful and deserving children, and lately, my parenting might not have been up to snuff.

I didn't want my children to feel the way I did about my mother at times: she was selfish and self-centered and so out of touch with reality that conversations with her inflicted pain on me. Dreams of the future often occupied my thoughts, a time when, as adults, the children still called because they wanted to, not because they felt obligated to do so. But to cultivate those dreams, I needed to be *more*. The kids should have a *fantastic* mother and *spectacular* childhood, one full of laughter and memories and traditions they'd want to pass on to their children, and only *I* could make it happen. If only I could figure out how to do that. If only I could figure out a lot of things. Tears simmered behind my eyelids.

Pickles regarded me with a sparkle in her eye as she leaned in close, the smell of the cinnamon scone coming with her. "You're not telling me something, young lady."

Her comment surprised me in many ways, but the tears had probably tipped Pickles off to my situation. One bite of strawberry scone later, I decided to let her in. "Maybe, maybe not. But for one, I've just met you..."

"That's true." She wiped her mouth with the napkin and poured herself another cup of tea before offering me a refill. The chestnut brown liquid cascaded into the cup much like I wanted to spill myself over Andrew. Argh. Where in the hell did that thought come from? The calendar pinned to the wall became my focus, allowing me to turn away from her gaze.

"And two, I wouldn't want to trouble you," I said.

That phrase had always bothered me, and yet there I was, uttering it myself. In my experience, a person used those words when she wanted the other person to ask questions, to pry open the lid of whatever Pandora's Box stood before her. They were to be said if I *wanted* to unload a burden but first had to probe the situation, to see if the other person would be receptive. Would Pickles change the subject and convince me she had no intention of listening, or would she offer to shoulder the burden and persuade me to open up? This wasn't a game I was playing, and I owed my new acquaintance more than a thoughtless phrase, though I wasn't sure why I felt that way.

"You're right," I started again. "I don't know you..." The gears of my mind turned, and I cut my gaze toward her. "Sometimes, we don't have to know one another to know one another, do we?"

Huh. The things that came to my mind when I didn't worry about what I was saying. Pickles and Andrew made me feel the same way: safe, comforted, content, and appreciated. She'd likely listen without judgment, and, if time allowed, become a best friend. Like I thought Andrew would do anything for me without question, provided it was within the confines of the law and didn't hurt anyone. Two different people, two different situations. Perhaps Pickles could help me with my issue with Andrew. Kate's words echoed in my ears: *Rewrite the stars, Sadie. You can shape that narrative.*

The first draft was finished. Now, I needed to tackle the revision.

"Can I be frank with you?" In that moment, the dialogue as written on a page sprang to mind, as if someone was reading a book in which I was the protagonist. Of course, it wasn't a romance novel, but something else more literary, something strewn with drama, joy, heartache, and humor. The ending hadn't been written yet, and I was picking up more characters along the way, one of them named Pickles. And why was she there? For a good laugh? Or a good lesson? It was time to find out.

"Of course, you can," Pickles said and sat back against her chair, as if she was ready to be in for a long haul.

Was she right? Could I unpack my life's baggage like I had the luggage in the cottage on Shoreview Drive? And should I? Before I spoke, I took in the little bits of Pickles' life that had been strewn here and there in the break room. Newspaper clippings and butterfly stickers clung to the walls, along with pictures drawn by children, and a paper vase full of dried wildflowers, probably something she'd picked in the late summer. The room burst with simplicity and happiness, two things I wanted so much to grab onto.

"I guess I'm having a tough time right now. With my life in general. I'm not sure who I am anymore, although that's not the case at work. Percoletti-Winn is about the only place that seems to be drama-free right now." I peeked at my new friend, afraid of what I might see in her face as she focused on me over her teacup.

"It seems that way," Pickles said. "Something in your body language spoke to me of being needy for something you aren't getting. Is that right?"

Pickles Martin possessed an uncanny amount of perceptiveness. Of course, her statement could be interpreted in many ways, and I'd just admitted to a discordant life. But perhaps she was more observant than the rest of the population....

The glint of the fluorescent light off my watch reminded me I didn't want to be late getting back home. Needing only a few minutes to walk back, I allowed myself a bit more time with Pickles, but any more purging of my soul wouldn't happen today.

"That's about right. Amazingly right. You're a discerning woman." I wondered about how to phrase my next sentence, not wanting to offend her or imply I was running away. "I'd love to fill you in, really, but I do need to get home. I told my family I'd be home by noon, and I don't want to disappoint them. This is supposed to be a vacation. A *family* vacation. I might have an odd—dysfunctional, even—family, but I do need to get back to them." That was as close as I'd get to telling her of all my thoughts and problems today.

"I understand. We can finish up another time, if you'd like. Most days, I'm here, unless my knees start to hurt too much, which is happening more and more the older I get. Then I call in the sub and sit at home, wondering what all my library friends are doing. But with the weather being as nice as it has been, I'll try to get here as much as possible."

It took but a few moments to collect my wrinkled napkin, plate, and teacup and place them near the sink, all the while marveling at the sound of Pickles' voice as she spoke about her life in her cottage next to the lake. A dream world that wasn't mine enthralled me, but I soon snapped myself back to reality.

"Would you like me to do the dishes before I go? I certainly don't mind—there are so few, it won't take long." I helped clear Pickles' place as well and then turned to find a dish rag in the drawer of the cabinet.

"Another person that doesn't mind doing dishes, huh?" Pickles moved to scoot her chair away from the table. "I never liked doing them myself, but my son, oh, he loved the dishes from the time he was a little boy. He'd play with the bubbles and get as much water on himself as he did on the dishes. So many times, I'd sit back with a cup of coffee or tea and watch him scrub those dishes clean. Twice in one day on days the weather was awful. His hands were small but somehow, he'd get those dishes cleaner than our brand-new dishwasher did." Pickles focused elsewhere and then broke into a huge smile. "Andrew. Such a fine boy. I wish I saw him more often. I really do."

Dizziness and heat engulfed me, wrapping my entire skin in an uncomfortable sleeve. I looked at Pickles square in the eye.

"Andrew? You said your son's name is Andrew?" Inside my chest, my heart hurtled, and I placed my teacup, still dirty, into the sink where it would be safe from my agitated body.

"Yes, that's right." Pickles nodded her head with a quizzical look on her face.

"Andrew Martin, right? You said your last name is Martin?" If Martin was her son's last name, I'd be okay. The sink felt cold and sleek against my hands as I gripped the side, trying to stop the shaking that had spread through them.

"Well no, Martin was Henry's, my second husband's name. MacKinnon was the last name of my first husband. So Andrew's last name is MacKinnon. Andrew MacKinnon."

The last thing I remember was feeling the loss of blood from my face and a tingling in my extremities.

Chapter 23: Sadie

Lying on the bed, staring at the ceiling, every muscle in my body tense, I questioned if something more sinister than emotion lay at the root of my fainting episode. Was something wrong with my health, and did I have something to worry about? Jackie would be in a meeting, so I called Kate to help talk me down. She might appreciate a phone call anyway, considering the last two times we'd spoken had ended less than favorably.

"Yes, you heard me right, Kate," I whispered into the phone. "I fainted while having tea and scones at the library with a little old lady named Pickles Martin. I even have a tidy little bump on my head to prove it. At least I didn't have to go to the ER."

"Pickles Martin?" Kate scoffed.

"Yes."

"*Pickles?*"

"Right? If she'd been a boy, it would have been Dill."

Kate's raucous laughter erupted on the other end of the phone. "Wow. Who knew tea and scones held so much danger?"

"Indeed." I arranged the coverlet around my legs, tucking the ends underneath my thighs in an attempt at some form of control, albeit a weak one.

"Well what happened? Haven't you been eating? You aren't pregnant, are you?" Kate asked in a conspiratorial voice.

"Watch your tongue, young lady. No, I most certainly am not. I'm not sure what happened. Am I worried? A little? Who faints like that? And if something is wrong with both me and Theo, the kids will need—"

"Wait. Back up, friend. Nothing is going to happen to you right now. You're young and healthy. Tell me the details."

So, I did. The entire story spilled forth, a few details repeated from past conversation, others news to her. From spending time with Andrew at Jackie's to running into him at the office and all over Kettering to his words about things not being right at this moment to my running away from him, hoping to find myself and figure out my future.

"That's crazy—a woman you just met is the mother of Andrew, your Grocery Store Man!" Kate said, restating what I'd told her. Did she think she had misheard me?

"Yes, apparently so."

"How random, right?"

"Yeah, but you know how it is sometimes." Despite no one being in the room with me, my level of discomfort rose. Most of the incriminating words were now on Kate's end, but I had no intention of revealing myself to Theo this way, in an overheard, hushed conversation. Theo deserved more, no matter how I felt about him.

"What are you going to do about this?"

"I'm not sure. I mean, I'd like to see where this thing with Andrew might take me, but—"

"But what?"

"Even he admitted things aren't good right now. I didn't let him explain, but I'm pretty sure he means I need to get my act together. Choose to let Theo go, so we can move forward. How can I start a relationship with Andrew if I have another man living at my house?"

"A relationship? You've already started that with Andrew."

"True. But you know what I mean."

"I do. And I can't say I have any words of wisdom for you right now. If you like him, then you need to talk to Theo, to get past this, this, uncertainty you're living in. He's not being fair to you, but have you asked yourself what he's doing? You might be finished with him, but is he finished with you?"

Kate's words ricocheted in my ear. I sniffled into the receiver, willing the tears to remain behind my lids. Kate tried to make amends on the other end of the line.

"I'm sorry, Sadie, but I've been thinking..."

I grabbed a tissue and huffed a few incoherent words before mumbling goodbye and effectively hanging up on my friend. The phone rang—it had to be her—but I let the call go to voicemail. When I was more put together, I'd call her back.

A bone-weary fatigue forced me to lean back against the feather pillow, and the ceiling fan caught my eye again. The rotation of the blades, as always, calmed me, almost like a mobile did to a baby. In seconds, my breathing evened out, and I wiped away the last of the tears with my wrist. But just because the evidence was gone from my face did not mean I had wiped everything away from my heart.

What Kate said, unintentionally, was one hundred percent true: while we decided divorce was the best option, I had to consider Theo might have had an ulterior motive in hanging on to our situation as it was. And even if he didn't, everything over the last six months or so had pointed me in the direction it was time. To let go of Theo, our life as it was. To let go of the past.

The muffled sounds of my family's actions slipped under the door: the roll of the dice and Charlie's sweet laughter. Every so often, Delia's or Lexie's tender voices projected my way. When I'd gotten back from the library, Lena agreed to stay while I rested. Instead of eating lunch, I'd crawled into bed, slept for a few hours, and then called Kate. And here I was, awake and ashamed to go out and face my family. Would my feelings show on my face? Or could I count on the fall to cover everything up? And if I relied on camouflage, wasn't that the easy way out, again?

The attached bathroom served as a distraction, and I splashed cold water against my cheeks. In the mirror, my face looked drawn and tired, much the way Theo seemed most of the time. I blotted the water up with a towel, hung it back on the hook next to the sink, and opened the door. The smell of something delicious floated my way, and my stomach rumbled.

As I reached the kitchen, I looked over to the living area, where I presumed everyone would be stationed. In fact, due to the temperate weather, the whole family, save me, had moved to the front porch. The front door stood partially open, and all the familial sounds traveled through the metal screens to the kitchen, warming my insides. The large plate glass window gave me a perfect view of the entire family.

Charlie and Delia sat on the wicker arm chairs, while Theo, Lena, and Lexie lounged on the porch swing. Theo rested his left arm on the back of the swing, almost up against Lena's shoulders, while she held onto Lexie, who had snuggled against Lena's other side, thumb in her mouth, blanket to her cheek. A beautiful picture of a happy family. A family like I wanted again, and probably could have, if I had the courage to let go of the past and grab the future. The beating of my heart stuttered, and bile rose in my throat.

A knock sounded at the rear door off the kitchen. Tearing my gaze away from my family, I gathered my wits together, then wiped my hands on the kitchen towel and strode the few steps toward the door. A pit formed in my stomach. Andrew stood there on the back porch with a bright smile on his face and a paper grocery bag in his hands.

"Thought you guys might need help," he said and walked toward me.

One beat, then two, and then without a word, I took the grocery bag from his hands and set it on the floor. Standing on tiptoe, I reached up, placed my hands on either side of Andrew's smooth face, and pulled it toward mine.

Chapter 24: Sadie

The moment before our lips touched, Andrew pulled back and removed my hands from his face. "Sadie," he said, shaking my hands between his. "You don't want to do that."

"Uh, yes, I do." After pulling my hands from his, I wiped a stray tear from the corner of my eye.

"No, you don't. And as much as I *really* want for you to do that—and I can't tell you how much I want it—I didn't come here for that," Andrew said. He retreated a couple steps backward, giving me space, giving himself some. "Plus, you're not even officially divorced, and I had no idea you came up here. When I went to see Mom about an hour ago, I heard the news."

His words were both shocking and expected. He wanted to kiss me? Was he having the same struggle I experienced? If so, why hadn't he said anything? Of course, he had mentioned he felt something for me as well, but this was Andrew we were talking about. The man people called an all-around good guy. A man who, evidenced by what just happened, seemed to have more morals than I did. But he was also a man who had trouble staying away from me. Was he a stalker?

"Are you stalking me? Because I find this a little creepy that you'd—"

He threw up his hands, palms facing me. "No! I swear I'm not stalking you. The first year I came up here, I ran into two families dressed in T-shirts from schools back in Kettering. I found it odd and surprising, but the norm around here. Lots of people from Ohio visit the lake. And I had no idea you knew of this place."

I backed myself up toward the cabinet holding the cleaning supplies, and after a quick glance to make sure no one else had entered the house, leaned against the door. "I had no clue you knew about Walloon Lake, either. I swear. To be honest, we came here to get away from you. Or at least I did." My gaze traveled up and down Andrew's form. He looked as great as ever with a clean-shaven face and a sparkle in his eye matching his mother's. "That didn't sound right, did it?" I dipped to pick up the grocery bag and turned toward the kitchen. "I meant I came to get away...to find myself again."

"I know what you meant. Here, let me take the bag for you." Andrew—chivalrous as always—reached for the grocery bag, and I let him take it, which clearly invited him to come farther into the cottage. "Where is everyone else?"

"They're out front. Had you come in that way, you'd have seen them." I motioned for him to follow me, a second, bolder attempt to lure him inside, perhaps? What in the hell was I doing? Having Andrew and Theo in the house might not be the best idea I had ever come up with. So far, Andrew had only seen the kids. What would Theo think, and why didn't Andrew say no and go away? Spider, fly. It was impossible to tell which roles we both played.

Andrew set the grocery bag on the granite counter and reached in, pulling out a carafe of orange juice, a sack of clementines, a bag each of flour and sugar, a pound of coffee, and a bottle of Tylenol, as well as an odd assortment of hard candies and my favorite chocolates. His purchases told the story of what he knew about me. My chest warmed.

A glance toward the living room window revealed everyone was still talking and laughing. "You can join them, I suppose. I'll be heading out that way, eventually." I waved my hand in the direction of Theo, Lena, and the kids and then snatched the paper grocery bag and folded it up before settling it between the wall and the refrigerator.

"Shouldn't we address what almost just happened?" Andrew asked.

"We should."

"You don't sound convinced." He lowered his voice and tipped his head. "You have no idea. No idea how much...I want...I'm tormented. When I first met you, there was something. I wasn't sure what. And then, we kept meeting. And even though I knew you weren't completely available...I don't...oh fuck!" He punched his fist on the counter, let out a hiss from his lips, and flicked a quick look away from the kitchen. "I'm not getting this out properly, but you know what I'm trying to say." Andrew closed his eyes and drew a deep breath in through his mouth.

"No. Yes. No. I mean, I know what almost happened back there at the door and why and what you're trying to say. We're quite a pair, aren't we?" The smirk on my face as reflected in the small mirror above the stove revealed my error. "Wrong choice of words there, eh?" I laughed and went on. "Well, I won't let it happen again, and I won't let that almost-kiss happen again, either. I was wrong."

I rubbed the back of my head, the part that had contacted the cabinet at the library. The bruised skin hurt when touched, but the pain grounded me and kept me moving forward in my quest to rid myself of this man. "But I'm going to be honest again here and tell you what needs to be done, which is this…" I looked him over from head to toe as I appreciated his whole being. His face, his arms, the way his eyes seemed to dance in the light of the day, the small dimple on his right cheek. Like a caffeine addict, I gulped one last, long sip of him and then continued. "I need to try and stay away from you."

Andrew fell back against the counter as if my words electrocuted him and threw his hand over his heart. "Ouch, Sadie. Ouch." Despite his words, the curve of his lips told me his ego hadn't been harmed.

"Yeah. But that's the truth. You and I both know it and based on that last action of mine there on the back porch, I can't be trusted." Here I was, falling into the same pattern of teasing and flirtation with Andrew, and it scared me. The slope was too slippery: either he had to go, or I did.

"I said it once already. We could be right, but I guess not right now, and I can see you're serious, so I'll go." He pushed his body away from the counter but was careful to maintain adequate space between us. "I just wanted to check on you. Mom said you took quite the fall."

"I did, but I'm okay." The throbbing at the back of my head wrestled with the pain inside my heart, and I rubbed again at the injury to try and gain focus and relief. "By the way, how long will you be up here?" Extending the conversation with small talk was stupid; my fascination with Andrew bordered on obscene. Go home, Andrew, I thought. Make this job easier on me, please.

"I'm just here for a day or two. I have business over in East Jordan, so I thought I'd swing by and see Mom. I come up this way a few times throughout the year. This is a tough place to stay away from." Andrew moved a few more paces toward the door. "And Mom hasn't been the same since Henry died. I swear she talks to him still, as if he were right there with her."

"Is that who she speaks to? I thought it was the dog, but the library doesn't allow dogs, and she was speaking to someone as she headed to the break room."

"Yeah, she says Henry's with her much of the day. She loved my dad, but she and Henry had something special, magical almost."

I imagined myself as old as Pickles, shuffling to and from work each day, chatting with my long-gone love. Theo? Or Andrew? Dampness settled in my eyes, again. I rubbed away the tears, not embarrassed but angry with my vulnerability. "Wow. What a love they must have had."

"Sure did." Andrew handed me a tissue from the box on the counter and then moved all the way to the door before looking back. "We'd all be so lucky to find a love like that."

Andrew's words—completely matter of fact—were in stark contrast to the look he gave me. The man needed to leave the cottage before my defenses crumbled, so I pulled open the door, a silent plea for him to exit. "Listen, I need to check on the kids. I'll see you later, okay? I mean, I won't see you later."

Andrew flashed me a grin so bright and broad, it reached all the way to his eyes, across the intervening space, and snared me. *He's the spider.*

"All right, I'm going. But if you need something, give me a shout."

Leaving no time for me to answer, Andrew spun on his heel, pushed open the screen porch door, and left the way he'd come in. He hadn't disturbed the happy family image that inhabited the cottage. But he had to guess our contentment and well-being had already been disturbed and life as we knew it was on the brink of breaking. Didn't he?

Through the porch window I tracked his movements as he ambled down the driveway and up the modest hill at the end of the street. The sound of his whistling met my ears and drew me toward him like the Pied Piper had done with the rats. But I was better than a rat. At least that's what I told myself.

"What ya looking at?" Theo, who'd taken off his outdoor shoes and replaced them with fleeced-lined moccasins, had come up behind me. Theo's ability to be stealthy increased when he wore those slippers.

I turned around to face him and stopped. Had he seen me watching Andrew?

"You okay? You look like you need a hug," he said and extended his arms.

It had been a long time since we exchanged such gestures, but I hesitantly stretched my arms around his mostly fit middle. The action felt off somehow, like my arms weren't sure why or where they should go and were awaiting instructions. But within seconds, they'd found their groove, and I rested my head on his shoulder, trying to figure out how to answer his question.

"Just looking at the gorgeousness of this place and thinking how much I love it here." My roundabout answer spoke the truth, but I hadn't been honest either.

"It is gorgeous, isn't it? I'm glad you introduced me. You missed lunch." He pulled his head back to look me in the eyes. "How's your head? Do you want to come out on the porch? The kids would love—"

The crunch of tires on the driveway pulled my attention toward the back porch, and I maneuvered out of Theo's arms and peeked out the door.

"Oh, you've got to be kidding me. This can't get any worse. What in the world is my mother doing here?" A tension hit my jaw, and I bit the inside of my cheek. Another conflict or another person to take care of was the last thing I needed.

"No clue. I didn't tell her we were here. And I'm guessing you didn't."

He was right. Vacation away from everyone included my mother in that *everyone*. "No, no I did not. Does any of my life look like a bad Lifetime movie to you?" My question bounced off Theo, who leaned against the counter with a confused look on his face. I swung my glance back in the opposite direction to check if Mom had finished parking.

"What's so bad about it?" Theo asked from behind me. "I mean, from where I'm standing, you have quite the life."

His words struck a nerve, to the point they hurt, because Theo was right. Down deep, I understood. But I still floundered with so much. "If you only knew." My voice ran thick with petulance, but the back of my head was not the only part of me that had taken a beating. My psyche was bruised and while helping it heal should take priority, I needed to find time to do that. With Mom around, I wasn't sure I would.

"Then tell me," Theo said as I twisted to look at him. His features—so uncharacteristically patient and composed—challenged me to be truthful, to open up and enlighten him. He was still a part of my life, a player in our unfortunate situation whether he wanted to be or not. He challenged me with his gaze. To tell him what was so wrong with my life. To tell him about Andrew, about what I wanted. My words might produce irreparable wounds, but it was time.

"Let me get my mom settled, and we'll talk. I promise." I reached out and touched his arm, hoping my gesture told him I would follow through with my promise. Then, I moved toward the door. My mother struggled with her seat belt; a long afternoon, it would be.

Chapter 25: Theo

Sadie's mom had always been more than I wanted to handle, so speaking with Sadie likely wouldn't occur until well after dinner. Maybe the kids would want to play a game or something in the meantime. The unseasonable weather continued today, and despite the early hour for a sunset, we'd have plenty of time for something fun. After slipping my shoes back on, I headed to the front porch. All three still lingered there: Delia on the swing with Lena, Lexie in the chair to the side of the swing. Charlie leaned against the porch railing, eyes closed, as if he was thinking hard.

The screen door creaked as I opened it, but only Lena looked up and smiled at me.

Delia thrust her finger toward her brother. "Dad! What's he doing? What is Charlie doing?"

Charlie had always been kind and loving to his little sisters, but the look that passed across his face—full of scrunched-up nose and clenched teeth—said this wasn't one of those times. But he had far more patience than I did.

"Can't I have time to think?" His eyes remained closed.

"Sure," Delia said. "But what are you thinking about?"

"Something."

"Charlie, come on! You have to tell me! Lena!" Delia turned to Lena for help. "Charlie's not telling me something, and I want to know what it is."

"What is it you want, sweetie?" Lena leaned down to take a decayed leaf from Lexie's hands. Lena had learned trash and other things always found their way into Lexie's mouth.

"I want to know what he's thinking." Delia's lack of true explanation—dead-on for a kid—caused Lena to smile. I snickered but cut it short as soon as she threw me a "better stop now" sort of look.

"Oh, honey." Lena patted Delia on the hand. "We can't always find out what someone else has in their mind. We're allowed to have our own private thoughts, those we don't have to share with anyone if we don't want to. And these," Lena held up the dry leaf and crumbled it between her fingers, "need to stay out of your sister's hands. I might need help with that!"

Delia frowned, a huge scowl that this time made me laugh out loud, and crossed her arms over her chest. I folded my arms over my chest and crouched in front of her, making sure she saw me, and then grabbed her little belly, tickling her until she begged for mercy. Lexie howled and hopped up next to Lena while Charlie just stood there, looking shell-shocked after opening his eyes.

When Delia had had enough, I addressed Charlie. "You okay?"

"Yeah. Just thinking," Charlie said.

I laughed. "Well you can do that better out in the backyard. Want to go play ball?"

"Soccer or baseball?" Charlie cocked his head and raised one eyebrow, an action not in my repertoire.

"Your pick. What do you say?"

He nodded his head. "Give me a minute to find the soccer ball, okay?" Then he glanced at Lexie and Delia and leaned in toward their small faces. "You will never know what I have inside here." He tapped his temple with his index finger. "It's all mine. Got it?"

The girls' eyes widened, and Delia's lower lip trembled until a bright smile broke across Charlie's face. "Gotcha!" he said before backing away and pulling open the front door. "Meet you near the shed, Dad."

Lena spoke quietly to the girls as I walked down the steps leading to the side yard, my back to them. "Let me tell you a thing or two about boys..."

By the time I reached the backyard, Charlie had found the soccer ball and set up a small net for us to use. He'd shown promise on the pitch, and as of now, Charlie aspired to play soccer even in college. Time would tell whether that goal would pan out, but if he put his mind to it, he'd reach his goal. Envy—at his youth, his optimism—filled me at times like these.

"So, what's on your mind?" I kicked the ball his way.

He stopped it easily with his foot. "Nothing...really."

"It's not nothing. It was enough to be rude to your sister. I'd have done that to my sister, but you...you don't normally do that sort of thing."

He sighed and returned the ball. "Yeah. I was just trying to figure something out."

"Well, can I help?"

"I'm not sure." A swift kick sent the ball to Charlie's right, but he lunged, connected with his left foot, and launched the ball over my head. It landed in a pile of dead hydrangeas behind me.

"Then at least try me."

Charlie hustled to grab the ball from the plants and looked at me. "When we were first on the porch, when you were sitting on the swing with Lena and Delia, I saw what was going on inside the house. And Mom was in the kitchen with someone."

"And?"

"And it was that guy Mom sometimes talks about...the one we met at the arboretum. And I guess I just wondered what he was doing here."

A guy? A thump ticked at the back of my eyes. Was Sadie seeing someone? Charlie wouldn't meet my gaze. I took a few steps closer to him. "What guy?"

"Mr. MacKinnon."

The thump swelled into anger simmering in my chest. "Mr. MacKinnon? You've met Andrew?"

Charlie swallowed and kicked his foot back and forth, ball secured to his hip with one hand. "Oh. Yeah. I just told you. Mom knows him. And we've spent a little time together. His kids are fun. He has two..."

Any further words receded into the background as a rush of heat spread throughout my body. My fingernails dug into my palms, and the need to move—anywhere but my current location—swamped me.

"Where did he go, Charlie! Which way did he go?" I gripped Charlie by the shoulder, shaking him with each word.

"No idea, Dad! I saw him walk—"

Before I did or said anything else to scare Charlie, I let go and stormed out of the yard in the direction he pointed. The Walloon Lake area was too big to investigate on foot, but I knew Andrew's car. If he was staying on one of the surrounding smaller streets near us, I'd find him. But as the minutes passed with nothing to show for my search, my mind drifted to Doc and her calming techniques. *Breathe in, breathe out.* One, two, three. Again. *Breathe in, breathe out.*

One, two, three. The chill in the air rolling in off the lake stung my nose, much like the dust in Afghanistan. I had to keep myself from going back there...

My phone buzzed in my pocket. A message from Charlie: *Please come home. I'm sorry.*

Thank you. I'll be right back. Charlie didn't mean to, but he'd just helped keep me here, in the now. And he hadn't done anything wrong. Even though I wanted to get answers to my questions—what was Andrew doing here, how did Sadie and Andrew know one another, and did he know Sadie and I had a connection? They'd have to wait.

Breathe in, breathe out. One, two, three.

•   •   •   •   •

Charlie was waiting for me on the side stoop when I arrived, shoulders slumped, gaze directed at the ground. As I approached, he lifted his head.

"I'm sorry, Dad."

"For what?"

"For making you angry."

I sat next to him on the cool concrete, lining my thigh up against his. A few more deep breaths, and I'd be fine. "Did you think what you were going to say would make me angry?"

"No."

"Then how is it your fault?"

"It just is."

I turned toward Charlie. "I'm not the best Dad all the time. I get angry too quickly, and I'm trying to work through my anger—" *Breathe in, breathe out.* One, two, three.

"I know you are, Dad." Charlie laid his head against my shoulder.

"But this wasn't your fault. Okay? I have things I need to speak to your mom about. That's all." My arm wound around his shoulder, pulling him close. It was one thing to be angry with Sadie but another to be angry with him. And I wasn't. But I'd made him feel like I was.

"But what about Mr. MacKinnon? Do you know him? You never answered me before." Charlie's eyes sparkled in the late afternoon sun.

"I do."

"Oh."

"And I thought he was a friend. Now, I'm not so sure."

Charlie tilted his head and squinted at me. "So why was he talking to Mom?"

"I'm not sure. Do you have an idea?"

A flush moved up Charlie's neck into his face, and he pulled away. Maybe I shouldn't have asked. Maybe I didn't want to hear the details. "Charlie?"

"You're going to get mad."

Doc's voice echoed in my head. "Your family is here to help you. Use them when you can, Theo."

Before I second-guessed myself, I took Charlie's hand in mine and held it up to my chest, just over my heart. "I won't get mad if you help me, Charlie."

"What do you mean?"

"Here. Keep hold of my hand even if my breathing changes. I'm going to focus on something cool while you tell me whatever it is you want to say, okay?" Would this work? Who knew? But it couldn't hurt.

"Okay." He wriggled his fingers against my chest. "What are you focusing on?"

With my eyes closed, I conjured a calming image. Last summer. A hike on the old trail that wound around the lake. "Remember our epic hikes? To the beach and back? Wading in the Bear River? And that one day, when we got really far, you remember what you did?" I smiled at the memory. "You ripped your clothes off and jumped into the raging river and—"

"She kissed him, Dad. Mom kissed Mr. MacKinnon."

Breathe in, breathe out. One, two, three.

Chapter 26: Sadie

"Mom what are you doing here?" I exited the porch, and the screen door slammed shut behind me, causing her to wince at the noise she'd always despised. Sadly, a rush of pleasure coursed through me for one moment, followed by a surge of guilt.

Mom had opened her car door but still yanked at the seat belt, which had somehow wound its way through her purse strap and back again. "Well, Sadie," she said, without looking at me, "I thought you might want the company."

"But who told you we were *here*?" I had no intention of letting the issue go.

"The receptionist at your office, of course. Who else would know? Who else would tell me?"

Suppressing an urge to get angry and slam the door shut, I gripped the edge of it. Was she serious? I thought I'd been clear when I informed the folks at work I'd be taking a family vacation. For *my* family. But the woman had driven close to seven hours to get here, no matter having endured twenty-seven hours of labor for my sake (or so she claimed), so I couldn't just send her home.

"Well, you can have one of the empty rooms upstairs or the one in the basement. Your choice." An overstuffed suitcase begged to be set free from the rear of the car, and I placed it on the pocked driveway.

"Which room is available upstairs?"

"The yellow one toward the front of the house. It's the one with the twin beds and the trundle, and it's got a fan. Don't be surprised if Charlie wants to bunk in with you, though." The next suitcase I grasped was lighter, but why had Mom packed two entire suitcases? How long did she plan on staying with us? We had less than two weeks to go here.

"That's fine. I don't mind Charlie." She pulled her purse to her chest and slammed the rear door of the car, turning her head to take in the surroundings. It had been a few years since we'd invited Mom up to stay with us. Her presence usually meant aggravation for me, which in turn meant aggravation for everyone else. What did she see when she looked at the cottage, the lake, the trees? Was it an idyllic space like we'd come to love, or was it something more feral and threatening? Based on our interactions here in the past, I'd have chosen the latter as her answer. The more I thought about my mother, the more my head throbbed at the spot where I'd hit it. Mom had to get settled, soon.

•   •   •   •   •

The next few hours passed smoothly as I dusted off most of Mom's micromanaging and assigned her the task of playing with Lexie and Delia. Charlie was with Theo, and Lena took a trip to the general store for a few perishables. At dinner, after I had placed the baked chicken, potatoes, and fresh veggies into the center of the counter for plating up, my mother turned to grab a bowl and then filled it with leftover soup from the fridge.

"You don't mind, do you?" My shock escalated as she placed the bowl in the microwave and pressed the start button. Was my cooking not good enough? As an uninvited guest, shouldn't she be grateful I hadn't sent her packing when she arrived? Before I answered, she jumped in again. "And where's Theo?"

He'd opted out of sitting with us for dinner, offering no explanation, and Lena, who had chosen to stay, regarded me with sympathy in her eyes. We hadn't had time to speak much, but I was grateful for her presence and her apparent understanding and placed her into the category of temporary ally. Her calming presence made me sorry about my rush to judge her the first night, although I had no plans on telling her. I flickered a quick smile in Lena's direction and stabbed my fork into my chicken; the poultry was clearly done, and so was I.

After the dinner dishes had been put away and Lena had gone home, I asked Mom to take care of the kids so Theo and I could cross the street and sit by the water. The time had come to purge myself, and a bench near the lake might provide the comfortable yet neutral setting I wanted. The old teak seat wasn't right on the shore, but it set close enough to enjoy the not-quite-frigid breeze wafting off the lake and to watch the late evening waves make their marks on the beach. The journey only used up four minutes on the clock, but by the time we reached the bench, Theo slumped onto the seat and leaned his head back, as if the walk had exhausted him.

Choosing to focus on the water's wake and the slow descent of the sun over the horizon, I didn't speak right away. Signs of the approaching evening filled the air, and months from now, my voice would compete against those of the crickets. But this was November, and most insects had taken shelter for the winter. The silence stretching between Theo and me became deafening, and I knew, in that instant, Theo had to suspect something or had to be questioning the mounting tension from the last couple months. Why he hadn't said something confounded me. Was he trying to push it from his mind and bury his head under the pillow?

In the buzzing quiet of my happy place, I asked myself, what is the best way to tell a man you used to love that you want to be free to love someone else?

I thought back to my conversation with Jackie, who encouraged me to write up my initial encounter. That had been months before, when the idea of loving anyone other than Theo was someone else's story, not mine. A lump rose in my throat, and I swallowed it, almost choking myself in the process.

In the end, under the eggplant-colored sky, I revealed almost everything to Theo. That I'd met Andrew, the state of heart, my talk to Kate. He was the third person to whom I told the story when he should have been the first. Tears welled up in my eyes as I concluded my litany of words, adding the reason I had fallen at the library was because Andrew MacKinnon happened to be Pickles Martin's son and—even worse—he had stopped by the cottage that afternoon.

My heart ached with my last admission, and if Theo had turned to me with fury and rage—even hate—written across his face, I would have understood. But he didn't. Theo's lack of response, his complete apathy, gutted my soul. I sat still, listening to the rush of blood in my ears as he said, and did, nothing. Finally, my resolve broke. "Say something."

His troubled gaze met mine. "I...I don't know what to say." Another turn of his head dismissed me and my problem. His viewpoint was now of the water— calm, strong, even—unlike our relationship.

We sat there in a thick, suffocating silence, but if I walked away, we would have solved nothing. "Theo?"

"Anything I say isn't going to make this any better." He didn't meet my gaze this time.

"I know. But what do you think?" Willing myself not to vomit from the pain in my gut, I placed my shaking fingers under my thighs to steady them and took a deep breath through my nose.

"What I think? What I think is the woman I loved is attracted to another man, and the thought makes me feel fucking awful. I think I don't know you anymore, and I wonder when you changed. I think I'm fucking tired, and I'm fucking angry this happened. That you *let* it happen."

"I didn't *let* anything happen! It just happened. I—"

"Seriously? Didn't let it happen?" Theo's cheeks blazed pink in the dim light of the streetlamp, and his fingernails dug into the wood of the bench. "Did you kiss him? Have you fucked him?"

His anger infuriated me, and I rose to my feet. "No and no. And even if I did, we're not married anymore, haven't you noticed? You live with us because you need us, because you need the help. But we're not an *us*. We're not what we once were. We aren't, and you know it."

Theo took a breath through his nose. "Technically, that is true. But what if I'm not ready to let you go?"

What? Why the flip-flopping of hearts? A year ago, I was ready to help him heal, to stay no matter what, but he fast forwarded the plan to dissolve. I didn't—

"Do you think I even look at other women?"

Against my thigh, I clenched my fists. "You should be, dammit! If we're not together, and we're clearly not, then why aren't you?"

It took Theo a while to answer, and I willed every muscle to unknot, every line of tension to ease, before the conversation took a complete turn for the worse.

"I don't know, Sadie. I don't know. Fear? Maybe I'm afraid of hurting another woman like I hurt you. Or I'm afraid I won't find anyone. Or I'm afraid after everything is said and done, I was wrong, and I still love you."

Oh God. An excruciating pain radiated throughout my entire body, stabbing my heart. "You...you can't say that now and expect me to pick up where we left off—"

He shook his head. "That's true. But tell me. Where'd you find him? And how'd you find him?"

I fell back into the seat, wanting to be anywhere but there, near the water, having that conversation, and I tried to explain myself. "I can't...one conversation at the grocery store...I can't explain it, I just found him. This PTSD is hard on you, but it's hard on me, too. I thought I could live with you in the house, but everything's different. Don't tell me you didn't recognize we haven't been the same."

He faced me again. "What do you mean?"

"We're not the same couple we were when we got married. We're not even the same couple who decided to split up and live together! We've changed."

"So you just decide to find whatever it is you're looking for elsewhere?" Theo rolled his eyes and looked out over the water again.

"You make no sense, Theo. We're separated, so I can go look elsewhere if I want. But this is a relationship, even if it's unconventional. There are *two* of us in it. It worked for a few months, but it's not working now. Not for me at least." I tugged on his sleeve, wishing to look at the face I used to read so easily.

"I'm not sure that's true. We haven't changed that much."

My anger blazed, and I rose from my seat again, staring down at Theo with a glare I hoped would fluster him. We'd had heated conversations like this in the past, and I usually found myself agitated and furious at how I ended up with someone so hard-headed and literal, someone who wasn't willing to consider my perspective at times.

"Theo, it's not always about you, is it? I'm trying hard not to be selfish here, but I just tore open my heart, the heart that has been twisted inside and out over the last couple months, and now we're back to you and what you think or don't. As if I don't have the right to anything besides what you condone. I'm sorry you have this, this, PTSD. I'm sorry about everything that happened to you. I'm sorry I've been the way I have been." Sobs overtook me. "But yes, something's not right and even though I'm fucking up big time, there might be a reason that hinges partially on you. Your future health and happiness are important, but mine are too."

Nothing more needed to be said, so I stood from the bench and walked away.

•   •   •   •   •

One of the persons most closely involved in my story finally knew the details, and in a way, a great relief settled on me, allowing me to sleep that night. But the next morning, I stumbled out of bed and opened the bedroom door. The cushions in the living room sat empty. The bathroom stood cold and dry. A still-fluffy pillow, a smooth comforter, and cool sheets greeted me in Theo's room;

he hadn't slept in his bed, and reality hit me. Perhaps I deserved this treatment—him leaving us—after walking out of the argument, but the fact still stung more than I thought it would.

Sadly, I wasn't surprised when I plodded through to the kitchen where a note reclined against the coffee maker, which was as barren as the couch. Empty coffee pots signaled turbulence in our house, the red flag denoting unrest. I flicked open the envelope and read the note, written on a thick piece of ivory stationery.

Dear Sadie,

I need time. I'm headed to the Inn since they're close, and they have an available room. I'll tell Lena where I'll be. I promise to take care of myself for the next couple days, but I need space to think.

Theo

I flipped the paper over, looking for more words on the back that didn't exist. Theo needed time and space, so he ran away; I needed time and space, too, and had performed an escape act by putting together a vacation to Walloon Lake. The kids were sure to be disappointed. Had he even thought of them before making his decision to leave?

In a move that surprised me, I slammed my fist against the countertop, pain slicing through and rippling up my arm upon contact. Mentally weary, I slumped to the ground. Taking in a deep breath through my nose, I counted to ten and sighed, letting out all the air caged inside my lungs. What to do? The sun slept on, as did the kids and Mom, which meant I had enough time to make breakfast for everyone and figure out how to tell them Dad had left. That he needed time, space. But how do you phrase those words to children? More lies would wear me out, but burdening Charlie, Delia, and Lexie with all our garbage wasn't an option.

My life's issues had never solved themselves before, so I rose from the floor and threw open the cabinet door. The bag of sugar Andrew had brought the day before stared me in the face. He'd lined it up in a row with the other staples, much like I would have attempted at our house. "Keep the order," I mumbled to myself with a shaky voice. "Keep the order. You can do this." I reached for the flour, the baking powder, the sugar, and the vanilla extract, plucked two eggs from the refrigerator, and started on a batch of pancakes. If my life was indeed a novel, then from-scratch pancakes could at least help this dilemma.

The aroma of the hot, steaming griddle must have woken my mom, because within the quarter hour, she padded down the stairs in her fleece bathrobe, looking rumpled and small, an astounding image. When had she changed from the woman I knew? Had *I* been so selfish and only aware of my life I hadn't noticed anything going on in hers?

Lines feathered out from the corners of Mom's eyes and across her forehead, and her gray hair had lost its luster. I considered how this visit would go and whether she and I would survive. But Theo was gone—who knew for how long—and I ought to be grateful she had decided to visit. As much as I didn't want her to think I'd be using her, someone would need to watch the kids if Lena wasn't available while I attempted to make progress on my projects. And God dammit, despite her faults, despite all the grievances I held for her and the way she raised me, she was my mother. I loved her. If nothing else, Mom deserved full honesty.

"Morning, Mom." I reached into the cupboard above my head for two mugs. "You want coffee?"

"Do you have decaf?" She lifted her eyes to meet mine. They looked dull and vacant; with time, her light green eyes had turned muddy and gray. Another detail I hadn't observed.

"Sure do. I drink a combination of decaf and regular these days." I placed one of the mugs in front of Mom, who took a quick sip before adding milk into her cup.

"Why?" she asked.

"Oddly enough, I get more tired by the end of the day if I drink a cup of fully caffeinated coffee in the morning. And I don't have time to be more tired than I already am. You know how it goes. It ain't easy having kids." A splash of regular coffee would round out my cup. Bringing it up to my nose, I inhaled the pungent scent of the deep brown liquid. In an instant, a placidity pushed at the despair and anger that had settled over me that morning.

"You do too much, Sadie. Why doesn't Theo help you?" Mom lowered herself to the seat at the breakfast bar, which squeaked under her light form as I slid a plate of steaming pancakes toward her.

The light from the low-hanging pendant lights highlighted my mother's face. It appeared she didn't understand what Theo was going through with his PTSD.

I scooped another cupful of pancake batter into the measuring cup and practically threw it against the bubbling butter on the griddle. "Mom, I've told you before. It's complicated."

"Well, I'm not so sure—"

Chucking any manners and respect for my elders, I held my palm up to my mom, interrupting her train of thought. The last thing I needed to do was get into another argument with or about Theo. The cottage was supposed to be my sanctuary, my slice of tranquility, and so far, nothing had gone as planned. "Mom, I don't want to talk about this right now. If you have questions, ask him. He's trying to get better but...Theo left." I put my hand up again and pursed my lips to signal the conversation was over. "Not sure for how long, a couple days, but again, our situation is...weird, to say the least. So, I don't want to talk about it, but when I'm ready, I will."

Perhaps the set of my shoulders told her I meant business or the salty tears clinging to my lashes, threatening to spill over the lower lids of my eyes because Mom looked at me and said, "Okay, what can I do to help?"

Had I heard her correctly? "First, why in the hell did you come up here?"

Mom sipped her coffee and placed the mug on the counter before answering my question. "Something was off, and I wanted to make sure you were okay. You've never hung up on me, and when you did that, it hurt. And it's so unlike you to take off for vacation during the school year."

"Yeah, it is. Did you ever ask yourself *why* I might have hung up on you? Did you replay the conversation in your head and try to figure it out?" That day stood out clearly in my memory. I'd felt so empowered with the simple push of a button.

"Yes, but I didn't understand it. I still can't."

"Then why did you wait until now to ask?" The bubbles in the center of the batter popped, and I flipped the pancakes over, one at a time.

"I don't know, honey. I just didn't." Mom placed her chin in her hands and stared at me but had nothing else to say.

"Then you're welcome to stay, but I don't have time to explain it to you." Shaking my head, I handed her plates. At the least, she'd bear a bit of my burden since I still had my *own* work to finish.

With Mom's help, I finished preparing breakfast and came up with a plan I thought was best for the kids. I'd shower and get changed while she woke the kids up and got them dressed for the day. We'd all eat said breakfast—Mom had already eaten—head down to the beach for a quick morning walk, and Mom or Lena would take them in the afternoon while I worked on my project. In that plan was buried the moment I'd tell them Dad was away for a few days. Pancakes, syrup, and a dash of "your Dad's not home, and we might be splitting up for good."

That plan would work for everyone but Charlie. He proved it later, when I revealed the news.

"Where is he? Why did he leave?" Charlie jabbed a piece of his pancakes—his second serving—and dunked it into a puddle of syrup collecting on the side of the plate.

"He's over at the Inn, honey. He's had a rough time lately, and I didn't think this vacation through...it's been a lot for him." Charlie's big soulful eyes stared at me, challenging and asking without words if I was telling the truth. Children did that to you, kept you honest. What I said was the truth, but I had to be more straightforward with Charlie.

Pulling one of the chairs at the breakfast bar right up next to Charlie, I looked him right in the eyes. "We had a discussion last night that didn't sit well with Dad. And so, he wants to be alone. Can you understand?"

Charlie sat back and thought for a moment, blinking his eyes. He placed his thin hand under his chin, a tiny caricature of Rodin's *The Thinker*. I thought at first he was playing around but then realized he was doing just that, thinking. And processing. And letting everything sink into that wonderful brain of his.

"Did he say anything about me?" Charlie asked.

"No, should he have?"

"Just wondering. And I get it. Sometimes I need to be alone, too, but finding alone time and space at our house is always hard." A thoughtful smile passed across his face.

My gaze turned toward my mom, who sat with Lexie on her lap, reading an ABC board book. Finding alone time and space of my own always took so much effort; I'd tried to get some here and look who showed up.

"So," I said. "We're going to give him time. He's got his phone. I'll text him later and see if you guys can go over."

"Will you come with us? When we go see him?" Charlie had a way of asking questions that by themselves seemed innocent, but if I read into them, I'd get mired in a load of trouble. Again, the kid was keeping me honest.

"Not this time, Charlie. Your dad told me what he wanted, and I'd like to respect his decision. But he loves you very much, and I'm certain he'll have time to see you today." So confident was I Theo wouldn't make the kids suffer for the sins of their mother.

"Okay." Charlie leapt from his chair and looped his arms around me. "What's the plan for today then?"

Thankfully, Charlie got caught up in what the shape of the day would be. He gathered the girls together, found Delia's and Lexie's wind jackets and sneakers, and with as much patience as he could muster, helped Mom and me prepare snacks for the afternoon. As we hauled everything to the wagon, I looked at my little man with warmth and love and wondered if this separate family would not become the new normal for us.

Chapter 27: Theo

Space. Is that what I'd called it? *Space to think*. Fuck that. Space wasn't going to help me any more than time would, and I'd used that word too. My wife wanted someone else, and I wanted to crawl under a rock and never come back out. Actually, that was too tame a description for what I wanted to do. A bullet to the heart would hurt less than this shit, wouldn't it? And a bullet to the heart at least would be instantaneous. Not like this. Liam might beg to differ, but he wasn't here to argue. Hadn't been for a while. My chest threatened to cave in, and I streamlined my breathing. *Breathe in, breathe out.* One, two, three.

A few more seconds passed, and I heaved myself off the bed before pounding the wall of my room at the Inn. Not enough to damage the wall but enough to scrape the skin of my knuckles. Again. *Shit.* Sleep hadn't been within my reach—flickering images of past and present Walloon memories featuring Sadie had kept me awake—and my reflection in the mirror told the story of a crazed man. Hair up at odd angles, shadows beneath his eyes. A man ruined by his wife's words, strung together into news she wanted someone else. Andrew no less. Andrew fucking MacKinnon. What the hell? Had he known all this time my complicated relationship involved Sadie? Talk about a Lifetime movie. Sadie didn't have all the details yet. What would she say when she found out?

But Andrew was here—I had seen him—and that meant finding him would be a possibility. My recon skills were second to none, and in this small village, it wouldn't take long. He had to hear me out because I had to know: Who would stab a brother in the back the way he did?

First: a shower. Second: a trip to the general store. Third: a lambasting of Andrew MacKinnon.

The steam from the shower did nothing to tamp my nervous energy, so I dried off, threw clothes on, and slugged a cup of coffee in the lobby of the Inn. Texts from Sadie would go unanswered—if she sent them. But I knew enough about her to trust she would respect my wishes. For time. For space. That word again. My fingers shook as I gulped the last of my coffee and slid the cup away from me. A bite of bagel, and my day began.

The bell above the door of the general store chimed as I walked through the entrance. Mike looked up, concern flaring on his face.

"You okay, man? You look like shit."

Mike had never been one to mince words. A decade of summer friendship had taught me that.

"Not my best day. Do you know a guy named Andrew MacKinnon? Tall, dark hair..."

"From around your neck of the woods. Yeah. He's the librarian's son, Pickles Martin. Great guy. Great kids too—"

"Well that's just *great* then. Any idea where I'll find him?" Thunder roared in my ears, and it took me a minute to realize it was the blood pushing through my body and not a late fall thunderstorm outside. I pressed a hand to my ear, hoping to lessen the noise.

"When he comes up, he stays with his mom. But he's probably out and about right now. Usually has work over in East Jordan to attend to. I don't have his number, but I'm pretty sure he's over on East Street. Are you sure you're okay? Can I help you with anything?"

"No. It's okay. You've done enough." Before I pivoted, I slapped the counter. "Sorry. Too much going on right now."

"Well let me know—"

Sticking around to hear the rest of Mike's words wasn't part of my plan. Instead, I pounded the pavement and made my way to the library. His mom might be there. She'd tell me where he was.

A lukewarm breeze from the vestibule met my face as I opened the door of the library. Posters advertising every event and service offered in Walloon Lake lined the walls. Once I'd made it into the lobby of the library, a general hush, a calming, settled over me. The thumping in my head waned, and the constriction in my chest eased. Looking right and left, I saw no one. Where was everyone?

"May I help you?" a voice sounded. Not a woman's voice, but a voice that sounded a little like Liam's, or at least my memory of his voice. It came from a man, who stood to my right. Deep-set eyes, dark with interest. "You look like help is what you need."

"Meaning?"

"Your aura is reaching out to me. You're lost. You're afraid. You're alone—"

"What gives you the right to say that to me?"

"Am I wrong?"

Having not slept much, I didn't have the energy to argue with this man. This man who, yes, was right, even though I wasn't sure *how* he was right.

"No, you're not wrong. I'm looking for someone and I—"

"You won't be able to speak to that person in your present state. Why don't you join us? We're practicing mindfulness right now. Over here, in the great room."

A quick glance to where he pointed revealed two folks stretched out on yoga mats. I'd never practiced yoga—the need to move incessantly inhabited my body—but the looks of contentment on the people's faces...they intrigued me.

"I'm here for a purpose—" I said.

"And so am I. Give me five minutes. It will make a difference."

"If I do, will you answer a question for me?"

"Yes."

"Is the librarian here? Pickles Martin?"

"Is that who you are looking for?"

"In a way, yes."

"She won't be in until this afternoon."

"Okay, well, then I'll see you this afternoon." I turned to leave, and the man touched my forearm with his fingertips. A jolt of warmth shot up my arm. What the hell?

"Please, stay. I can help."

An image of Doc in her chair, pen poised over her ever-present notebook, jotting a list of items that might help me: breathing techniques, meditation, yoga.

Minutes later, I was stretched out on a blue yoga mat, eyes closed, random, fractal-like pictures blooming behind my eyelids. My mind wandered away from my thoughts of revenge or whatever I was trying to do with Pickles...how many digits of pi could I remember? Why had Sadie just walked away? What the hell am I doing here in the library? Did the Higgs Boson particle really prove the interconnectedness of the universe? Why do I feel so good right now? What would Doc say to—

"A few more minutes, and we'll be finished here. Let go of your thoughts or don't. Whatever is good for you. Now find the tingle in your right shoulder and concentrate on it."

Tingle? In my shoulder? What did he mean?

"Follow the tingle to your left shoulder..."

Finding the tingle proved to be a problem, but I at least focused on my shoulder.

"Then the right bicep...and the left bicep..."

Yoga Man's voice droned on, lulling me back again to a state of calm. A bell rang four times. "And come to seated."

I looked at the clock. Forty-five minutes had passed, and I felt great, hadn't felt this good in years, as if nothing mattered. Sadie and Andrew? No problem. We'd work through it, just like—

"How do you feel?" The man stood, hands on hips, bare feet against the floor, eyebrows raised, waiting for me to say something as the other folks rolled up their mats and walked away.

I stood, connecting my gaze with his. Something I rarely did these days. "Actually, great. Better than I thought I would."

"Good."

"Don't get me wrong. I thought you were crazy when you asked me about helping. But I guess you did."

"That's wonderful. You just need to take time for yourself. To figure out what you need. To be selfish for yourself." He tapped his chest. "It's all in here. Everything you can control. It's in there. Don't allow yourself to get upset by what's around you."

"That's easy for you to say."

He folded his arms across his chest. "You're right. It took me a long time to be where I am. Years. And I'm just trying to help people like you, so it takes you less time than it did me."

"People like me?"

"Those who see themselves as damaged."

"But—"

He held up a hand and then let it fall, gracefully, to his side. "I know. I've worked with veterans for years. Some with PTSD and some without. Now maybe that's not you—"

"It is."

"Well then, all the better. And I always say, use this—what I've given you—but also use what you have. Your support system. This—what I do here—can help but so can your resources."

"So, I should call my therapist?"

"I can't tell you what to do, but if that's what you want to do, then...maybe. By the way, do you want me to leave a note for Mrs. Martin?" He squatted near a bin full of yoga mats, rooted around inside, and pulled out a notepad and pen.

I wasn't angry at her, just her son. Would the man give me her address? Wouldn't that look odd?

"Nah, it's okay. I can handle everything from here. Thank you."

"You're welcome." The man put the pen and paper back and then stood in front of me. Silently, he placed his hands together in front of him and bowed. "Namaste," he said.

I'd heard the term but never had any opportunity to say it. Despite my discomfort, the word fell easily from my lips. "Namaste." I rolled up the yoga mat, placed it in the man's bin, and turned to leave. I glanced back once, when I'd neared the door, but the man had already disappeared.

Chapter 28: Sadie

"It's bad. Seriously, it's bad."

Pickles and I sat in the library break room for a second time that week, after I'd put in a few more hours on my project and decided staring at the computer didn't mean the work was getting completed. Mom had said to stay as long as I needed, and I planned on taking her up on her generous offer. She'd handle the kids easily, Lena was on backup alert, and I required deep reflection. A sea of uncertainty and unknowns threatened to drown me, and finally, I truly understood how Theo might view a future. This no longer involved only an uncomfortable lust and attraction for a man who wasn't mine; Andrew and I possessed a spark that might be more, if we let it. On the other hand, Theo had almost admitted to not wanting to follow through on the divorce, something that involved both of us. The time had come for me to grow up, make mature decisions, and think about my future, my happiness, and what might be best for the kids. Sooner rather than later.

"What a pickle you're in, huh?" Pickles said as she giggled.

"Really? Now?" But I laughed, and it felt so good to ease some of the anxiety, to let myself go and pretend that, while I was here, ensconced in the Crooked Tree Library, everything outside the library either didn't concern me or could be easily ironed out.

Sometimes, the universe works in mysterious ways, and I sensed Pickles wasn't there to judge what I had to say. Even if she didn't understand or approve of my situation, she'd listen. For some reason, I trusted her, and while a week ago I might have called Jackie, now, in between sips of tea and bites of shortbread cookies, I shared most of what was going on in my life, including exactly how her son was involved.

"Oh no." Pickles shook her head, a slight scowl marring her face when I revealed Grocery Store Man and Andrew MacKinnon were one and the same, that we'd seen each other off and on since our first meeting, and he and I, well, had more than just a passing interest in each other. Her tone of voice and the softness in her eyes told me the truth: my words had touched her. But had I been right to confide in her? What would she say? How would she react?

"Oh yes," I continued. "The whole situation started out as the beginning of a tawdry romance novel and now, well, it's gotten out of control. I'm stuck in the plot of a heartbreaking book-club book, and the ending is still murky. It sucks, pardon my French."

"No offense taken." Pickles stacked a few of the shortbread cookies into a sugar-infused tower that began to lean. How long would it be before it tumbled? What if I asked myself the same question?

"And one more thing. Theo left last night."

Pickles cocked a thin eyebrow, much the way Jackie would have, as she extended her hand to my right forearm and patted it several times. "Oh Sadie, really?"

"Yes, really." I leaned back in my chair, removing my arm from under Pickles' fingers with care. Before I went on with my thoughts, I needed space, even from such a gem of a woman. "That's what I get for being honest with him. I mean, I knew what the consequences might be if I unloaded the truth on him. I *knew* he might choose to leave, which oddly enough is what I've been trying to get him to do, right? I owed him the whole story, a no-holds-barred discussion, but I should have spoken to him sooner."

"But did anything actually happen with Andrew?" Pickles pointed her index finger and shook it at me. "I raised him better than to prey on a woman!" The expression on her face cut the tension within the limited space of the break room, and a glimpse of the mother I wished I'd had peeked through. The type I might have had, if Mom had been more confident, more present.

"Oh, no, no. Nothing physical happened. In fact, once I told him I had feelings for him, at least what I thought were feelings...no they are...I need to keep being honest...they are." I took a breath. "Anyway, no, Andrew didn't do anything. At all. He's been honorable for the most part, trying to fight his feelings. You did a great job."

This time, I patted the old lady's hand and marveled at her smooth skin. Despite the liver spots and veins lining the surface, the skin was as soft as a baby's bottom. It reminded me of the hands of my grandmother, who used to visit for weeks at a time, keeping me company and providing comfort when I found none from Mom or Dad. A few tears welled up in my eyes.

"Oh, I didn't mean to bring up anything that would hurt you." Pickles placed her free hand on top of mine, young alternating with old, sandwiching our hands and simulating the weave of a basket. Even an amateur basket maker would tell you overlapping the materials added strength to the actual basket itself. Hoping to gain fortitude from my new friend, I clung to her hands and squeezed them.

Despite my tears, I managed a small smile. "You didn't do anything to hurt me. You're making me feel better by being here. And there's nothing you can say to make any of it any better." Unlike my mother, who in my shoes would be blaming Theo or Andrew or the people who built Bloom Market, the only person I should castigate was myself; I had to stay accountable. "I'm not confident about what to do. The kids will have a few weeks of school and then Christmas break. All that time, if Theo's not back, they'll be looking at me, condemning me, I'm sure of it. And we can't stay here. As much as I'd love to stay, working remotely will only pass muster for so long. Plus, Charlie has his presentation day at school soon. I promised we'd go. I can't break that promise. I've already done enough harm to my family." I pulled my hands out of the configuration they'd been in and twisted them in my lap.

Pickles' gray curls bobbed back and forth as she shook her head. "Don't take this one on by yourself, Sadie. I don't know you well, but it *always* takes two to tango. That cliché rings true almost every time. Your situation...it's up in the air right now, but you know what you want, what you've wanted since you both agreed to divorce in the first place. This is a minor setback, but figure out what you want, even if this new information from Theo changes things, and then move forward. Remember, he's as much a part of this dilemma as you are."

Stray crumbs from my cookies had landed in my lap, and I brushed them away. "I know. I've known this. I thought coming up here would be a way to fix things. That getting away from home might allow me to see clearly, to figure out what my future should look like. And I never thought Theo would be angry about me being interested in someone else. Uncomfortable? Sure. But his admission? It came out of nowhere."

"It did, or it didn't. Maybe he can't deal with the hurt and is clinging to what he can, to make his life seem more normal." Her sparkling blue eyes connected with mine as she straightened the tablecloth.

"True, but I'm stuck in a rut...not sure what to do or where to go and my mind spins the same damn thoughts all the time, and nothing gets fixed. I'm still broken. We're still broken."

When neither of us said a word, I listened for the call I hoped was out there. Was I just not hearing the answer? Was the solution in front of me all along, and I'd chosen to ignore it? The plink of a water droplet dripping from the faucet to the stainless-steel sink reverberated, and the constant hum of the heater filled the room. Everything else must have been on mute.

Pickles looked directly at me then, her face stoic and unmoving for a moment. Kindness filled and projected from her eyes, and I imagined what sort of mother she had been, and still was, to Andrew. He was a lucky man—that was for certain.

"I heard something recently, dear, and I've thought about it often since then. It went like this: 'One day someone is going to hug you so tight all your broken pieces are going to stick back together.' I'm not sure who said it, but in my opinion, it's true for you."

The opportunity to respond to her words never arose; her break time was up. She got caught up in helping one library patron after another, and I had to get back to the family.

As I cleaned up the break room table and packed up my things, my thoughts performed pirouettes. Who could hug me that tightly, to fix everything and put me back together? And while I willed my mind to imagine Theo, his face as I once knew it, not the tight indifferent one from the night before, the picture never appeared. Instead, the kind, soft face of Andrew bubbled up from the deep and floated to the surface. It stayed there.

•　　•　　•　　•　　•

We didn't hear much from Theo that week, and Thanksgiving passed by without a word from him. I hoped his silence implied a start on his road to emotional healing. All the texts that eventually arrived were short and cordial, but cold, the words like little icicles piercing my heart each time I read them. The children visited the Inn at different times of the day, and I relished the quiet that ascended and allowed me time to ponder the situation when all the little feet were away.

My mind swam with questions. Did Theo think about us, about me, at all? Did he place all the blame on me? What was going to happen to everyone? Again, and again I returned to the question, *What did I want to happen?* As much as I longed to ride off into the sunset with Andrew, it was clear my circumstances required much thought. My life was one, hot, complicated mess.

A few days before we were scheduled to return to Ohio, I decided a quick jaunt to the village bakery would force me out of the cottage and provide a different set of walls for at least the day. I'd been wallowing in self-pity; I knew that, and apparently, so did my mother. She had been kind enough to point it out to me the night before, after dinner.

"Sadie, your behavior lately...it's so...so crass," she'd said when we were cleaning up for the night.

Her words stopped me in my tracks. "What are you talking about, Mom?"

"You have a good life and one you need to *live*. Stop the wallowing. Stop the blaming."

My gut heaved as I grappled to find the appropriate words, those that would say what I intended without hurting her in return. "Why didn't you leave the subject alone? Did you have to call attention to my 'crass behavior' as you call it? I realize I'm behaving this way and ashamed of it." With anger inside me, I practically spat the words at my mother, but I turned my voice down so my voice didn't carry to the kids. "And really, Mom. That's like a case of the kettle calling out the pot."

Why didn't Mom let me do what I needed to do to heal, to find my way? It was a good question to ask, but the night before wasn't the right time. However, that morning, after I'd thought about my rude behavior, it dawned on me Mom's words held truth to them, and I'd been out of line. My mother and I might be entrenched in a quagmire of unresolved issues, but she still deserved my respect. A whispered apology accompanied my request for her to watch the kids for the morning. She accepted my apology, gave me a hug, and agreed to help, maybe to gain back my favor.

A promise to bring a box of fresh pastries upon my return brought a smile to the kids' faces as I said goodbye. The wind skimming off the water along the street pebbled my skin, and I tucked a few stray hairs behind my ears, straining my eyes against the sun to see the lake before me. A delinquent seagull squawked and circled the marina, and a person on a motorcycle honked as I strolled by. The glare from the sun kept me from seeing who it was, but I waved back anyway.

In the distance, as the pathway rounded the curve toward the main thoroughfare, the facade of the bakery came into view. My mood lifted at the sight, and I drew in a large, fortifying breath. The aroma of fresh-baked goods and coffee trailed out the door and pulled me to the wide, boxy building. Once inside, I chose a cup of coffee and a mini-cinnamon bun and pulled the newspaper from a wire basket against the wall. Buying the box of pastries could wait until I was ready to go back to the cottage.

I opened the newspaper and held it up in front of me, a simple shield against the daily grind of my life. I didn't mind engaging in conversation with anyone; but a few moments of isolation would be good for me, a kind of anonymity I sought in times of despair. Even though many of the folks here were familiar, if anonymity could be found anywhere, it would be at Walloon Lake, where the people respected you, your life, and your desires.

As I sipped the hot coffee, my thoughts drifted to life back in Ohio. I had no idea what was going on there or anywhere else in the world; keeping up on the news hadn't been on my to-do list when connected to the internet at the library. It was my way of hiding in the sand. Or it was that damn pillow again. My laughter bubbled at the expense of my mother.

I tilted the newspaper to watch customers stream into and go out of the popular bakery. A few stopped to say a short hello while others moved on their way after a quick nod. Here, so many miles from home, my network still existed—friends, those I enjoyed spending time with, even if I was in a foul mood. A network of support. My mind leapt to my Mom, who didn't have that same group of people. And while Dad was with her, he didn't have that either. For a few moments on a sunny autumn day, these strangers helped me appreciate my life and what I had—not what I didn't—and that was something my parents never had. I grabbed a tissue from my purse before the tears started to course down my face. The paper would blot away the traces of sadness, and I sat there for a moment or two, gathering my wits and blinking my eyelids.

A gentle hand grazed my back, and I looked up: Andrew. He silently took the seat across from me, sipped from his cup of coffee, and waited for me to speak. Pulling my gaze from his, I tried to come to terms with what I wanted to say, what I needed to say, to articulate what was wrong. This time, it wasn't about him though.

"I seem to cry each time I'm in your company," I said, my eyes still brimming with tears.

"What does that say about us?" Andrew teased and then continued. "I wanted to help, but...Perhaps I should go. I thought you might be here—it's one of your favorite places, but I'm not trying to stalk you or—"

My personal alone-time moment had changed for me with Andrew's presence. Instead of the craved isolation from minutes before, I didn't want to be alone. The company of someone I knew more than the folks who wandered in and said hello sounded heavenly. Oh, who the hell was I kidding? I wanted the company of *Andrew*.

"No, please don't." I reached out to cover his hand with mine. The coffee mug had warmed his fingers, and while I didn't want to let go of them, I did.

"Do you want to talk about it?" His voice held concern, and a realization hit me: I'd turned into someone needy. How was he attracted to a needy woman? What did he see in me?

"If you can believe it, this has nothing to do with you and me. Sort of. I came here for a bit of peace and time to be alone, and my always-churning mind began to work overtime. Looking at all these people I care about, even here, far from home, I began to think about them."

"This place is like that, isn't it?" Andrew glanced around the bustling bakery and beamed. "They care about you. About me. About people in general."

"They do. And if I wanted to, I'd unburden myself to them. They'd take my troubles and help me walk in my shoes. I know that." A rogue tear escaped down my cheek, and I swiped at it with my finger. "I have all these friends, the people I turn to, to help me make it, day by day. My parents didn't have those people. They took care of me, and we had what we needed, but Mom and Dad never took care of themselves." I thought about what else I wanted to say. "Well, I guess my dad did when he left. But my mom will say she tried to take care of herself and make friends, when in reality, she didn't. She never stepped out of her comfort zone to meet people and cultivate friendships. And if she had friends, she didn't try to keep them. You need to meet with people regularly, give of yourself and take in what they say. Listen to them and let them listen to you. Neither one of them did that."

"That's why you're crying? For your parents and what they didn't do?" Try as he might to hold it back, the confusion appeared in his furrowed brow.

"Women are complicated, aren't we?"

"You have no idea." The look on his face indicated he stunned himself with the statement, as if he hadn't meant to be so honest in his reply.

I chuckled. "But no, I'm not crying for my parents. It's that I don't want to end up the way they did." A fresh round of tears began its trek down my already warm and tight cheeks.

Andrew passed me another tissue, a soft smile warming his face. "But you said it, Sadie. You won't. You have friends and are willing to make more."

"Yes, except my mind doesn't stop at that juncture. I always go the extra mile. And so, when I say my parents didn't take care of themselves by way of making friends, I can stretch that to their marriage and how they didn't take care of themselves there, either. My parents' marriage...well...from my point of view, it wasn't the best fit. And that right there is something I understand. Sitting here, I look at you and what we have the potential for." I sniffed, almost choking on my next words. "And I'd rather have that than what I've got. *That* is why I'm crying." My honesty surprised even me, and I lowered my head, ashamed and confused.

Andrew took my fingers in his and held on tightly. The warmth of his hands spread across my skin, throughout my body, to my brain, where the heat tried to soothe my soul. There were no words to ameliorate the situation—we both knew it—and I was grateful when he didn't even try to say anything to make me feel better.

Chapter 29: Theo

"Why did you choose not to tell Sadie what Charlie told you about her and Andrew? What purpose did that serve?" Doc's voice over the phone sounded the way it did in person. Nonthreatening and kind, something I needed to hear. I sat in the wing-backed chair, staring out at the choppy waves on the lake. Despite the mindfulness experience from a few days ago, my turmoil still bubbled and boiled, and the day before, I'd woken up in bed, covered in a sheen of sweat, heart beating wildly. Anger coursed through my body. Sadie's admission had cut me, and no amount of "finding the tingle" was helping bring me back to center. So, I took Yoga Man's advice and called Doc.

"I'm not sure why I did what I did. Denial? Charlie told the truth, but..." What had I been thinking? The patterned wallpaper instead drew my attention, and I considered it, trying to find my words. "I was trying to convince myself I was imagining something that wasn't there."

"But it was."

"Yep. Come to find out it was. It was."

"And we know how that made you feel, but my question to you now is, *why* did it make you feel that way? You've been on the verge of divorce for a long time. You've hashed out the expectations for living with Sadie. You're the one who—can I say this?—pushed for the divorce."

Doc wasn't telling me anything I wasn't aware of, and she was right. But her questions required introspection, and I'd never been that guy. If Doc wanted introspection, she should speak to Sadie, and there'd be no reason to do that. She'd made up her mind already. I had to live with it.

Or not.

"I don't know. Sometimes Sadie and I don't communicate well. Like she says one thing, but I hear something else. And everything gets mixed up."

"That's easy to do, however, hasn't she been the one encouraging you to sign the divorce papers?"

"Yes."

"And again—you're the one who started the process, right?"

"Yes."

Doc stayed silent for a moment, the sound of the furnace the only accompaniment to the beating of my frantic heart.

"Theo, here's the thing. I want to help you manage everything you're going through, so we need to set boundaries and realistic expectations for you. I was wrong by not encouraging you to move out. In a way, we've all enabled you to be where you are—"

"But—"

"No wait. We've enabled you to take your time, which you've needed, but at the end of the day, you're an adult. With adult thoughts and feelings. The problem is, we're not helping you deal with those right now. Somehow, I thought if we concentrated on all that had happened in Afghanistan, the rest would fall into place. But it hasn't. I said it the last time I saw you in my office, and I'll say it again: you have unresolved feelings for Sadie. I should have pushed more then and I didn't."

Where did that put me on my path to healing? Doc's words seemed ominous, like she might beg off treating me and send me to someone else. She'd been a mainstay in my life for a while. I wasn't sure I could take losing Sadie fully and Doc all at the same time.

Beads of sweat collected on the back of my neck. "What are you going to do? Send me somewhere else?"

"No, not exactly. Or not right away. I'd like you to head back and come see me in the office. In the meantime, I'll put together a strategy that might be more advantageous for you. I'll also say again you might consider in-patient therapy. You've been good about keeping the anger out of your reactions, but I worry about you. Very much so."

"I know, Doc."

"You do. And I have to say, this phone call has been enlightening."

"Ha! Every once in a while, I come through, don't I?"

"Oh Theo. You have so much to offer, and I want you to get better. Your children want you to get better; even Sadie wants you to get better. And I *know* you can do so. We all have setbacks, and this might be one of those. But someday, when you've moved into a healthier place, you'll look back and understand everything. Before we end though, how are the dreams, the flashbacks? Any more episodes?"

I'd expected being away from my normal routine might throw me into a tizzy, but Walloon Lake had worked its charms on me, at least a little. Except for the dream I had the night Sadie and I argued, my nightmares hadn't increased— at least they weren't any worse than the few weeks prior. I had even felt mostly in control while talking to Sadie, almost as if Charlie's reveal served to prepare me for that conversation. Heads up, it said, which had helped. And Doc didn't need to hear about my trip to the library or what had spurred it on. Revenge? Anger?

"Actually, they haven't increased. I..."

"Yes?"

"Who knows what I want to say. Probably nothing. I appreciate your time, and I'll be back soonish. You have to visit this place to understand how hard it is to leave."

"Ah, yes, so I've heard." The smirk in her voice stood out to me; she'd listened to me sing the praises of Walloon Lake too many times. "But you need to remember your health is top priority. The longer you stay there, the more you're running away, which will be detrimental in the long run. Plus, it will keep you away from the kids. Those kids make you happy."

A smile tugged at the corners of my mouth. Those three made my heart grow bigger, something I rarely held onto these days. Sadie would say I'd become a huge softy when it came to them, but no matter. Placing the three of them at the front of my mind would be a good thing for me.

•   •   •   •   •

As much as I often hated to admit it, talking to Doc helped clarify my station in life. Even though I could be in a better place, I had made progress, right? Anger and depression had always been my go-tos in the past, deliberating about what might have been but wasn't, and this time, I felt healthier somehow. Maybe the lifeline to Doc helped just by existing—who knew? What we hadn't talked about was confronting Andrew, and I wondered about taking that route and busting open that can of worms. Did he know about Sadie and me? He didn't seem the type to mess with lives. Maybe Charlie had witnessed one solitary, weak moment for Sadie. Maybe they didn't have a relationship. But all the maybes in the world wouldn't give me Sadie back. If that's what I wanted, I had to make it happen.

What did I want?

I sat back against the chair in my room and contemplated the fringe attached to the blanket draped over the arm. It reminded me of the fringe on Sadie's snow hat, the one her aunt made for her when she was in college. The hat, long packed into a box or given away, held fond memories for us both. It had made an appearance on each winter date Sadie and I shared until it disappeared: I had hidden it from her in my garage, hoping she'd forget about it. Sadie hadn't, and in true Sadie form, she'd gotten back at me—she convinced her aunt to knit a matching one for me. Sadie made me wear it, *and* she sent a Christmas card out that year with a photo of us in striped hats. I hadn't thought of that hat in years; taking it to Afghanistan would have been a mistake. No sense wearing a winter hat in the heat, and I'd have stood out too much from the crowd.

That hat had also seen bad days, though. The winter after my first deployment, the hat played a starring role in giving Sadie a reason to doubt my health and happiness. It had been missing for days, and Sadie wanted to wear it. Tired of hearing the incessant, "Where is that hat?" I snapped at her. In a big way. (Doc would call it a major tantrum.) The fear in Sadie's eyes still showed up in my nightmares sometimes. I had started to question my abilities, my love, and my life that night.

Thoughts about Sadie now caused an avalanche of emotions. What gave her the damn right to walk away from us? What about talking to me about new feelings for someone else? And why would she allow me to live in the same house if she didn't want to repair the marriage? An itch began in the bottom of my feet and worked its way up my entire body. Pacing would help, so I pushed up from the chair and wore my usual treads on the carpet floor. My fists clenched at my sides, and soon, a deep anger surged within me, and a thumping in my forehead took on a life of its own. Increased breathing calmed the storm: in, out, in, out. Progress? What progress?

My phone rang: a call from Sadie, which meant it was probably the kids. In this agitated state, I didn't have the heart to speak with them, so I let it go to voicemail. Another indescribable jitteriness overtook my entire body, now full of the need to do something, be more active in this situation. Even in this state, senses overwhelmed, I considered what Doc would say: "Be an active participant. Keep your anger in check and talk to the other party."

I'd easily found where the librarian lived—a quick search had popped up her information. I hoped Andrew was home.

It didn't take long to get there, and the walk did nothing to dampen my rage. With each step, my thoughts swam: Whose fault was it? Was Andrew a friend or not? What would I say to him? How could he do this?

He opened the door, an unassuming smile on his face. "Theo? What are you doing here?"

"Coming to see you."

Andrew stepped back, opening the door wider, as he furrowed his brow. "Are you okay? Do you want to come in?"

Rational and irrational at the same time. A downward spiral of control. I did everything wrong. My anger was so raw, so electric, the first punch to his face had him falling backward, onto the floor of his small foyer, his head landing with a gigantic thud against the tile floor.

"That's for messing around with my wife." My fist connected again with his jaw. "That's for not being a true friend." Despite the blood, I went in for a third time, right for the eye. "And that's just because, you son of a bitch."

I left Andrew there, unmoving on the tile, blood dripping out of his nose, and walked back to the cottage, nerves still frayed and all cylinders firing. Sweat poured off my skin, and I was grateful for the empty house. After a quick splash of cold water to my face, I hunted in the freezer for a bag of frozen veggies and placed them on my throbbing hand. Then, I took the keys to my mother-in-law's car. She had never been my most ardent admirer, but Marjorie wouldn't mind me taking the car either. I needed to get out of there. Pronto. A quick note explaining my actions would need to be enough.

A jumble of thoughts twisted in my head as I peeled out of the neighborhood and drove away. From my life. My family. From anything and everything. The scenery flew by, and I'd never been more thankful for the rural life: two-lane roads with a fifty-five mile per hour limit. With little water on the streets, I pushed the limit, pressing my foot to the pedal with force. Sixty. Seventy. Eighty. Eight-five. The old car shuddered as the speed increased, and my fury unleashed. Sadie. Andrew. The tension in the almost-moment Sadie described; I embodied it. What the hell? It was all too much. Too much. Reflexes took over, and the car lurched as it tried to keep up with the demands of the hill.

A glance in the rearview mirror showed the lake behind me. I'd left them all there, removed myself from their lives. Removed myself from *my* life. That was the answer: removal. The tires squealed as I wrenched the steering wheel, barely making the quick jog onto the road running along the river that lay to my right. The river, with its slow-moving, clear water sparkling in the sun. Placid, peaceful. The perfect place to rest...

Chapter 30: Sadie

Based on Theo's departure from the cottage and my breakdown with Andrew at the bakery, I decided to leave Walloon Lake early. Truncating the fun and disappointing the kids was never my intention. My mom pulled those stunts; I did not. But to gain perspective and figure out where to go and what to do, immersing myself back in reality—which included going into the office and taking the children to school—had to happen. I held a certain confidence in myself, although some would call it a delusion. Releasing the full truth had lifted the burden. Now, I'd put my best foot forward and turn things around. A future with Andrew might be possible, if that's what I truly wanted. But I needed to do Theo a favor and pull the plug on our relationship for good. I hadn't heard from Theo for a good thirty-six hours, so I imagined he planned to stay up in the area for a bit longer.

With a heavy heart, I told the kids Theo was going to remain at Walloon Lake for a few more days. As expected, the news about Theo affected Charlie the most. After I had spoken to the children, he placed his hand on my arm and stared at me.

"Mom, can I stay here with Dad? Please?" Charlie said. The planes of his face contorted with sadness, and the tone of his voice, full of hope and longing, hurt my ears. An arrow pierced my heart as I denied his request.

"Charlie, you can't. You have school to get back to, and we have Christmas shopping to do. This was a surprise vacation anyway. And we had a good time, didn't we?" A curl sprang away from his forehead, and I smoothed it back while holding my eyes steady with his.

"Yes." Charlie's quiet voice spoke volumes.

"But I've already put the deposit down for next year. Okay?" A hug and a smile might be able to wipe away his sadness, at least for a little while. He looked up at me through the mop of hair flopped over his forehead.

"Okay," Charlie said, leaning in for a quick squeeze.

I told him to get packing and then headed to the laundry room to finish up the wash. The piles would take at least two hours, so we'd aim to leave after lunch. I sorted the clothes into lights, darks, and towels and set a few pieces aside to be hand-washed later at home. Something about the monotonous act of laundry soothed my flustered self. I was happy to be doing it and was glad I'd asked my mom to take care of the kids.

When I stooped to pick up the rest of the bath towels, a pair of Charlie's pants—tucked behind the door—caught my eye. Checking the pockets, I laughed when my fingers encountered a Petoskey stone and a bottle cap on the right side, along with a wrinkled piece of tin foil. And in the left pocket a piece of paper, folded into eighths. Charlie the collector, we'd always called him. If we didn't watch it, he had the potential to become a hoarder. The items found a transient home on the bathroom counter because if I threw them away without asking Charlie about them, we'd have a real problem later.

A load of wash took twenty-five minutes, so with the kids occupied and a few minutes on my hand, I jogged over to the library to say a quick goodbye to Pickles.

"She's not here today," the substitute librarian told me. "Something about her knees. Would you like to leave her a message?"

Pickles didn't have a cell phone, and while I could knock on her door on the way back to the cottage, I left a message just in case.

And that was a good thing: when I got to her house, the blinds were drawn, and no one answered the door. Was she okay? Despite my reservations, I texted Andrew.

All okay with you and your mom? She's not at work, and I wanted to say goodbye. I'm leaving today.

Andrews's reply—short and curt—cut to the quick.

I'm under the weather, as is Mom. I'll give her your goodbyes and make sure she has a cell phone. Safe travels.

It lacked the warmth of his past texts and interactions. Was something wrong? I didn't have time to dwell on that thought.

Back at the house, as I stood transferring clothes from the washer to the dryer, the front door slammed, and the sound of little feet echoed across the living room. My mom's lighter footsteps crept behind them, then she encouraged the kids to wash their hands and get a cool drink of water. The patience in her voice astounded me, but once the kids caught their second wind, Mom would be ushering them my way. My pace picked up, and I headed toward the bedrooms to check for any more stray pieces of clothing.

A white T-shirt of Theo's had been left on his closet doorknob. I pushed the fabric to my nose and inhaled, reveling in the scent of him: deodorant and the light aroma called Theo. Tears sprang to my eyes, but I wiped them away and jammed the clothing in my suitcase for safekeeping. I might have made my decision about him long ago, but old habits die hard; that could be the only piece of Theo I'd have for time moving forward.

Mom interrupted me. "Uh, Sadie? Have you seen my car?"

"You mean it's not in the driveway? I haven't been using the back door. I assumed it would..."

"It's not there. And neither are my keys."

"That's odd."

"Did Theo take it?"

I sighed. "He's not supposed to drive by himself but hold on. Let me text him." He knew better than to drive alone, but maybe he took someone with him. Mike?

Delia ran into the room, paper in hand. "Look what I found! A note from Daddy."

Mom looked at the paper and read it aloud. "Marjorie, I'm borrowing the car. I'll keep it safe. Sorry you weren't here to ask." She met my gaze and raised her eyebrows.

What? "I'm—"

"I'm not mad," she said. "I understand some of what he's going through. If he needs the time away, so be it. I can stay up here for a few more days—if you're okay with it. In fact, I'm happy to do so. Lake life agrees with me."

An uncharacteristic connection emerged in my chest. Walloon Lake had worked its magic on Mom too. "We'll get to the bottom of this, but if you want to stay, the place is yours."

We spent the last few hours at Walloon Lake hiking the trail along the lake, swinging at the empty playground, and ordering double scoops of Superman ice cream. The soundtrack of the kids' voices brought happy tears to my eyes, and I stored it for later, when I needed to hear utter joy and contentment. Theo hadn't returned my text yet, but Mom wasn't worried about her car—Lena offered hers when needed—so the kids and I packed up and swept the house. Then, we left for home. The kids might have sensed something, or perhaps it was the sadness they felt from leaving Dad at the lake, but none of them quibbled at the sandwiches I doled out or how few stops we made on the return drive. Charlie and Delia read to themselves and chatted with Lexie in the back seats, interrupting me only when necessary.

At the last stop, I texted Jackie and Kate, telling them of our change in plans, practically begging them to come by sometime after we arrived home. I didn't give either of my friends the details, just that I needed to talk. It was no surprise, then, to see them in the dark, lounging on the porch of our house back in Kettering. Jackie held a bundled but sleeping Clara on her chest, and Kate sported a bottle of white wine in the crook of her arm. A levity bloomed inside my chest that hadn't been there before. Glancing in the rearview mirror at the three sleeping children, I put the car in park. It wasn't too late, but all the activity of the past few weeks had caught up with the kids. If I was lucky, Kate and I could get them to bed while Jackie manned the baby and the wine.

It didn't take long to deposit the kids in their beds and get the baggage and outdoor toys into the laundry room. A quick closing of the laundry room door served its purpose: I wouldn't see the mess, and Brooke wouldn't try to tackle it the next day when she arrived. Jackie and Kate had come over for me, to help *me*, and everything else could wait.

In the living room, Kate had set up the wine and glasses, and Jackie had pulled in an old pack-n-play. Clara lay there, snug and asleep, and I laughed. Not so long ago, I'd been seated in Jackie's living room helping her with *her* life problems. And here she was, coming to help me. The ebb and flow of friendship; I smiled at both my friends and was grateful they'd arrived at a moment's notice. How lucky was I?

"Thanks for coming to rescue me, ladies. If you hadn't come, it's likely I'd be here drinking by myself." I poured the wine into one glass and nodded my head in Jackie's direction, a silent question as to whether she wanted any.

"Go ahead, but just a little. I don't want to have to pump and dump this precious stuff." Jackie gestured to her chest.

"By the way," said Kate. "I'm happy to rescue you. Of course, I don't like having to rescue you, but you know what I mean."

"Yeah, I do." I passed the glasses to my friends and slumped onto the couch. My body language must have said something.

"Is it that bad?" Jackie asked, taking a small sip of the wine and leaning in to listen.

My actions mimicked Jackie's, but my swallow turned into a large gulp. "Probably not, but sometimes, it is." I stood up from my seat. "Good evening. My name is Sadie, and I'm a horrible person. I haven't divorced my husband yet, but I want someone else." After a quick and clumsy curtsy, I sat back on the cushion, placing my hand to my head in dramatic fashion. Holy cow, the wine had just started, and already my tongue ran loose. The night could only get better.

We sat in the living room and drank wine by the streaks of moonlight filtering through the blinds, faces glowing in the dark. Jackie and Kate distracted me from my life with topics ranging from the kids to recent movies to the lack of parent volunteers at the elementary school. From time to time, they interjected a question or two about Andrew and Theo and what had happened, and I supplied a few, simple, but terse, answers; for the most part, I wanted to stay as far away from the subject of love as possible. The minutes and then the hours passed. Sitting with friends was something I hadn't done in a long time, and I realized how much fun I was having. A few minutes after eleven, a wicked thought came to my mind.

"Hey," I said, "Why don't we text Andrew?"

"What is that? Like drunk dialing?" Jackie asked. She yawned. Our little party would soon have to wrap up. I wasn't too drunk I couldn't understand my friend. She still had work to get to next week and her holiday preparations to take care of.

"I guess. Wouldn't that be funny?"

"Yeah, until tomorrow, when you check your texts and realize what you did. Don't do it. For goodness sakes, let's have some dignity here," Kate said.

Kate's gravelly voice reminded me so much of my mother's, the voice I grew up with, the voice that criticized and made me feel inadequate. Whether or not she had meant it the way it sounded, her words brought me back to earth, to my reality. To the fact I was behaving like a kid, and I wasn't one. I had responsibilities, and for a brief time, somehow, I'd forgotten them.

Straightening up in my chair, I brushed at my lips. "You're right. I don't want to lose any more dignity than I already have. But in my opinion, you're being a wee bit judgmental." I held up my hand and put a small amount of space between my thumb and my index finger. "Try walking in my shoes for a change."

Kate's eyes grew wide in response to my words, and her face blanched. But I'd never been in this situation before and truthfully, I felt judged by her. She got up from her chair and approached my seat. She knelt in front of me and extended her hand to my arm. "You can get through this slight bump. With my help, with Jackie's, with a therapist, one who isn't your friend. I don't..." Kate let her voice trail off, but she continued to stare at me.

"I've thought of that," I said. "It's why I went to see you in the first place...thought you'd suggest therapy." A mist gathered in the corners of my eyes. "I've had a lot of time to ruminate about this, though, and now, I'm convinced I don't *want* to get through it. I'm keeping myself stuck in this middle because it's my way of punishing myself." I placed my hand on top of Kate's. "There's a therapist's response for you, eh? I'm not doing anything but spinning my wheels because being in the middle, between wanting to be with Andrew but not wanting to leave a person who might need my help...it's punishment. Self-flagellation if you will." I hadn't thought much before I said those last words, but they sounded right to me.

"Don't you see though?" Jackie interrupted. "You're concentrating on the wrong part of the problem. Sure, Theo has issues—who doesn't?—but you aren't looking elsewhere because of his sickness. You and Theo made the decision to end things before you met Andrew. And, even if Theo didn't have PTSD, what's to say you'd be together now?"

The conversation had turned deep so quickly, my mind sobered. "I see your point, Jackie, but please, if you weren't my friend, would you be sticking up for me? Or would you be on the side of the sick man, pitying him because his rotten lifeline wants to leave him?"

Holding up a shaky hand, I didn't let her answer. "I'm so glad you came over. I needed girl time, time away from my troubles, and you gave that to me. I'm not ready to face this right now, and it's late." I hugged my friends and placed a kiss on Clara's fuzzy head, then turned my back and walked on wobbly legs to my silent bedroom. Kate and Jackie would be kind enough to let themselves out and let me wallow in my sorry state.

That night, I tossed and turned in my bed, half expecting to hear a car pull up on the driveway and for Theo to walk in. Being there, in the house we'd lived in for the last thirteen years, made me miss him—his smell, his laugh, everything about him. I pulled what had been his pillow to my face and inhaled, trying to capture his essence even though it had been a long time since he'd been in the bed. Desperate for warmth and sleep, I took his fleece bathrobe from the hook on his bathroom door, wrapped myself up in it, and folded myself onto the big armchair in the corner of his bedroom. My phone sat on the side table, and I contemplated calling Kate. She'd be home by now, and while we had our differences, her experience as a therapist had its benefits.

After grabbing the phone, I clutched the device in my fingers, my predicament staring me in the face. Not long ago, I'd vacillated between wanting out of my marriage and wanting to stay in. I'd chosen to sort of stay in, for Theo's sake, and now, a different kind of vacillation presented itself. Pursue my happiness or make sure someone I used to love got what they needed? Where on the continuum did my feelings lie? I knew only one thing: I had to get my act together. Sadie Rollins-Lancaster played the roles of partner, mother, employee, and more, and people depended on me. Before Theo came back—*if* he came back—I hoped I'd align myself again and find a conclusion to send me up the right path, whatever that might be.

Chapter 31: Sadie

When Theo and I decided to separate, he still couldn't admit to being wrong. Or admit even though he'd been dealt a bad hand in life, he'd *chosen* to join the service and go to Afghanistan. Or admit he'd played a role in how his life unfurled. He'd been that way since I'd met him, but I'd had no reservations about the characteristic. Because I loved him; because he *got* me; because he cared for me more than anyone else; because he was my best friend, and I could imagine growing old with him.

After Theo started seeing a therapist, I thought he'd become more willing to admit his weaknesses, and he'd let me help him more on a day-to-day basis as his mental facilities fluctuated, not battle me each time he needed something. I naively thought he'd say, "You're right, honey. This situation is stressing me out, and I'd love to go for a walk right now. Thank you." I imagined PTSD would humble him and make him more compassionate for those who were hurting. But it never happened. I didn't know why he was the way he was, but his inability to ask for help played a part in our separation, and the need to be right meant this time away for Theo could be long. I'd have to buck up and deal with it because Theo might take all the time he needed and then some, despite the children.

But why hadn't he at least checked in with us? I'd left messages for him, asking him to call the kids, to speak to them and inform them he'd be home for Christmas. Nothing. And by Monday morning, two days had passed, and my ire had grown. "You can stay somewhere else if you have to," I muttered to myself, "but the kids need you. I'm the one you're angry with, not them."

That morning, a distant headache and thoughts about how to sever the family successfully joined me on my way to work. I also thought about the kids and if splitting completely with Theo when my relationship with Andrew wasn't a sure thing was the way to go. But even if Andrew and I never became a unit, this same problem might arise again at some point. I needed to be proactive and try—what?—I didn't know. Perhaps Theo's therapist held the answer.

As I entered my office, enormous doubts plagued me. But the plant on my desk from Andrew —amaryllis, one of my favorites—put a smile on my face. And the files on my computer and the monotony of the morning took me away from my thoughts. I spent the first half of the day holed up, drowning myself in the unremarkable tasks that had piled up while I was away. They proved to be therapeutic in a surreal way, and I made my way home extra early, ready to tackle the afternoon and evening with the kids.

But the illusion of happiness can be fragile. Right after lunch, I stood in the kitchen, finishing up the odd dishes as Lexie frolicked outside in the front yard. The unseasonably warm weather had surged once again and being able to send my youngest outside was a godsend. Brooke sat on a chair in the driveway, making sure Lexie didn't run into the street. Their laughter filtered through the window I had cracked, and the sound tickled my ears. Amongst the loud noises came the crunch of tires and a squeal of delight. Had Theo returned?

I rushed to the bathroom to check the state of my appearance and stood shocked, looking at my reflection. It had been months since my hair had seen the inside of a beauty salon, and I'd lost my Walloon Lake glow, but I was the same Sadie he'd seen for the past fifteen years. No better, no worse, just myself. Why did I care? My legs began to shake, and I held myself against the wall to keep from crumbling.

I waited long enough to gather my courage and then approached the front of the house. Andrew, not Theo, stood there speaking with Brooke, a look of concern on both their faces. My entire being reacted in the usual way: a quick flutter in my stomach and a flood of warmth throughout my chest. The phone in my pocket buzzed, twice, and I pulled it out to check the message. The first, from my Mom:

Have you spoken with Andrew?

The second, came from an unidentified number:

Mom, it's me. Charlie. The presentation has been moved up to today, this afternoon. Can you get here?

Before I had time to reply to any texts, Andrew was in front of me, sadness flaring in his eyes, fingers gripped against my shoulders. A large, purple bruise lined up along his nose, and his right eye didn't open fully. I reached out with my fingers to touch the battered skin.

"What the—"

"We need to go. Theo stopped by mom's place days ago, he was angry with me, with us, and—" The words rushed from Andrew in a manner I hadn't experienced since Delia had taken a terrifying plunge down the hill in a neighbor's yard, and Charlie was trying to explain what had happened. My pulse quickened, and this time, fear, not lust, caused it.

But something in Andrew's face, part defensive, part guilty, confused me. "Wait a minute—you know Theo? What the hell? *How?*"

"We met a while ago now—at the gym. I didn't know you two were a couple. Listen." Andrew caught my chin in his hand. "Theo stopped by Mom's house, and he didn't even give me a chance to say anything. Punched me a few times before I had the chance to explain anything—knocked me out, almost—and walked out the door. I stayed silent for a few days and didn't want to speak of it, even when you texted me, but then...well I didn't think anything of his behavior until I got notice from your mom saying they found her car and Theo had been in an accident."

"Oh, God." I fell back against the car and placed my hands over my ears. My body and soul couldn't handle hearing what might come next. "Why didn't she call me? What—"

"Stop." Andrew pulled my hands to my sides and leaned in toward me. "She put a call through to you, but when you didn't answer, she went into crisis mode and got help. I'm pretty sure he loves you—still. *Loves*, not loved. He's alive. Pretty bad off, but alive." Always the gentleman, Andrew helped steady me against the hood of his car while tears trekked down my cheeks.

"Theo? Where is he and—"

"He's at the hospital. Here. I called in a favor with an air ambulance company, and they flew him over. I'll take you there."

Muddled thoughts took hold of my brain, not letting go even with a shake of my head. "I texted him less than an hour ago, asking if he'd care to tell us when he'd be home...I haven't heard from him in days. No wonder he hasn't answered—" I rummaged in the pocket of my sweatshirt for a tissue.

"I know. He left his phone at the Inn, didn't even have it with him. Apparently, he's been in the ditch for a few days. He's lucky someone found him and that the weather has been so good too. I didn't want to tell you this over text or with a phone call. Mom managed anything that needed to be done in Petoskey for him, and I left to come back here. Your mom is on her way too."

"How?"

"They're not sure what happened yet," Andrew continued. "But he needs you. We should get going."

Clutching his fingers in mine, I looked up at Andrew through a watery haze. "Thank you," I whispered.

"You're welcome."

• • • • •

Andrew and I didn't speak much as he drove me to the hospital, mostly because what was there to say? And, I had other things on my mind. My interest strayed to my phone, where I first responded to Charlie's text with a quick, *I'll try*, and then checked and rechecked the messages I'd sent to Theo over the last week or so. The thread was mostly one-sided, but an exchange from earlier in the month, before our trip to Walloon, caught my eye.

How's it going? I had texted.

You want to know?

That's why I'm asking.

I want peace.

We all do.

I know.

Something in Theo's text sliced through me like a sharp blade and goose bumps broke out along my arms. Had I missed something that day he sent this? Was this truly an accident or— A compulsion to continue reading overtook me. This new lens could reveal so much.

Okay, what do you need from me? I had asked.

I'm not sure, but you once said you weren't made of steel. But you are.

And, I love you.

Holy shit. I had not seen that last addition to the thread back when he sent it. A simple no-frills *I love you*. What did it mean?

Now, my fingers automatically wanted to text back *I love you too* because I still did, in my own way, but he wouldn't receive the reply, and the response seemed so contrived, inadequate, and to be quite frank, dishonest, even if I had sent it back then. An enormous deluge of emotions engulfed me as I gathered my shirt in my fists and held back a huge sob.

Andrew followed my lead, saying nothing while he extended a tissue toward me, allowing me to sit with my thoughts and memories. All the times in my life when I counted on Theo to be there flickered through my mind: how deep our love had once been, what he had meant to me and the children. My fingers dug into the skin of my chest, as if to hold in a heart that might burst through the flesh at the thought that Theo wasn't okay.

Andrew deposited me at the hospital's front doors, asked me to stay put, and then left to find a place to park. A compulsion propelled me to begin the hunt myself, and winding my way through the maze of hallways to the ICU, I found him. My lunch lurched into my throat at the sight of Theo tucked into the white sheets of the hospital bed. How his health had gone downhill so quickly stymied me. What had I missed over the last week? My face must have registered its shock, for the attending doctor cut into my thoughts.

"Don't blame yourself for this. He's a grown man."

The words confused me; had I heard him correctly? "For this? What are you talking about?" I looked over to Theo and back to the doctor, whose face had turned a stark shade of pale.

"We don't have all the details, but the authorities mentioned he meant to drive off the road. He wasn't found for two days' time. Theo had to have understood the repercussions of his actions."

Ice breathed down the back of my neck, and a shakiness overtook me. "Oh my God. Are you kidding me?"

"I'm afraid not," he said.

"But...how the hell did this happen?" I dropped into the metal chair next to the bed and placed my head in my hands, pulling at the roots of my hair to manage the pain ripping through me.

"Listen, clearly this is a plea for help. We'll do what we can, but I'm not sure if he'll recover at all..."

Did the doctor think I wasn't smart enough to understand a cry for help when one presented itself?

"Yeah," I said, unable to keep the rancor out of my voice. "I see he's sending me a message. His kids can't handle this. I can't handle this." I hauled myself out of the chair and snatched at the doctor's arms, grabbing his shirt in my hands. "Who else knows?"

He pried my fingers away from his clothing but continued to hold them within his hands. "Listen, it's not my place to tell anyone. As far as I'm concerned, no one besides a few folks here and the sheriff's office know about the suspicion."

The bell of the breathing machine to which Theo was attached made its ascent upward and then downward, and the vitals monitor beeped its signal. My strong and formerly still-capable partner couldn't even breathe by his own accord. Why did he do this now? Had our argument and my admission instigated this? My breathing rate picked up, and I clenched my fists against my sides as an indescribable anger rose within me. In a small hospital room, my fury would have no outlet, so I slumped back into the chair next to the bed and stared at Theo.

His face, so pinched and drawn, looked like the product of an epic battle he'd barely come out of alive. *Epic battle, indeed.* For the last several years this man had taken up a fight against an opponent that perhaps, he'd never beat. And years before, with his dad? Theo fought an enemy for far more years than anybody should have to.

The doctor took a piece of paper and a book from the bedside table and handed them to me. "The team found these in the coat Theo had on him. They're meant for you, obviously, but they may need to be seen by the police. The note is important enough to let you see it before it gets lost or taken. I'll leave you two alone now." The doctor's slow stride took him closer to the door before he glanced back once, pity on his face.

Flipping the book over, I gasped at the cover: Dante's *Inferno.* Was this a sign? What was Theo trying to tell me?

My fingers traced the edges of the same thick, ivory paper Theo had used back at Walloon Lake, and my stomach turned at the thought of what the paper had represented that day: detachment. And now, this huge attempt—if that's what it was—at complete separation. When had he decided this? Why hadn't he spoken to me? The tears pooled in my eyes, and my lips quivered. Fearing what I'd find inside the folded-up square of paper, I turned it over several times before plucking up the courage to face those fears. With trembling hands, I lifted the top half of the paper.

Dear Sadie,

You tore my heart into a thousand pieces with your admission, but once I thought about everything you'd said, I realized you were right. We had been damaged for a long time before we agreed to separate, and I was partially to blame. My inability to want to seek help and my lack of confidence in my abilities—both played a huge role in our demise. My choice wasn't fair to you or the kids or to me or to our marriage. I understand and accept responsibility for that.

Life can be hard; marriage can be hard. Those statements are true. And you, Sadie, would have worked your tail off to make this marriage work, had I let you. But I didn't, and then, I didn't let you go either. And that's not fair. To you or to the kids. Or even to me.

It took a long time to realize, but I'm not made like you. Each day, I step toward a life I never wanted and one I'm having trouble accepting. There's a way to change the path, a way to make life less difficult, but choosing that route won't help anyone but me.

And then there's Andrew. It's clear he reveres you. He made me realize I should have held tightly to you and never let you go. He also made me realize the two of you could be happy together, really happy. Imagining you and him in the cottage almost kissing was like experiencing Dante's inferno the whole time. All seven fucking levels.

Just remember this: I loved you then, and I love you still.

Yours, Theo.

I crumpled the paper in my hands, threw it to the floor, and stomped on it in a fit of rage so full of heat, it took my breath away. When had he written this? Its presence implied he'd *meant* to drive off the cliff, and I turned toward the window, trying to calm myself with the early December Ohio sky, mottled with thick, gray clouds and dotted by a group of birds headed south.

But my mind was quick to pick up the fury again. The Theo I married would have been stronger than this! How could he leave his kids this way? "They'll remember you as a coward, not as the strong character you wanted to leave them as. Why couldn't you see that?" I whispered.

Tears streamed down my face as I leaned in toward him, extending my fingers to his pale cheek and tracing the line of his jaw. I longed for him to open his eyes, move his jaw, and begin speaking. I'd listen to anything: the weather, his job, baseball stats, fractals, current events, anything. *Just talk to me.*

The hinges of the door creaked, and I sensed someone behind me. Glancing over my shoulder at Mom, my eyes watered. She clutched her hat in her hands and an expression of deep sorrow lined her tired face. She'd gone through a lot on this last day, and how she managed to get here so quickly—I'd address that another time.

"How are you doing?" Mom said.

"How do you think?"

"Not so good, I'd say."

"You've got that right, but what did you expect?"

"True. I only came to sit and listen. I thought it might help." She pushed a second chair close to the one I had been sitting in and settled into it. Then, she leaned down, picked up the letter, and silently handed it to me.

Letting go of Theo's hand, I sat next to her, our shoulders touching. The physical connection stood out to me as an indicator I should let her listen, let her show she cared. In my book, she'd be the prodigal mom who went away and came back, and we'd be the mother-daughter duo who reconnected and forged a new, healthier relationship.

"You've caught on to most of everything that's happened over the last half year or so, but recently, I've been comparing my life to a book," I said.

The lines of Mom's face danced upon hearing my words. "Oh, why am I not surprised? You always were a voracious reader, even when you didn't have the time to be. And with your job..."

"So, I got to thinking. What sort of book would my life be? And while I couldn't quite decide—because I kept getting more thrown at me: men, drama, laughs, you name it, I got it—I also started wondering about the character I'd be. It's clear now I'm the flawed heroine, if I can even call myself a heroine...look what I'm doing with my life. But who wants to read about a person with flaws?" I pressed my back against the chair and felt the steel rod up against my spine, which forced me to sit up straighter than I would have preferred.

"We all have flaws," Mom said, a simple quirk to her lips.

"I know that."

"And some of the most well-written and highly regarded characters are flawed; it's what makes them human. But this isn't a book." Mom extended her hand to mine, and I didn't stop her from taking it. "This is your life, and you've always been the type to take what you want from it. Decide what you want and then go for it." She pressed our fingers together, a gesture I chose to interpret as unwavering, yet surprising, support.

"That doesn't apply right now does it? Theo is dying here."

"Not to be crude, but he's been dying for a long time, Sadie. You've just been hanging on for the ride. And is he really what you want?"

All this time, and I thought Mom hadn't noticed. Her words felt like pins to me, and I removed my hand from hers. "You aren't married anymore. How can you understand? It doesn't matter I've wavered back and forth, and I've been inconsistent. I thought Theo was going to try and make things better for himself. That's what we agreed on. Plus, I told him I'd be here for him."

"But are you *here?*"

This time, her words slammed into me like a linebacker taking out an opponent. I gasped, shook my head to rid myself of the offensive feeling, and concentrated on the floor, which couldn't spew verbal barbs. "Your words hurt, Mom. They really hurt." For once, I wanted to be completely honest with her, plus I didn't have the energy to throw anything more offensive her way.

"I know. I'm sorry I'm the one who had to say them. But I am your mom. And always will be."

For so long, Mom and I had spoken words that served as slings and arrows, and now, only now, when I was in the crux of a crisis, did I realize this time she probably *was* truly sorry.

"It's okay, it's what we do...as mom and daughter anyway. We have this knack for injuring one another with a single word."

"Well then, I might as well go ahead and mention you're reacting like I would."

"What? Like you? How?" I stared into Mom's eyes. I'd never seen truth shining from them like I did that day.

"You can't see it? Being indecisive, going back and forth, trying to find a reason for everything that's happening and trying to find a place to put the blame. You, only *you*, are accountable for your actions. No one else.

"But if you really wanted Andrew, if you *want* Andrew, if he's the best option for you, you're the only one who can decide that. Screw what everyone else says, it's your life. But be sure of what you're doing, because once you do it, you can't go back."

Tight silence hung in the air, punctuated only by the sounds of Theo's machines.

"You're a little late, Mom." I had decided to at least try a new future involving Theo far off to the side and Andrew in the new supporting role. "Theo seems to want to call the shots right now. I'm not sure I can deal with anything else at this point."

The cavalier way the words spilled forth surprised me, but my entire being flooded with fatigue and exasperation. Was Theo going to die? If he did, how would that affect me and the kids? I'd anticipated a sense of relief when Theo signed the papers and moved out because even though I hadn't originally wanted to divorce, it became clear it was the correct path. But this would be a sudden happenstance, an abrupt loss, a shock to both me and the kids. I gripped the arms of the chair, so cold beneath my fingers, and fought against the sobs wracking my body once again.

"I want Andrew, but I also want Theo back. Is it possible to want them both?"

"Yes, but not in the way you've been going about it. You've been trying to balance both for a while now, right? And has it worked?"

Just because Mom told the truth didn't mean I had to like it. But I knew better this time and thought about what she said, absorbing the words and giving my honest answer.

"No, it hasn't worked at all," I said.

"Then dig deep. Get inside your head and heart and soul and take the time to listen to what they're telling you. And figure the whole goddamn mess out."

Chapter 32: Theo

The sun's rays streamed through the plate glass window next to Doc's desk as I sat in a chair in her office. The slivers of light hit the brown carpet, highlighting a dark oval that didn't match the surrounding fibers. A rust-colored cast. What had happened there? And why didn't I remember how I'd gotten here?

"Do you feel better now?" Doc said, smirk on her lips, legs crossed in front of her. She'd bought a new pen—ruby and black, the kind that clicked—and she'd been pushing the end up and down since I'd shown up. Normally, Doc knew better than to try and set me off, but today, she had a major problem. Click, click, click.

"Do I feel better? I'm not sure. How did I get here?"

"You mean you don't know? You don't remember?" Click.

"I remember talking to you on the phone when I was at the Inn. But the rest of it. All hazy. Am I on new meds?"

Doc's phone rang, and she lifted a finger, silently telling me to hold on before she answered it. What the hell? She never answered her phone during one of our sessions. In fact, the phone had always been silenced...

"That's right," Doc said to the person on the other line. "Dinner party at eight means you'll need to be there by six. I could use a bit of help cooking." Click. "I'm not going to serve anything fancy, but you know how I am." She giggled and glanced at me. "No, no. That's okay. I'll be sure to have something you can eat...chicken? I'd much prefer something a bit darker, shall we say..." Click.

Giggling? Doc? The lift of her eyebrow...I shoved my hands against my eyes, rubbed them, and blinked. Click. Doc had switched positions. She now stood in front of me, arms across her chest, fire blazing from her eyes. A normally calm fixture in my life, she'd become an imposing and daunting figure.

"You're not as forthcoming as you need to be, Theo. I'm worried about you. It's time to consider new alternatives."

"Like what?"

Doc reached for my hand and pulled me to standing. We faced one another, her breathing in tune with mine. Click.

"Can you please stop?" I asked, my entire body pulsing with tension, a slight humming moving up and down my legs and arms.

"Stop what?"

"The clicking."

"I'm not doing anything."

"But your pen—"

She held up her hands. Both empty. Click.

I blinked again, grit stinging my eyes. When I opened them, Doc had moved to the corner, and the Yoga Man had appeared, lying on a thin ochre mat next to my feet.

"There's still hope for you, Theo," he said.

"What do you mean, hope?" All of me fought to push up from my chair, but something otherworldly tethered me to the seat. My feet. No luck there either. My arms—stuck to those of the chair.

"I mean you're looking for something. For a connection. I can feel it, in here." The man touched his chest with one finger and turned his head my way. His dark pupils glittered in the light. "What is holding you back from moving forward?"

"I'm not even sure what forward means anymore." An image of an empty road, split down the middle by a broad, yellow line, formed before my eyes. The line splintered in two and the road divided, then vanished, taking the man with it. Darkness enveloped the whole room.

His voice remained. "Your body needs to be in tune with the Earth."

"You mean like Liam's body is in tune with the Earth?"

"Was that critical tone intentional? Where did it come from, friend?"

His voice—soft and smooth as the newest of skin—moved forward, caressing my ears, moving down my neck, propelling me to speak, even though I didn't want to.

"From inside, where I'm broken," I whispered.

"At least you admit it."

"What else can I say?" Each moment brought a breath, and then another, not slow and steady like Doc would have wanted, but choppy, as if I'd run a long way through water or sand. One, two, three. In through the nose, out through the mouth. I had to be dreaming, didn't I? But this...this dream was indescribable, eccentric, maddening, all at the same time.

"Have you thought that the love has changed? It's still there, but different. Might you be better off separate?"

A light flicked on, and the man again sat on the mat at my feet.

"The love? What love? Are you talking about my relationship with Sadie?"

A burst of color pulsed beside him and broke into a thousand shards of light, all of them settling into the man's hands. He blew against the pieces, and they vanished. "I am."

"How do you know about my relationship?"

"Because I'm in tune with the Earth, and you're a part of that Earth...and so I'm in tune with you." He gestured for me to lean down as he stood, holding his palms up, cupped like a bowl.

Between his fingers, what looked like a single atom hovered. The cloud of electrons parted, and the nucleus cleared. The subatomic particles thumped and swirled, grew bigger and bigger, and then began to change. Shimmers of images scrolled before my eyes: memories I'd made with Sadie and the kids.

"What? How?"

"Life changes, Theo. But how do we react to those changes? Only worry about what you can control...do not spend energy on everything you can't. Are you looking?" He raised his arms upward, toward the ceiling. "Are you really seeing?" Now, he brought his arms down before placing them crossed over his heart. "What's inside you?"

"My body? Organs are."

"And inside those?"

"Blood, cells, nutrients..." The particulars were easy to list, but what did he want?

"Yes, but more specifically...it's your life force." A starburst of yellow light popped behind his head as he spoke the words, and a distant hum began to grow louder.

"I'm not sure what you're getting at."

"Well then, when you figure it out, let me know. You have everything you need, Theo. You have everything you need, Theo. You have everything you need, Theo." His voice reverberated around the room, but came back each time to my eardrums, piercing them.

"Stop!"

Click.

Andrew. Blood on his face, in his eyes, trickling down his neck in rivulets, leaking on to his shirt. A drop and then a bloom of scarlet against the white fabric.

"What are you doing here?" I reached my hand toward him. He needed my help, but what could I do?

"You're looking for a connection, Theo." Andrew's voice, thin and shaky,

"He already said that."

"*Who?*"

"*The man. Yoga Man.*"

Andrew turned his head. "*I don't see any man, Theo.*"

"*And stop saying my name! Why is everyone saying my name all the time? Who talks like that? I know who I am, and I know who you are and who Doc is. Stop it!*" *I closed my eyes and placed my hands over my ears, but his voice still rang loud and clear.*

"*I'm sorry if I was doing something wrong. I'm just trying to remind you of who you are.*"

"*Why?*" *Having my eyes shut meant I didn't need to focus on the red blood, the truth of the situation. That I'd hit him and hurt him because I couldn't handle myself. That's who I was. What did I need reminding for?*

"*Because if you remember who you are, Theo, you might come back to us.*"

The words targeted my gut, and I opened my eyes. Andrew no longer stood before me. Instead, Sadie. The kids. They looked lost, broken.

"*Come back to us, Theo. We'll figure everything else out.*"

"*Come back? Come back from where?*" *I shouted.*

Click.

Chapter 33: Sadie

I made it to Charlie's school with a couple minutes to spare, in a state that probably didn't look good. My eyes had to be puffy and red, and my hair—I was sure it had seen better days. Charlie stood in front of his poster board presentation as I approached. Did he wonder about Theo? This program was something Theo shouldn't be missing. In the distance, Charlie craned his neck, looking around at the large group of people hanging out at the gym. My stomach dropped.

Thanks to video calls, I'd witnessed one of Charlie's conversations with his dad right after he'd moved to the Inn.

"I have a lot going on in my brain, Charlie," Theo had said when Charlie asked him about why he moved out. "I guess I have so much going on in there," and he pointed to his skull with his index finger, "I haven't been paying much attention to what's going on out here."

Huh. At least he admitted it. But now, here I was, left to my devices, having to tell Charlie about the man he loved and called his dad. Along with a bellyache, my hands began to shake.

Once Charlie caught sight of me, he dashed a couple steps away from the booth, almost crashing into me.

"What's wrong?" His voice, small and low, shook with his words.

"Dad's in the hospital, and you need to visit him, now." My clipped words always meant business. Charlie knew that.

"Okay. I can show you this later," Charlie said. As he packed up his folder and binder clips, slipping his things into his backpack, the title of the poster grabbed my attention: *My Dad, My Hero* stood out at the top of the board. As I moved closer to the board, I thought back to our summer and our discussion of the project. Charlie hadn't been forthcoming with details about what he'd planned to say. Come to think of it, I'd never even seen a rough draft, something unusual for Charlie. What had he written? I leaned in closer, trying to catch the details on the board—

"Mrs. Rollins-Lancaster, how nice to see you again!" The principal of the school interrupted me. "Charlie has been a pleasure all semester long. You have a real gem here."

"Thank you for saying that. I'm sorry I have to pull him away from here, but we have a slight emergency."

Who was I kidding? Charlie needed to see his Dad, in case—

"Well, I hope you were able to view his final presentation. He worked very hard on it, and we're so pleased to hear that things are going so well for Mr. Lancaster."

I felt the color drain from my face as I swiveled my head in Charlie's direction and stared at him. So well? For Theo?

"What?" I leaned in toward the principal, but Charlie pulled on my sleeve.

"Well Charlie here said..." The principal stopped talking and looked back and forth between us. She flipped through the pages on her clipboard, looking for the list of presentations. "I thought..."

Charlie didn't let me finish. "Mom, let's go. We *need* to go."

"Yes, we do." Charlie could explain later. He *would* explain later. In the meantime, we needed to get to Theo.

•　　•　　•　　•　　•

After throwing Charlie's bags in the trunk, I slammed the lid and walked over to the driver's side door. Gripping the handle, I flung the door open, then pulled that same door shut with such force, the coins in the center console jumped. As Charlie buckled up in the back seat, I counted to ten, breathing in through my nose and out through my mouth, just like Theo. The crisp air tickled my nose and worked to refresh my bad attitude. What a shit day. But Charlie had never responded to anger, so calming myself before speaking took priority. I twisted around to face him and tried my best to paste the most loving and peaceful smile on my face.

"All right, Charlie. Are you going to tell me what happened back there? What did the principal mean that things are *going well* for your dad? I've never been one to condone lying."

A million ideas swam through my head about what Charlie might have said. He'd most likely written that Theo didn't have PTSD, or he'd beaten it with no issue. He might have gone with a full-fledged lie of something outrageous, like he'd been promoted to—what? I didn't even know. Instead of jumping to conclusions, I waited for Charlie to speak.

His voice, small and weak, cracked as he told me what he had done. That while his father *had* been his hero, back when he was younger and before Theo had developed his condition, he wasn't any longer, and so he'd lied. The more I listened, the more despondent I became. Neither Theo nor I had any idea this subterfuge had been happening. What sort of parents were we?

"He didn't ask for PTSD, honey," I said.

"I know, Mom, I know." A hiccup broke though Charlie's words. "But a hero is someone you want to grow up to be like. I don't want to be like Dad, ever." He cast his gaze downward, and a few tears fell toward the floor of the car.

Poking around in my pocket, I searched for a semi-clean tissue to give him and thrust it into Charlie's waiting hands. He nodded his thanks.

Charlie's point of view made sense, and for a moment, I paused, taking in the entirety of my son, the one who looked much like Theo did as a child. Charlie would have to remember the good parts of his life with Theo because there might not be more happy memories to make. He had to fully comprehend his complex father before we visited the ghost of the man in the hospital.

"Charlie, just because Dad doesn't look like a hero to you right now doesn't mean he isn't one in his own way. For these last few years, he's gotten out of bed and tried to take on what the day brings him, whether he was strong enough to do it or not. He's moved forward every day, hoping his therapy might help, even knowing it might not." Balancing whether the next words that popped into my mind deserved to be shared, I hesitated. "He's fought his demons with extreme honor and courage every day, Charlie. And for that, he *is* a hero."

More tears slid down Charlie's young face before he wiped them away with the back of his small hand. He blinked a couple times and sniffed, shaking his head up and down, as if he was contemplating what I said. Charlie had no words to give me in return and truthfully, I shouldn't blame him. Everything I'd mentioned was a lot to take in for an eleven-year-old.

I twisted back around toward the steering wheel and placed my head on the cool center of it. Despite my better judgment and the fact that I always tried to stay calm in front of the children, I wept then, harder than I had in a long time and so much I had trouble catching any air. Amid my breakdown, Charlie climbed over the car seat and wound his arms around me. We sat for a long time, entwined in a hug.

•　　•　　•　　•　　•

Once we'd cleaned our faces and found our equilibrium again, Charlie and I visited the hospital, but I let him spend time alone with Theo. My son needed to resolve his feelings for his father, and I wasn't sure having me in the room would have been helpful. Instead, I sat in the hallway outside Theo's room, processing everything: the letter, the book, Theo's initial detachment, his most recent actions, and how everything fit together. *Dante's levels of hell.* What did he mean? And when did he write the letter? How long had he been thinking of doing what he did? Biting my lip to keep me in the moment, I thought about his words. *He reveres you. The two of you could be happy together. Really happy.*

An idea formed in the forefront of my mind. Did Theo take himself out of the mix prematurely, so to speak? Did he think he was doing me a favor? Acid rose in my throat, and I charged for the nearest restroom, barely pushing open the door before everything I'd eaten that day came rushing out.

As I splashed cool water against my heated cheeks and rinsed out my mouth, I knew it was time to go get Charlie. The words I had spoken to him in the car held the truth but were all lies at the same time. Charlie didn't know anything about what Theo had done. Not being privy to the same information I was, about Theo's probable act of cowardice, Charlie might be right: Maybe Theo wasn't a hero. At least not of his own life.

December marched on, and Christmas came and went. Despite my full days, I had plenty of time to reflect on what had happened in the moments leading up to what Theo had done. I knew the why of it, thanks to his letter, but I still wasn't sure if I'd missed something. Running through the details with a fine-tooth comb, I mulled over actions I thought I remembered and snippets of conversation that had occurred at Walloon Lake. My mind floated back to daily interactions: the smile on Theo's face when he played with Lexie, the serene lines and mellow angle of his jaw as he sat with Charlie and Delia. Even though he had seemed somewhat detached when he'd been at the cottage, I'd checked in with Theo. "Good day or bad?" I'd asked. And on most of those days, he'd lift his thumb and nod his head.

But in his letter, he revealed he'd known about Andrew and me and the almost kiss, an event that came *before* my huge revelation to him. That explained his initial apathy when I told him. He must have been furious, but instead of lashing out at me, he'd turned inward and let the wound fester. Almost fatally. But what had finally set him off?

The days inched by. Theo had moments where his vital signs seemed stronger, and at one point, after the first of the year, we even took him off the ventilator. He survived, shaky and tenuous, but still on this side of alive. At other times, as people filtered in and out of his room, it seemed as if only a gossamer thread tethered him to this world. Coworkers and neighbors streamed in and sniffled their greetings, many of them saying silent goodbyes with a single nod of their heads. They didn't know about Theo's last act—or if they did, they didn't let on—and I didn't correct them otherwise. No one needed to find out the courageous serviceman had, in the end, not been so courageous after all. The only people outside of Kate, Jackie, Andrew, and Mom I informed were Rick and Laura Sullivan. If anyone would understand, it would be those two. But I'd taken the easy way out and written them a letter, and I still hadn't heard back from them.

We hadn't drawn up a living will, so I wasn't quite sure what to do about Theo's condition, should I need to decide. If the time came to make a choice, I hoped my family and friends would help me consider the options and make the right one.

I thought about taking a leave of absence from my job but instead requested to work remotely. Some of my workload would fall to Jackie, who had found her groove both at work and at home. She juggled being a parent and an employee with grace and poise and told me to take as much time as I needed, as much as the company would give me.

"Thank you, Jackie," I said, my voice muffled against her hair as I hugged her. "I have to do this. There is no way to stay at the hospital much of the day, be there for the kids, and get to work. I'm not doing a very good job of being a mother, but at least they have one parent mostly present this way."

"Don't worry," Jackie said. "The boss won't give that office to anyone else."

And I was grateful. For the boss, the employees, the clients, and the pace my job lent to my life, the rush of getting through a book or a project and moving onto the next one. I'd miss every aspect of the office, partly because being at the hospital was difficult and being at home was even harder. I'd look at the kids and try to approach the subject of their dad. Most of the time, I failed.

Lexie and Delia had it the hardest, in a way. Both were young, and neither understood why Theo wasn't home or how he was clinging to life in a stiff hospital bed. They'd never dealt with death before, and watching my girls hurt made me realize I hadn't prepared them fully for when Theo and I would part ways. Lexie had come on the scene after Theo's symptoms had escalated. She never knew the strong and healthy Theo, but it was clear that while his lack of health was the norm for her, she'd never contemplated he wouldn't someday be there. How could she have done so? Now, our decision to live together without living together seemed so wrong.

Charlie knew a bit more, but by the looks of it, he was living in a state of denial. The pile of books on his nightstand now included books on veterans, PTSD, and coming back from heaven. Tears welled in my eyes as I stumbled to find words to speak to Charlie, but even when I tried, he shut me down.

"I love you, but I need to read," he'd say. And I let him.

On the nights I made it home from the hospital before the kids went to bed, I'd climb onto each of their mattresses, and we'd send an extra positive vibe out into the universe for Theo. Would the universe be there for a man who tried to end his life? Did Charlie have a good book about *that* topic?

After the kids were tucked in and the house was quiet, I'd leave Brooke in charge and return to the hospital for an hour or two. Staying in our house ripped at my insides; Theo might never come back to that place. At least at the hospital, despite the beeping of the machine and the antiseptic smell, a small ray of hope existed.

Chapter 34: Sadie

One morning, after getting Delia and Charlie onto the school bus, waving with a smile I pulled out of nowhere, and finding my large travel mug so perfect for coffee, I kissed Lexie goodbye, thanked Brooke, and headed back to my perch next to Theo's bed. My head throbbed from lack of sleep: the prior night I had rolled myself into a fetal position and cried for so many reasons, only one of which was for Theo. For once, the last person on my mind was Andrew, so color me surprised to hear he'd been by to visit Theo. Not seeing Andrew near the rooms or the nurse's station, I took my seat and pulled out a tattered copy of a *People Magazine* Kate had given me. Too much idled in my mind to do anything but read trivial news.

Andrew and I hadn't spent as much time together as I would have liked, but we'd somehow come to an unspoken agreement: get through this time right now, and we'll address us later. Of course, we'd exchanged texts, but anything more took too much of my energy, and he understood. Did he still feel the same way I did about us? Despite the too-tight feeling that comes with being stretched so thin, my heart still raced when Andrew came to mind. Could he say the same?

As I sat with the magazine in my lap, flipping through the old Kardashian non-news of the day, wondering how much everything in my life might change before I had a nervous breakdown and when I should speak with an attorney, my phone pinged with a text from Andrew.

I'm here.

Okay. Come on up.

I'm in the hallway.

Then come on in.

The old, fleece sweatshirt and the flyaway nature of my hair didn't worry me. Andrew didn't care, and so many other things were more important. Like the fact that Theo was still in this hospital bed, unaware of the moving world around him, and that he had friends and family who would give anything to have him back on this side of consciousness. I included myself in that group of people. My love for Theo might not be the same as it used to be, but I certainly didn't want to live in a world void of all things Theo, especially Theo, the person.

The door squeaked, and a rush of stale hospital air came into the room with Andrew; he shut it behind him, saying nothing as he looked my way. He pulled a chair over and lined it up with mine. His voice did not disturb the silence until I turned toward him, as if my movement acknowledged his existence and gave him permission to speak.

"Hey. Anything I can do? Anything at all?"

Andrew had already done so much. Brooke had told me a few weeks prior that Andrew had been stopping by the house when I was at the hospital, helping with the kids by taking them to the indoor playground or seeing that the homework was getting done before I got home. He'd been careful to explain his presence, reminding the kids he knew both their mom and dad and wanted to be helpful, to do something nice for the family, because we needed a little help.

"It's obvious the kids enjoy his company and they love his kids. They've taken in the two new playmates almost as if...as if they're siblings," Brooke had said.

I had recoiled at her words. She didn't outwardly admit to acknowledging my feelings for Andrew, but her insightful comment said a lot about a potential future. Approaching this subject with Andrew before now might have been the smart thing to do, but dammit, I was tired. Too tired to mess with a good thing.

But the time had come to pull myself out of the mud pit of my thoughts.

"Sadie?" Andrew tried again.

"Yeah, sorry. I was off in space." I drew my right leg up toward my chest and hooked my arms around it, securing my body to the chair. Every inch of me craved restraint, something to anchor me to the place, as I was so close to trying to escape my life again.

Andrew leaned in and placed a hand to my face, which caused me to turn my head toward him. His warm fingers gave energy to my cool cheeks, but I wasn't sure how to interpret the gesture.

"What's wrong?" A look of concern clouded his eyes.

So many thoughts lined up, one behind the other. My conversation with Mom or thoughts about Theo. And the possible future—it weighed heavily on my mind.

"How did you meet Theo? And did you know he was connected to me?" Life had moved forward, and I hadn't thought to ask for more details before.

Andrew drew back in his seat. "We met at the gym and hit it off. I'd see him a couple times a week, text every so often. We've even met at the Kennedy Grill a time or two. But I swear I had no idea he was part of your life."

"And when he knocked on your mom's door and punched you, why didn't you call me? I texted you."

Andrew inhaled and looked away. "I was embarrassed. We were friends, almost. But had I realized he was hung up on you, well, I'd have walked away."

"And now? What about now? What are your motives—"

Andrew narrowed his eyes and lowered his voice. "My motives? What are you talking about?"

The din of the hospital rang in the background, grinding into my head. "Sorry, sorry. That came out a bit...not how I intended. But you've been coming over to my house, taking care of my kids..."

Frustration flared in Andrew's eyes. "I'm just trying to help. I run my own business, and I have the time to help. Plus, I like kids. I like Theo. I like *you*."

"Ditto. Is that a problem?"

"Is it?"

The next words to come out of my mouth would make all the difference. My breath hitched as I stumbled over them. "Remember when you said that bit about us being right, but it wasn't the right time? Theo is barely holding onto life in there, and I...he's not what he used to be to me but...that's what I need to concentrate on, okay?"

Andrew's thumb traced the line of my jaw. "Okay. I can't imagine how difficult this is for you, and that's the truth. I want to help and dealing with the kids is the one thing I *can* do to help you. You should be here with Theo."

"Do you mean it?"

"I do," he said, his face stoic and serene, in sharp contrast to my inner turmoil and the bustling of the hospital staff out in the hallways.

Andrew's lack of emotion cut into my heart and soul, but I believed what he said. After all these months, it wasn't just attraction that connected us. He was my friend, a good friend. And he'd be more, if I said the word. I owed him something, didn't I? A word or two, an explanation?

"I hadn't planned this, Andrew. My world turned upside down the day we met at the store. Do you realize that?" My hands shook as the moment in June, only half a year earlier, flickered in my mind. "A simple conversation in a grocery store line busted up the life I thought I had, the life I thought I was content with." I placed my hand on Andrew's arm and lowered my voice level. "Let's be clear here. I'm not blaming you at all. But I *am* saying all that has happened since then, our frequent encounters, our texts, our learning about one another, our admissions, realizing my situation isn't quite working for me, the fact that I have wanted you through all that...everything has led me to the conclusion I need to be accountable for my life, but also that I...I am one fucked-up woman."

Andrew opened his mouth to say something, but I held up my hand to stop him. I had to be selfish, to let the words flow, to find a cathartic release in the moment lingering with the near silence. He sat there, almost still, dropping his hand to my back and then my waist, pulling me toward his warmth, toward him. Barely touching me and yet touching me all the same. Unspoken words appeared in his eyes, and while I wasn't sure if he meant to let me see them, I did. *I can take care of you*, the words said. *If you let me.*

●　　●　　●　　●　　●

Andrew must have contacted Jackie because hours later, long after he had left me to my thoughts, she tiptoed into Theo's hospital room, pulled me into her arms, and handed me a letter.

"I'm not here because of this letter," Jackie said. "But Brooke told me to give it to you. Looks like it's from Rick and Laura."

Too few positive messages had come to me lately written on stationery like this, and I feared what lurked inside. Would they judge Theo for his actions? Even though I had judged him, I wasn't sure I'd survive reading a letter full of condemnation.

"I know what happened, and Rick and Laura have always served as rays of hope. Open the letter. It might make you feel better."

Turning my back to Jackie, I pushed my finger underneath the envelope's flap before extracting a square of blue paper. The writing—the product of a steady hand—was Laura's, but Rick had signed the letter from them both. My gaze found Jackie's. "These two are such beautiful examples for all of us, working in concert together, all the time. If only..." My sentence hovered, unfinished. Instead, I lowered my body into a waiting chair and attempted to read the words swimming before my eyes.

Dear Theo and Sadie,

Thank you for contacting us and for being so honest about the situation. If we could, we'd head down for a visit. But with the weather forecast being what it is, it isn't possible at this moment. Theo and you and the children are in every thought we have. We hope, so much, that Theo pulls through this trying time.

Sadie, I also want to say that what Theo did has indeed crossed my mind before. When I was given the diagnosis, my first thought was I had been handed a life sentence, and I wouldn't see my children grow up and have grandchildren. I'd have to leave Laura behind before I was ready because I wouldn't be able to live with PTSD. But something in me made me want to stay and fight, and I'm not sure I can even articulate what that something is. If I could bottle it, I'd send it down to you and Theo in a heartbeat.

If there is anything we can do to help you right now, please let us know. We are only a phone call away.

With much love and hope,

Rick and Laura

I read the letter twice and then folded the piece of paper over and stuffed it back into its envelope, hoping Theo would one day be able to read it himself. Drained of energy, I crumbled against Jackie and clung to her as if my life depended upon it.

"I'll talk when I'm ready," I said into my friend's shoulder.

"Okay, Sadie. But I'm dragging you to the cafeteria. A change of scenery, even a small one, will be good for you."

The slap of our shoes against the squeaky tile floor of the hospital distracted me from noticing much about our entrance into the cafeteria. To my surprise and delight, Kate and Pickles Martin sat at one of the old Formica-covered tables. My mood lifted the moment Pickles and I made eye contact, and I hugged the older lady with strong arms, not letting go for what had to be at least a minute. When I pulled back, Pickles smiled, took my hand, and escorted me to one of the coffee kiosks.

I filled my paper cup to the halfway mark with the hospital-grade decaffeinated brew and then poured in strong, regular coffee. Pickles fiddled with her tea bag and returned to the table as I splashed the cream into the cup, covered it with a plastic lid, and extracted a tall coffee stirrer from the container. The line behind me was mounting, so without looking at my beverage, I went back to the table the ladies had secured.

"Thank you for bringing me here," I said as I pulled out a chair and placed a hand on Kate's back. "This'll taste so good today. It's been too cold around here, and the warmth is lovely." Peeling back the lid of the coffee, I plunged the stirrer into the cup. To my horror, large chunks of curdled cream floated on top of the coffee, like miniature icebergs. I grimaced, and pushed the cup toward my friends, all of whom leaned back with pained looks on their faces.

"Ewww, you better go get another one," Pickles said.

With a huff in my heavy steps, I emptied the cup in the trash and progressed through the same motions again, filling the paper cup with coffee and pouring in the cream. For the second time, the cream curdled, a sickly ivory against the sea of brown. Annoyed with a simple act that went so wrong, I sat at the table and sighed.

"You can ask them to replace the cream," Jackie said as she glanced into the cup I should have, but hadn't yet, thrown away. "Actually, you *should* ask them to replace the cream. That," she waved her fingers in the direction of the offending cup, "is just awful."

I shook my head and chuckled. "I know. I will." I rotated the cup sitting before me and scrutinized how the chunks swirled and bobbed in the brown liquid. The cream had one job—make bitter coffee smoother and richer—but it was tainted. Like me. The cream *was* me: I, too, had a job to do, but I wasn't certain how to take care of my family at this point. My mind turned somersaults while my dear friends sat and waited for me.

"You okay, honey? What can I do?" Pickles leaned in, a frown on her face, a light touch from her fingers to mine.

"I'm okay...doing the best I can. But..."

"But what?"

"But..." Somehow, the normal clamor of the hospital seemed to fade away as I unpacked everything bothering me. Confused but stoic much of the time since the previous June, when I'd envisioned something different and wasn't sure what I wanted, I'd done a decent job hiding behind almost anything. But there, in the hospital cafeteria, despite the muddled appearance of my coffee, or because of it, everything came to a head and somehow, a clarity descended on me.

I'd always been the sort of person who, once I'd articulated something, moved forward. And at this point, I'd spoken to all the people involved in my melodrama and those who stood on the periphery. Venting, purging, clearing my thoughts—all done. Though there were words left unsaid between Theo and me, I had to decipher the right path for me and follow it because I might have three kids to love and raise, all by myself.

My view of Jackie, Pickles, and Kate, women I was so lucky to have found, showed three beautiful and strong souls I could choose to emulate. I would take the best of everything and everyone in my life, mix in a dash of hope, and make progress toward a life worth living.

Somehow, my rumination over curdled cream had shown me the way, and I wasn't torn any longer. Yes, I loved Andrew. Even though I hadn't spent much time with the man, something within his being spoke to me so loudly and clearly, I'd love a piece of him forever, if possible. On the other hand, though, I also knew I'd always love Theo, even if our life had taken a detour and turned into something so unexpected. Two different kinds of love, but I was deserving of them both.

I didn't tell my friends of my epiphany, simply because of a need to protect my heart. It had been repeatedly attacked and wounded and would take a long time to heal. Instead, after unloading myself and a cursory "Thank you and I'll see you soon," I returned to the hospital room, clear-headed and content.

After settling into the chair next to Theo's bed, I pulled his letter out of my pocket. The one Theo had written, explaining his reasons for doing what he'd done. Finding sympathy for the place Theo was when he wrote the letter was easy, and I could forgive him. But would he forgive me before he passed through to the great beyond? Dishonesty and I had played together too much in the past, and had I any respect for him or for myself, I would have approached Theo the moment I felt the draw for Andrew. Hell, I should have said something when I noticed *we* had become *he* and *I*. What if I had pushed him to sign the papers earlier? But just like I hadn't wanted my life to be a series of *if-then* statements, dwelling on the *what-ifs* of life would accomplish nothing.

I stroked Theo's lifeless arm and brushed my fingers against his wan cheeks. Tears dropped against my face, and I sat there, my mind tangled in everything that had transpired in the last year. Back when I'd watched Clara for Jackie and Pete, I had yearned to be free of so many responsibilities of my life, including Theo. Now, I was reminded of Jonathan Stroud, one of Charlie's favorite authors, who had once written, "Freedom is an illusion. It always comes at a price." If only we understood the price before we had to pay it.

Leaning in close to Theo's ear, I told him how much I missed him, and I hoped he had found his freedom and his peace too. "I at least need to tell you I don't want you to go, Theo. I want you here, with us, in some capacity."

Reaching for his hand, I turned his fingers over against mine. The translucence of his skin worried me, as did the dryness of his palm. I traced the lines there, musing about his long lifeline and wondering how many years he'd have lived, had he not attempted to leave this earth. My tears fell onto Theo's bedsheets when I thought about how much history we had together.

My lips brushed against his cheek. "And I was wrong. Yes, we were both to blame for letting our relationship drift, and our future might not be together the way we had once imagined, but we need you. Come back...please."

Of course, Theo didn't respond, and I sat there for a few moments, savoring the silence, trying to find clarity in what wasn't being offered. And right then, realization descended: If he didn't wake up, I'd always keep him tucked away in my heart in a special place only he'd inhabit. If he did wake up, I'd keep him tucked away in my life in a suitable way for everyone.

•   •   •   •   •

The next morning, stationed in my usual spot next to Theo's bed, the doctor on duty arrived to speak to me.

"It might be time to talk about what to do with Theo." The doctor pulled up the chair next to me. "He's languishing. How long are you going to let him do that?"

His words twanged in my ears, but they formed a valid point too. Should I let him languish? What would Theo have chosen? But I wanted no hand in Theo's demise. Instead, I wanted him to die a noble death, not the one he had decided, shrouded in whispers and secrecy.

Words escaped me, and I simply shook my head as heat bloomed in my cheeks and acid surged in my belly. The doctor rose, patted me on the shoulder, and walked away without a sound. I sat for a long time, willing myself to calm, listening to the sounds of the hospital staff as they chatted about the breakfast offerings and flavored coffees, the squeal of the medical cart wheels, and the swish and whisper of the automatic doors. Sniffing, I pulled my sweater around myself, wishing for guidance from somewhere. When I couldn't stand any longer to be there, I texted my mom.

Gotta run home. Can you come be with Theo? I don't want him to be alone.

Sure thing. Give me twenty minutes.

The doctor stood near the nurses' station. "I'm going to head home. Mom's going to come stay with Theo. I'd like to take care of a few things and speak with the kids. They should all go in and see him before..." I didn't meet his eyes as I spoke to him. I *couldn't*. He'd see the truth behind mine if I did. "You're right. It is time, as you say, but...please give me a few days."

On autopilot, I drove home, thoughts swirling in my head, everything I might say to Theo if he woke up. Only after I'd reached my driveway did I give in to the sobs threatening to overtake my body the entire way home. With white knuckles, I gripped the steering wheel and then placed my forehead against the cool, hard leather. It didn't matter what I said in my head; it was likely Theo would never hear those words. After a few moments, I reached for a tissue, wiped away my tears, and gathered my purse and mug. Charlie and Delia weren't home from school yet, and Lexie was out with Brooke for the afternoon. If all went well, I'd have a few hours to myself before I shattered the worlds of my children.

As if not to disturb the peace even further, I tiptoed into the house, placed my things in the kitchen, and meandered to the bedroom. The open arms of the rocking chair in the corner of the room gathered me close and helped me fall asleep. Andrew found me there later, and like the gallant man I knew him to be, did nothing but pick me up, hold me tight, and lull me back to sleep.

Chapter 35: Theo

Darkness, complete and suffocating, for hours, too many to count. Time could be anything right now. Or nothing. Time. What is time? How much time has passed? And what is darkness, but the absence of light? And then, a single pinprick of white, until the edges of blackness began to recede, and light filtered in, little bursts of color against a backdrop of ink. Flashes like those in Afghanistan, but this...this place...wasn't it, I couldn't be back there, right? The noises didn't match. Instead of a rush of thunder and cacophony of screams, a gentle lull, a steady clack, a swish, and a squeal lingered nearby. Try as I might to open my eyes, they stayed shut. Willing my mind to make connections, everything diffused away.

Later: Time standing still, speeding up, slowing down; long time, no time, did time exist? What was this place, and when would I go back home? Could I go back home? More flashes, red, green, purple, black, twisting in front of me, hammering me from all sides. That damn ink again, pushing at me, my chest, my heart almost exploding inside my body. A shroud overtook me, and I breathed again.

Voices—high-pitched, low-pitched, young, old. Snatches of whispers. If I craned my neck, could I hear them better? Did they know I was awake? What did I look like to them? A jab to the arm, fucking painful, and a milky white shroud flooded my senses. Peace. Quiet.

I sat up, taking in the gray clouds lingering in the air. Mountains hovered in the background; small wisps of smoke curled up, dispersing as they rose. In the distance, people approached. Sadie, Charlie, Delia, and Lexie. "I'm here!" My voice reverberated off the scattered boulders. My family marched forward, faces unseeing, and passed right through me, despite my waving arms. When I turned around, they'd long gone into the mist, dissolving into a million tiny particles.

Then: The fuzzy edges pulled back and he was there. Charlie. In a room with white walls, Christmas cards attached. A framed picture of us—Sadie, the kids, me—stood on the end table. And there I was too, in a bed, covered with white sheets and a blue blanket. Eyes closed, purple circles like twin moons underneath them.

"How's he doing?" Charlie's voice, tinny and quiet, lured me in, and my view shifted, as if a lens had been changed. Now Sadie, standing next to Charlie. Me—my soul?—in front of them both. Did they see me?

"There haven't been any changes, Charlie," Sadie said as she rubbed the arm of the man—me—who lay in bed.

"He's not getting worse, is he?"

"No."

"But he's not getting any better, either, right?"

I tried to laugh, but no sound came out of my mouth. Charlie had always been so astute.

"You're old enough for the truth," Sadie said.

"No, he's not!" I yelled. Or tried to.

In slow motion, Charlie moved toward me, and I threw my hands in the air, covering my face, ready for the impact. But in a single breath, he walked through me—completely unencumbered—to the cards on the wall.

"Why can't you feel me, Charlie? I shouted. I'm right here!"

Charlie turned back to Sadie, tears on his lower eyelids. "I thought we'd have a Christmas miracle, but it's past Christmas. And New Year's has already happened too. I've hoped and prayed for Dad to wake up, but I doubt it'll happen."

Sadie crumbled into the chair next to my bed, gasping as she wept, extending a hand to Charlie, who tugged her fingers in his grip.

"When you picked me up from school and said we'd be going to the hospital today, you meant it as a time for me to say goodbye, didn't you?"

Goodbye? What did he mean?

The scene flickered for a moment, and I tumbled next to Sadie, crouching on the floor, trying to grasp her hand. Like a holograph, points of color shimmered as my essence moved through her body.

"Mom, I'm not sure how to say goodbye to him or what I even want to say, but I'll try. Can I climb up on the bed with him for a few minutes?"

"Yes!" I yelled. "Yes!" But Charlie didn't hear me, and darkness fell again.

Finally: A familiar weight, the scent of a boy. Back in my body, I felt it all. A warm hand against my cheek and along my chin. Charlie on the bed, tears on his face, redness to his nose and eyes. Is this how he felt, so full of abject sadness? What was he thinking now? The torment I felt inside—did it compare to what he felt? He rested his head on my chest. Did he feel it rising and falling?

He moved his mouth, and I leaned in to hear the words. Nothing. But Sadie left the room then, a haunted look in her eyes.

A heat burned within me, tremors erupted along my spine, goose bumps on my arms and legs. Straining to hear, more words, more nothing. I watched as Charlie looked around the room. What did he see? My essence moved to linger right behind his back, taking in the view he had: white walls, beige tile, and a corkboard full of medical information. A bathroom with a wide door, but one I probably didn't use. A large, plate glass window that looked out on a cloudless winter sky. I did a double take. The curtains were closed, and yet, I saw behind them, a gray of both building and sky, a reflection of winter sun that seemed bright, almost too bright. But what did it matter if the light came in? My eyes weren't open.

As if Charlie knew my thoughts, he got up from the bed, opened the curtains, and then curled up again next to the man in the bed. As he settled in, the sleeve of my gown lifted. Charlie grabbed my forearm and traced his fingers over it. Tears fell onto my skin, the bed, Charlie, the floor. A trickle, then a stream, then a tidal wave coursed up the walls, reaching the top of my mattress, my head, covering my form. My body did nothing, but I pushed against the force, and I was snapped back into my skin. Cracks spread from my toes to my knees to my middle to my neck to my face. Deafening silence and darkness once again.

Then, cutting through the muted world, a voice so sweet and clear once again, Charlie's.

"Dad." He whispered into my ear. "It's me, Charlie. In case you didn't recognize my voice. You can't see me right now. Or maybe you can. I want to tell you I love you."

More tears began to drop onto the sheets, and Charlie pushed his head against my chest, much like he did when he was little. I tried to remember the days when I was at home with him, playing ball or listening to his Minecraft stories. I'd always told Charlie to concentrate on something else when he was upset. Would he do that now? If I willed him to envision his friends or Big Nate or Walloon Lake or summer camp, would those thoughts help him get through this? Would it help me? A flicker of Charlie's face. His body. Me as a young kid.

"Okay, Dad, I'm ready." Charlie lifted his head again and looked at me. Everyone said he and I were two peas in a pod. Would he look like me when he got older too? I touched his cheek with my ghostly fingers and moved them toward his chin, just as Charlie did the same to me.

"I like feeling the prick of your stubble against my fingertips, Dad. It means you're still alive." Charlie swallowed and sniffed and then continued. "This is going to sound weird, but Mom said you might be hanging on for something. She didn't tell me, but I heard her say it to the nurse. I'm not sure, but are you waiting for me to say it's okay to go? Because it is okay."

Go? Go Where? I reached for him again, my fingers still moving through his flickering image. A thud sounded in my ears, covering the words that came next. I pulled back and watched again as Charlie lay his head against the chest of the man—me—in the hospital bed. Tears ran from his eyes, landed on my blanket.

A snippet: "...you're tired..."

Another: "I miss you…"

He began to fade then, first his fingers, then his arm, his shoulder, trunk, and down his legs, crumbling to dust and floating away, into a haze hanging before me. Another tightness gripped my chest, making me gasp for air that didn't exist.

And then, from out of the haze, his voice one more time: "No matter what, Dad, you'll always be my hero."

Chapter 36: Sadie

The shrill beep of my cell phone reverberated against the tile of the kitchen counter and interrupted my morning bowl of toasted oats.

"Sadie?" Doc's familiar voice said. "We need you at the hospital."

My heart thudded in my chest. "What's wrong?" I was finishing breakfast, with plans to head over in a few hours to say my final goodbye.

"Nothing. Nothing at all. Theo woke up."

I stumbled from my seat, ran up the stairs to Charlie's room, and gently laid a hand on his arm. He'd only been in a light sleep, for with a few taps of my fingernails against his skin, he blinked his eyes several times.

"I need you to hold down the fort until Brooke arrives." Confusion crossed Charlie's face, and I explained about the phone call. "I don't have any details." Whispering against his forehead in a rush of excitement, I then placed a kiss there. "But I promise to call as soon as possible."

•   •   •   •   •

At the moment I left the hospital elevator and entered the hallway leading to Theo's room, an overwhelming surge of love for Theo coursed through me. My heart pounded in my chest as I approached his door, both fear and longing warring with the other. I didn't know what I'd say or what Theo would say or how the next few months would go or how arduous of a journey it would be, but once I grabbed his hand, I had no intention of letting go of it until he was ready.

The sharp squeak of my shoes against the floor fought for attention with the hospital's daily grind and alerted Theo to my presence. A slow smile stretched across his tired face, and he waved his fingers, urging me to go forward. Slipping onto the seat of my chair, I threaded my hand with his and squeezed. His hand had felt so cold for so long, the sudden warmth against my palm surprised me. For a moment, I couldn't speak, and I sat there, watching Theo as he watched me. Once I'd composed myself a little, I dared to speak.

"How're you doing?"

"I've been better. But I can't complain. Though a sip of water would be good."

A cup sat on the table next to his bed, and I held the straw to his lips. "Here. It's good to see you awake."

He swallowed. "Is it?"

I understood what he was asking. Leaning in, I brushed my lips against his forehead. "It is. We're going to figure this out, and yes, I'm glad you're back."

While the nurses and doctors took over for the next few hours and swept me to the side, I texted Andrew, my mom, Kate, and Jackie and told them the news. That day, as I sat in the hospital room and Theo's face flushed with color we hadn't seen in a long time, peace, contentment, even hope, stirred within me. The road would be long, and we'd have bumps, all of us. But we'd figure out our way around them, together.

A fortnight passed before he was able to leave the hospital, and during that time, our friends and family worked as a team, despite the cold weather, to help Theo, to help us. Jackie and Pete, Kate, my mom, coworkers of Theo's, even Andrew, drew up and executed plans so that from the moment Theo stepped foot out of the hospital, life would run more smoothly.

A two-bedroom house had been rented three streets over from ours. The group had arranged for furniture and appliances, and the kitchen had been fully stocked with everything Theo might need. They'd also included a computer system, for when Theo returned to his full-time work as a web developer, as well as toys, books, and beds for the kids. Upon hearing the details, Theo smiled. "I don't exactly know what to say," he muttered.

I didn't have a reply.

But with all the buzz about Theo and his recovery, I may have pushed Andrew to the side, and I wasn't exactly sure where we stood. Our texts still connected us and meant something significant, at least on my end, and several of our exchanges contained more heat than I'd remembered. But I hadn't spoken to him specifically about our future, about us, about our expectations. I had to speak to him in person—not between furniture shopping or painting shifts—and owed him that much, at the minimum. After a quick phone call, he said he'd meet me in the hospital courtyard after work the evening before Theo was due to be released. The somewhat neutral setting he chose worried me.

When Andrew approached, a tight anxiety seized my soul, and I stood from the wrought iron bench. We'd known each other long enough to recognize certain tells, and his smile, normally wide and round, twitched at the corners, a true sign indicating unease. And when he wrapped his arms around me and pressed his lips to my forehead in a comforting gesture I knew so well, my unease skyrocketed.

He stepped back and gestured for me to sit once again. "Sadie, I'm happy for you, for Theo...really."

"Really?"

He nodded his head and paused before he spoke. "It seems so odd to be having this conversation. Here and now. I've had a lot of time to think over these last few weeks. Even with this...this thing between us...you still loved Theo."

"You thought that?"

"Yes." His breath came out in a puff of icy air. "I didn't want to admit it."

"Oh." The zipper of my parka held my interest, as looking at Andrew was difficult.

"And if I were in the same situation, with a person who needed me and years of love behind us, I'd fight for my marriage too." Andrew extended his hand to my shoulder and squeezed it. The gesture could have imparted concern for a friend and nothing more.

I cocked my head and looked at him, at his eyes, at his soul. I wanted *him*, plain and simple. Yes, I still loved Theo, and yes, I'd fight for him to some degree—his health and happiness were important to me—but I was ready. I'd made my decision. I wanted a future with Andrew. Did he not understand?

"We should have had this conversation before now," I said.

"Yes." Andrew shrugged. "But I was being selfish. I've enjoyed every moment of being with you. You made me feel more alive than I have in a long time." He quirked his lips, and his hand fell to his lap.

"I...I can say the same." A heat spread through my chest, and I looked around the courtyard. In the spring, the space would be overrun with every type of flower imaginable, and the birds would flit in the flowing fountain. But now, the harshness of winter's reign belied the life that had just come back to me.

"Then maybe that day at Bloom Market was supposed to happen, and we can both walk away from each other as better people." Andrew's flushed face and tentative smile contrasted with the muted gray tones of the evening.

"That's a rosy way of looking at the world." A tear sprang to the corner of my eyelid, but I willed it away. It was clear he was confused, unable to understand exactly how I felt.

"Yep, but it's the only way I can deal right now." He nudged my shoulder with his but didn't linger. "This hurts...this nebulous area we're in. If you didn't know it before, I wanted you to hear it now: I love you."

Andrew's words floored me, and the blooming hope in the pit of my stomach unfurled. His moment of truthfulness deserved one in return. "I...I'm not—"

Andrew held up his hand. "I needed to get that out there. I don't expect to hear it in return. But I didn't want to let you go without telling you. Now—" Andrew lifted himself from the bench, grabbed my hand, and pulled me up with him. "Go back to Theo, tell him I said hello and welcome back. We'll figure out how we all fit together another time."

"Shit, Andrew." Tears streamed down my face. "You're more like your mother than I ever realized."

"And that's a good thing?"

"Yes, but what if...we walked away *together*, as better people?"

Under the dim light, Andrew's chocolate brown eyes twinkled, much like they had the first day I met him. "Is that possible?"

Visions swam in my head: a house full of children, his and mine; holidays with Pickles, Theo, Jackie, Pete, Clara, and Kate; vacations at Walloon Lake, high school graduations, college diplomas; Theo and Andrew, passing a new grandbaby from one to the other. Maybe I was being naïve, but somewhere deep within, I knew I was being realistic. All of that could happen if we wanted it to.

"I do," I leaned into his side and placed my head on his shoulder.

"I like the sound of that," he said, right before his lips met mine.

Chapter 37: Theo

Lying around in a hospital bed made me cranky. Hence, no one called me a model patient. But after I woke up, and after the doctors and nurses had poked and prodded me and determined a couple weeks in the hospital would fix me up—physically anyway—my mood lifted. At least a little. Doc had been careful to come in each day, gauge my temperament, sit for several minutes to half an hour, and then walk away. I knew what was next: a thorough, in-depth session to get to the bottom of my behavior.

But my behavior was reckless, impulsive. I hadn't thought about not being here before I decided to do it, had I? Mulling over the past hurt my head too much, but little bits and pieces did come to me as days crept by. Snippets of times I'd been snarky or flippant in my response to Doc's questions. And of course, Doc confirmed them with her damn notebook, which she arrived with five days after I woke up.

"April sixth, May twentieth, October fifth."

"What are those?" I rubbed my forehead as the window drew my attention. Even the dull gray sky of Ohio winter held more appeal than the beige cinder block walls and white curtains of this dungeon.

"Each of those is a date when you said something about being worthless, invaluable, and so forth."

"Of course they are. Do you have the times on there too?"

"Glad to have the snark back, Theo. But yes, I do. And I have others, further back. Sometimes, I'm good at my job."

Her words made me physically sit back against my bed. "What does that mean? Sometimes you're *not*?" I cocked my head and narrowed my eyes, trying to take on the doctor role in this twosome.

"We're not going there today, Theo. I'm here to check in on you and only you. And we need to come up with a game plan." Doc tapped her clipboard twice.

"For what?"

"For what you need to do." She tapped the clipboard again. If she didn't stop soon, the tapping would drive me over the edge. Didn't she know that?

"What I need to do is get out of here and go home."

"Yes, but it's not that simple," she said.

Doc had always been savvy and good at her job, regardless of how she felt now. Which meant she was probably right: I had every intention of heading back home and doing what I had been doing, didn't I? And according to Doc, that wasn't the right approach.

"But why not? Why can't I just go back to the way it was?"

She sighed and looked out the window, a thoughtful grin on her face. Then, she turned to me. "Do you believe it's a possibility? To just get out and go home?"

"Well...why not?"

"*You* need to answer that."

Argh. Classic Doc. She hadn't changed in the time since I'd seen her, which felt like eons. She patiently waited, pen in hand, poised over the clipboard, as if ready to strike again, and a thought hit me. "Do you have a *clicky* pen?"

"A *clicky* pen?"

"Yeah. The kind you push down on and the tip comes out."

"Ah, retractable. No. The sound of the click can annoy patients. I try not to have those. Why?"

"No reason." I went back to looking at her, and she waited for me. She might wait for me all day. As much as I enjoyed a bit of company, I'd rather see the kids. Or Sadie. Crap, anything at this point would be better than being subjected to the detailed and honed eye of Doc.

"You're waiting for me to answer the question, aren't you?"

"You know me well." She brought the tip of the pen up to her chin.

I sighed. "Well, can I just admit I don't have an answer? I'm smart enough to realize if you're asking me the question, life should not go on as it did before.

But I'm not sure what to expect or what changes I need to make. My head hurts. Can I say that?"

"Yes, you can. But can I trust you to listen? To think about what I'm saying and to come up with a list of action items, together?"

"Pfft. Action items. That sounds funny. But yes."

And over the course of the next hour, we came up with the list of things I would need to do: 1. Work on a resolution with Sadie; 2. Apologize to Andrew; 3. Find a place to call home; 4. Check on my place of employment; 5. Reassure the kids I wasn't going anywhere (or at least as far as I could help it). I didn't say it out loud, but I felt the need to apologize to Doc too. She'd trusted me, and my actions made her question her talents. While I was often an ass, it wasn't something I aspired to daily.

Doc left me with my list and a homework assignment: to listen to calming music and contemplate the items we discussed. Had I placed them in order of priority? What would I need to do to get started on them? And how long would they take? Would I—

A knock sounded at the door, and Andrew poked his head into the room. "Have time to see me?"

A quick uptick in my blood pressure at the sight of him. Did I have time? How rude would it be to say no? I clenched my jaw. But then: "Are you sure you want to?"

"Yes. Even after all this, you're my friend." He moved toward the bed, pulled up the chair, and sat next to me. "Listen. I had no idea you and Sadie...you had a history. None at all. I've wracked my brain, tried to recall our conversations. Nothing. I came up with nothing. And she never said—"

"She never talked about me?"

"Not never. She just didn't use your name. And I met her as Sadie Rollins. How was I to know?"

Could I fault Andrew for his feelings? The thought of him and Sadie still hurt like hell inside, like a splinter that wouldn't go away. *Breathe in, breathe out.* One, two, three.

Andrew tapped the arm of the bed. "I won't be here long, but I wanted to at least say hello. Glad you're back."

Was he really? I wasn't ready to speak with him for much longer, and while I could feign fatigue, with him there, marking one item off my list sounded like a good idea. "I'm glad you came by. I'm not going to lie. I feel like hell when I think of Sadie and you. But I have to apologize for what I did. I shouldn't have—"

"Don't go any farther—"

I held my hand up. "I have to, per Doc's orders. Regardless of my fury, I shouldn't have taken it out on you." My voice cracked on the last word.

Andrew nodded. "Well, I don't know what I would have done under the same circumstances. But I'm okay and you are too. So, apology accepted."

"Well, thanks, but—"

"Mr. Lancaster?" My least favorite nurse entered the room. "It's time for me to check your vitals, and to get you to the restroom. Would you—" She looked at Andrew, and he stood.

"Say no more. I'll see you around, Theo." He tipped his chin up. "I hope you'll be back at work soon."

"You and me both, buddy."

Later that same afternoon, Charlie and Lexie stopped by. Delia had a cold and had been banned from my room, but I spoke to her via video call after the kids arrived. I was strong enough to hold Lexie on the bed next to me, arm wrapped around her little waist. She snuggled her head into my armpit and fell asleep while I chatted with Delia.

"Lexie hasn't been sleeping well lately," Charlie said when I'd ended the call. "But we haven't had much of a routine these days."

"You sound like your mother. Which isn't a bad thing. Just mature, I guess. When did you get so old?"

"I haven't changed, Dad. Have you?"

What did Charlie mean? In his mind, did I need to change? Had he spoken with Doc or Sadie? The kid missed nothing; I knew that, but...this...I shook my head and smiled at him, laying a hand against Lexie's head. "I guess we'll find out if I've changed, won't we?"

Charlie wrinkled up his nose and seemed poised to ask a question when the pesky nurse came back in.

"Seriously? Already? I feel like my room has a revolving door with you all."

"I get that a lot," she said and then gently picked up Lexie, placed her into Charlie's arms, and shooed the two of them to the side. "This won't take too long, but someone looks like she could use a better nap than what she might get in this hospital."

"Mom's right outside," I said to Charlie. "Let her take you two home. I'm not going anywhere."

"You promise?" Unlike the overly mature kid he was only moments ago, Charlie's voice sounded young, unsure, and shaky.

"I promise."

While one promise would not reassure the kids for long, it was a start.

•   •   •   •   •

After dinner had come and gone—emphasis on the *gone*, because rubbery roast turkey with lukewarm gravy, canned peaches, and red gelatin was a dinner I could seriously do without—Sadie stopped by. Brooke was at home with the kids, allowing us time to sit and chat. The last time we'd spoken had been at the cottage, that night she revealed all the details of her turmoil, Andrew, the life she was leading. And while I wasn't over her—that would take a while—what she'd done wasn't anything bad. Being attracted to another man when you're anticipating divorce? Nothing wrong there. My hands shook as I admitted as much to her.

"I've been selfish," I said as she took my hands and squeezed them, probably to calm my nerves. "I won't get better overnight, and it won't be easy because I love you and I always will. But you're right, and I was wrong. We weren't working, and why the hell was I holding on? I don't know. Comfort? I know what I need to do. But doing it will be difficult. And that starts with finding a place and moving out."

Her eyes twinkled, and she placed one of her hands against my cheek. "All in due time. You're not the only one to blame. The fault is mine too. I've been busy—too busy—to consider what we were or weren't doing. And I loved you— enough that I wanted to help you in whatever capacity you'd let me. But now, it's time to break it off for good. Don't you think?"

My chest didn't break when she said those words, and panic didn't rise inside my gut. I nodded my head, slowly, but steadily. "When I get out, we'll talk to the attorney."

"Together."

"Yes. Together."

Chapter 38: Sadie

Two weeks after he awoke, Theo came "home."

His eyes glowed with happiness on the afternoon we drove up the snow-spattered driveway of his new rental place and stopped at the top. The icy porch sported mylar balloons and tissue paper flowers, and the door handle donned red, green, and blue crepe paper streamers. Pink doily hearts adorned every available window.

"Who did all this?" He scanned the entire length of the small house. There it was, almost February, and the Christmas lights had never been taken in by the previous tenant, and a random tree ornament still hung in one of the dormant dogwood trees flanking the garage. A smile twitched at his lips, and moisture glistened at the corner of his left eyelid.

I reached my hand out to his forearm as he took in the scene. "Friends, family, colleagues."

His Adam's apple bobbed, and tears fell freely now down Theo's scruffy cheeks. "I don't quite know what to say...it's all—"

The arrival of the kids at the front picture window interrupted Theo, and he grappled for the interior door handle. By the time he'd hauled himself out of the car, with a bit of help from me, even Lexie had made her way to the edge of the driveway—arms spread wide, snow boots unfastened, huge smile affixed to her cherubic face. Carefully grabbing all three children into his arms at once, Theo rested his head on top of Charlie's hair and stood there, looking stronger than I'd seen him in months. He stayed there for a long time, in the moment, smile on his face, head tipped to the sky. Tears continued to fall, and he didn't wipe them away.

Theo's return to the world could have been difficult, and the pre-accident Theo would have made it that way. But the post-accident Theo seemed like a changed man. And because he had changed—or at least was making a concerted effort to do so—my confidence soared. In who I was. In who we were. And in who we might be moving forward. And if my confidence waned, he found a way to bring it back.

Three weeks after he'd returned, during my favorite task of washing dishes—he'd spent the dinner hour with us—he called me out on my behavior.

"What's with the silence from time to time?" Theo asked from behind me in the dining chair.

I grabbed the dish towel and dried my hands as I turned to face him. "What?"

"I'm still mostly the same guy I was when you met me, and you're mostly the same girl you were when I met you. We might have added a few new characters to the plot," he inclined his head toward Andrew, who sat in the family room playing a board game with the little kids, "but there's no need for awkward silences, my dear."

The grin on his face spoke more than his words, which, just like that, restored my trust in the idea we'd chosen wisely, and we'd make it, whatever our odd circumstances might be. That night, I finished dishes all the while chattering on about my day—the good *and* the bad—and Theo conversed with me in full. And after Andrew and his family reluctantly headed home, the kids drifted in and out of the kitchen. Charlie needed help with science homework he'd forgotten about, and Lexie wanted a book read to her before bedtime. Theo helped them both without reservation while I worked with Delia on her multiplication tables before taking on the bath duties and getting everyone to bed. Those mundane, ordinary actions became the cornerstone of our lives, and we performed them together on many nights.

And soon, we'd crossed the days off on the paper calendar and another Father's Day was upon us. Unlike the year before, I planned to cook something special to commemorate the occasion. A few days prior to Sunday, the kids and I gathered in the kitchen to make a list for our celebratory dinner.

"What would Daddy like to eat?" I asked the kids.

"Pulled pork!" Charlie shouted.

"He likes strawberry pie," Delia said.

"Peas! And potato chips!" Lexie chirped.

Charlie scowled. "Peas? For Father's Day? Are you kidding me? Dad isn't going to want peas."

I ruffled the hair on Charlie's head and then pulled him in for a side hug. "Hey, watch the tone, please. Lexie is still little. If she thinks Dad will want peas and chips, then that's what we'll do. Pulled pork, strawberry pie, peas, and potato chips it is."

"And what about Andrew?" Charlie put a finger to his chin in his classic pose. "He'd like the pork, but he loves baked beans, corn on the cob, and éclair cake. Can we add those to the menu, too?"

Charlie's words and acceptance of Andrew tugged at my heart. Unconventional family we were, but apparently, it worked for us.

"And one more thing," Charlie continued. "What about a present? What are we—never mind! I have it. Delia, Lexie, come with me."

The three kids ran for the back room and didn't come out again for the rest of the afternoon. When they did, their eyes twinkled, and their mouths twitched.

"What did you do?" I asked.

"You'll see," they all said.

On the day of, the kids and I, along with Andrew's children, donned our aprons, pulled out all the necessary ingredients, and began chopping, grating, measuring, and mixing. Theo and Andrew wandered in and out throughout the morning and reached over to each child in turn, tickling bellies and backs, or, in the case of Charlie, lifting fists up for a bump. By the time late afternoon rolled around, the kids and I were wiped out, all of us on kitchen chairs, waiting for the timer to ding.

Theo's lopsided grin spread across his face as he and Andrew once again came through the kitchen. "It's okay."

"What do you mean?" I sat back against the chair, confused for a moment.

"I mean, it's okay if Andrew and I serve dinner, considering all you guys did for us. Right Andrew?"

Andrew flashed his smile and winked at me. "Right."

"And I mean *we're* okay. I'm standing here, looking at you, at me, at all of us, and I'm happy. We'll always be happy."

Swallowing back emotion, I gripped the edges of my apron. "How can you say that?" Theo had always been the confident one. Did he know something I didn't?

"I just know, Sadie, and I'll leave it at that." He took my fingers and squeezed them against his palm for a moment and then moved toward the chair. "I'm right where I want to be."

Theo glanced at Andrew, who took two steps toward me and pulled me up for a hug. Not caring what the kids or Theo thought, he placed his hands against my cheeks, moved my face forward, and planted his lips against mine. After a quick nip he whispered, "Truer words have never been spoken."

"Oh Mom, really?" Delia said.

"You're blaming this on me?" I said. "What about Andrew?"

Delia blushed and smiled. Charlie, also laughing, stepped toward Theo and pulled on his shirt.

"Dad?" Charlie said.

"Yes?"

"Would you mind going to the den? Can you grab the two bags sitting on the desk?"

Theo looked at me, but I shook my head. I had no idea what Charlie had up his sleeve. When Theo returned, two small gift bags in hand, Charlie said, "Give one to Andrew, please. And open them." Charlie's wide smile, one of my favorite things about him, spread across his face.

The two men opened the bags and pulled something out wrapped in tissue paper.

Theo turned the object over in his hands, tracing an edge with his fingers, and furrowed his brow. "Is this—"

Charlie, still beaming, jumped up. "It is!"

Theo held up the gift. It was a framed photograph of the kids standing in front of the cottage we rented each summer at Walloon Lake. A picture of a happy time, an innocent time, taken two summers before. I looked closer at the photo and the frame, a clear glass rectangle with a blue tint to it, and recognition drew tears to my eyes. It was a salvage piece, formed from Charlie's favorite cereal bowl—the one that had broken suddenly, the one I thought was still waiting to be repurposed.

There'd been enough scraps of the bowl to go around twice, for Andrew held a similar frame with a photo of his children and mine, standing at the Steepled Tree, and my heart clenched. I picked up the frame, marveling again at the new structure that had been created from something completely broken. Somehow, Charlie had managed to fit the pieces of blue glass together almost seamlessly, as if the bowl knew it had to transform so it could live. Those pieces had survived a death and been reborn and no one, unless they were privy to the information surrounding the incident, would have known any better.

I blinked away tears of contentment and reached for Charlie's hand, pressing it to my lips. Theo was right: we'd be okay.

The End

Author's Note

Theo Lancaster isn't a real person. He's based on hours of research on post-traumatic stress disorder (PTSD) and depression as well as information freely given from friends and family who have firsthand experience with PTSD. But he could be real. He could be your friend, your neighbor, your grandson, your brother. He could be your spouse. He could be you.

Prevalence rates of PTSD in service members returning from combat vary by service era. Studies have shown the percentage to range from 11 percent to as high as 30 percent. But PTSD is not a condition exclusive to the military, and it can happen to anyone. In fact, the National Center for PTSD estimates the number of people with PTSD in the United States to be about eight million.

Treatments for PTSD *can* work, but it's up to the those with PTSD or family and friends to pursue treatment. And many people who have PTSD do not seek the support they need. Often, that's because the person living with PTSD is too ashamed to admit they need help, or loved ones might not recognize all the signs, or they may be afraid to speak up. But that's where we all can help. By understanding what PTSD is and raising awareness of it, we can help minimize its devastating effects on everyone.

If you think you're suffering from PTSD or know of someone who might be, say something. You'll be glad you did.

Post-traumatic Stress Disorder
National Center for PTSD: U.S. Department of Veterans Affairs—ptsd.va.gov (1-800-273-TALK); veterans press 1 or text 838255
Coaching Into Care: U.S. Department of Veterans Affairs—mirecc.va.gov/coaching (1-888-823-7458)
Make the Connection: U.S. Department of Veterans Affairs—maketheconnection.net
Substance Abuse and Mental Health Services Administration—samhsa.gov (1-800-662-HELP)

Suicide Prevention

National Suicide Prevention Lifeline—suicidepreventionlifeline.org
(1-800-273-TALK)
IMAlive—imalive.org
American Foundation for Suicide Prevention (AFSP)—afsp.org
Suicide Prevention Resource Center—sprc.org

Related Reading

The Things They Carried by Tim O'Brien
Down Range: To Iraq and Back by Bridget C. Cantrell, Ph.D. & Chuck Dean
Rule Number Two: Lessons I Learned in a Combat Hospital by Dr. Heidi Squier Kraft

Acknowledgments

This story started in June 2012 as a wisp of an idea, and it took a circuitous route to become the book it is today. Many thanks to the team at Black Rose Writing for giving my story a home and making my dream come true. And while words are not enough to express my gratitude for everyone who played a role in shaping this story, they will have to do.

The Plot Sisters: Cindy Cremeans, Ruthann Kain, Jen Messaros, Traci Ison Schafer, and Jude Walsh. You helped bring this story to life, and I am convinced fate had a hand in our meeting.

The early, middle, and late readers; those who provided resources, information, and character inspiration; and overall supporters of my dream: Sarah Anderson, Julie Ballin Patton, Tara Consolino, Gina Consolino-Barsotti, Sandra Doninger, Diane Dougherty, Erin Flanagan, Stefanie Griffin, Awad Halabi, Barbara Halabi, S.B. House, Janet Irvin, Jenny Jaeckel, Katrina Kittle, Andrea Kuperman, Meg Lammers, Laurel Leigh, Dan Loofboro, Kelsey Madges, Fred Marion, Darren McGarvey, Brooke Medlin, Emmanuel Nelson, Amy Galloway Roma, Scott Ross, Bob Schoeni, Gretchen Schoeni, Krista Sheehan, Tess Sherick, Sharon Short, Carrie Taylor, Penny Timmer, Anne Valente, and Father Pat Welsh. Your willingness to answer questions, give feedback, cheerlead when necessary, and provide unwavering inspiration and encouragement propelled me forward each day.

The writing communities: Antioch Writers' Workshop, Literary Mama, Miami Valley Writers Group, 10 Minute Novelists, Women's Fiction Writers Association, and Word's Worth Writing Connections. The education I received from you is invaluable, and I can only hope I'll pass as much information to other writers as you do to me.

My mom and dad: Each day of my life, I learn something new from you. Thanks for passing on the love of reading (and writing) to me.

All the wonderful fur companions, past and present: Arnold, Benedict, Ferdinand, Heathcliff, Lucy, Patty, and Shadow. Your quiet company in the early morning hours means more than you'll ever understand.

My children: Zoe, Talia, Aaron, and Melina. There's no way this book would have made it to print without the support of these unique and always-inspiring people. Remember you can reach for your dreams and attain them, and it's never too late to start on a new dream.

My husband, Tim: Who knew a meeting at Elbel Field would turn into such an adventure? Knowing you believed in me even when I didn't made all the difference. Thank you.

About the Author

Christina Consolino is a writer and editor whose work has appeared in multiple online and print outlets. Her debut novel, *Rewrite the Stars*, was named one of ten finalists for the Ohio Writers' Association Great Novel Contest 2020. She serves as senior editor at the online journal *Literary Mama*, freelance edits both fiction and nonfiction, and teaches writing classes at Word's Worth Writing Center. Christina lives in Kettering, Ohio, with her family and pets.

To keep up-to-date with the latest news, check out her website at www.christinaconsolino.com or follow her on social media.

Note from the Author

Word-of-mouth is crucial for any author to succeed. If you enjoyed *Rewrite the Stars*, please leave a review online—anywhere you are able. Even if it's just a sentence or two. It would make all the difference and would be very much appreciated.

Thanks!
Christina Consolino

Thank you so much for reading one of our **Women's Fiction** novels.

If you enjoyed the experience, please check out our recommendation
for your next great read!

The Apple of My Eye by Mary Ellen Bramwell

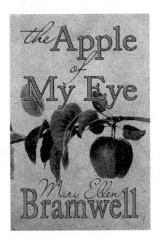

"A mature love story with an intense plot.

This book has something important to say."

–William O. Shakespeare, Professor of English,

Brigham Young University

View other Black Rose Writing titles at
<u>www.blackrosewriting.com/books</u> and use promo code
PRINT to receive a **20% discount** when purchasing.